TEMPING FATE

ESTHER FRIESNER

Temping Fate

DUTTON CHILDREN'S BOOKS

DUTTON CHILDREN'S BOOKS / A division of Penguin Young Readers Group

PUBLISHED BY THE PENGUIN GROUP / Penguin Group (USA) Inc., 375 Hudson Street, New York, New York 10014, U.S.A. / Penguin Group (Canada), 90 Eglinton Avenue East, Suite 700, Toronto, Ontario, Canada M4P 2Y3 (a division of Pearson Penguin Canada Inc.) / Penguin Books Ltd, 80 Strand, London WC2R 0RL, England / Penguin Ireland, 25 St Stephen's Green, Dublin 2, Ireland (a division of Penguin Books Ltd) / Penguin Group (Australia), 250 Camberwell Road, Camberwell, Victoria 3124, Australia (a division of Pearson Australia Group Pty Ltd) / Penguin Books India Pvt Ltd, 11 Community Centre, Panchsheel Park, New Delhi - 110 017, India / Penguin Group (NZ), Cnr Airborne and Rosedale Roads, Albany, Auckland 1310, New Zealand (a division of Pearson New Zealand Ltd) / Penguin Books (South Africa) (Pty) Ltd, 24 Sturdee Avenue, Rosebank, Johannesburg 2196, South Africa / Penguin Books Ltd, Registered Offices: 80 Strand, London WC2R 0RL, England

This book is a work of fiction. Names, characters, places, and incidents are either the product of the author's imagination or are used fictitiously, and any resemblance to actual persons, living or dead, business establishments, events, or locales is entirely coincidental.

Copyright © 2006 by Esther M. Friesner

All rights reserved. No part of this publication may be reproduced or transmitted in any form or by any means, electronic or mechanical, including photocopying, recording, or any information storage and retrieval system now known or to be invented, without permission in writing from the publisher, except by a reviewer who wishes to quote brief passages in connection with a review written for inclusion in a magazine, newspaper, or broadcast.

The publisher does not have any control over and does not assume any responsibility for author or third-party websites or their content.

CIP Data is available.

Published in the United States by Dutton Children's Books,
a division of Penguin Young Readers Group, 345 Hudson Street, New York, New York 10014
www.penguin.com/youngreaders

Printed in USA / Designed by Heather Wood
First Edition 10 9 8 7 6 5 4 3 2 1 ISBN 0-525-47730-6

This book is dedicated to the members of The Cane Club of Naples, Florida:
Riley Gilley, Lou Massa, John Mosele, Jake Stutzman, Carl Traeger.
With respect and affection. A few very *good men.*

TEMPING FATE

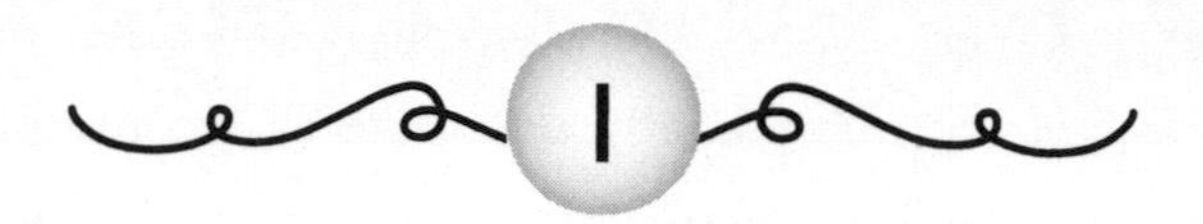

HOW TO GET A SUMMER JOB

Ilana Newhouse checked the business card in her hand one more time, then looked at the gleaming office door in front of her. The letters on the frosted-glass panel—big, black, outlined with gold—left no room for doubt. This was the place.

D. R. TEMPS, INCORPORATED
R. ATATOSK, MGR.

Ilana glanced at her wristwatch: 10:45 A.M. Her appointment was at eleven o'clock. She nibbled her lower lip and sighed. Dad said it was good to arrive early for a job interview. It showed your prospective employer that you were a willing worker, eager to be hired, eager to please.

Willing? Eager? More like last-ditch, all-other-bridges-burned *desperate.* So pathetically desperate to get this summer job that she wondered if maybe she should have shown up for this eleven o'clock even earlier. Like, oh, say, nine o'clock. Yesterday.

D.R. Temps was housed in a quaint, old-fashioned office building near the New Haven Green, a place where time had decided to get off the train in the 1940s. Ilana loved it from the moment she came in off the street and entered a world where frigid air-conditioning wasn't necessary because thick stone walls kept the summer heat at bay. The polished, veined granite floors with their black and brown and gold and white kaleidoscopic patterns, the elevator with its fold-down seat for a long-redundant human operator, the transoms over every office door, she loved it all.

What she didn't love was the way the high ceilings made her voice echo up and down the deserted corridors. It left her with a creepy feeling, a crazy suspicion that all the offices she'd passed on the way down the hall were empty, that she was the only living soul on this floor, if not in this building.

It feels like it's Sunday in here, she thought uneasily. *But this isn't Sunday; it's Thursday. People do* business *on Thursdays.*

As her hand closed around the hefty brass doorknob, she could hear her mother's cheerful, annoyingly chirpy voice in her ears: *Don't worry, darling. If you don't get a job this summer, it won't be the end of the world. Daddy and I will come up with* something *for you.*

That was what she was afraid of. There was nothing half as frightening as parents who promised to come up with *something*.

Ilana took a deep breath. *This is it,* she told herself. *This is your last chance. Stow the attitude, keep the smart-ass zingers to yourself, and for God's sake, do* not *push your hair back behind your ears! If you don't get hired after this interview, you're D-as-in-dogmeat doomed.* With that mental pep talk, she turned the doorknob.

Tried to turn the doorknob. It didn't turn. The door was locked, the knob frozen in place. Ilana jiggled it left and right. The massive oak door rattled on its hinges, but otherwise didn't budge.

There had to be some mistake. She knew she had an appointment for eleven o'clock today. She'd even gotten a phone call from Mrs. Atatosk yesterday, reminding her about it. The D. R. Temps manager sounded enthusiastic about having Ilana come in. *We can't wait to meet you,* she'd said. *We need lots of extra help, especially bright, imaginative, energetic young people. Gracious, can you believe that June is almost gone, school's out, and we* still *haven't filled all of our employment vacancies? Summer is our busy season. Something's always popping up in the summertime.*

That didn't sound like the sort of person who'd forget about an interview and lock the office door. There must be some mistake.

"Hello? Mrs. Atatosk? Can you hear me in there? The door's locked." She rapped lightly on the frosted-glass panel and tilted her head, hoping for a response from the other side.

Nothing. She knocked again, harder.

"Helloooooo? Anyone in there? I have an appointment."

The echoes died, and then, out of nowhere, a strange sound pierced the silence so suddenly that it almost made Ilana jump out of her skin.

"Oh God, what was that?" she whispered, eyes darting down the hall. As if in answer, the sound came again, a high-pitched, chittery sound of . . .

A giggle? Ilana frowned. *Great. Now I'm so spooked that I'm hearing things.*

Maybe Mrs. Atatosk had to run out of the office unexpectedly. Maybe she'd left a secretary behind, someone who'd locked the door because she felt just as creeped out as Ilana by the surrounding emptiness of this floor, this whole building.

But it's not *empty; it* can't *be empty!* Ilana reasoned. *Not the whole building! There's got to be other businesses here, other people working. It's stupid to lock doors when there's nothing real to be afraid of.* As if to make herself believe that, she banged so hard on the door that the glass panel rattled.

"Come on, open up, it's okay! I'm not a freelance ax murderer, honest. I'm Ilana Newhouse, I've got an eleven o'clock interview with Mrs. Atatosk."

And there it was a second time: that piercing, staccato giggle. It echoed through the hallway, but it came from behind the stubborn office door. Someone was in there, all right; someone who was playing games.

Not with me, *they're not!* Ilana thought. Now she was angry.

She banged on the door again. "Yeah, very funny, I'm scared, you win. So can we *please* play something else? I did *not* drive all the way to New Haven for nothing! E-lev-en-o-clock appointment, got it? *Not* twelve, *not* your lunch hour, *not* kidding! Open this door!"

Oops. And there *it* was again: That Attitude Thing. Ilana swore under her breath and switched her prayers from *Please let someone hear me and open the door* to *Please* don't *let anyone be there!* Blowing a job interview before she came face-to-face with her potential employer would be a new record, even for her.

It was That Attitude Thing that had cost her summer employment opportunities at almost every independent retailer in her hometown, that stronghold of white-bread-and-vanilla values, Porlock's Landing, Connecticut. From the town's ten antique dealers to its seven coffee shops to the one sad and lonesome bookstore, no one seemed willing to take on a girl who answered the question *Why do you want to work here?* with:

I'm glad you asked. See, I think venomous snakes are really cool, so I'm saving up to get my tongue split. I want to pursue a career in retail sales and I think something like that will give me a big advantage, marketing-wise. It's a proven fact: Nervous people make the best customers. The more you throw someone off balance, the more they're willing to spend just to get the heck away *from you! Will that be great for business or what?*

It was supposed to be a joke. No one got it. No one got her.

Joke or not, the whole tongue-splitting thing was relevant to why the remainder of the local businesses wouldn't hire her: appearance. Porlock's Landing catered to conservative consumers, whether year-round residents or Summer People. For most of them, wearing paisley was dangerously edgy, though certain brand-name floral prints for women were acceptable only because the jarring hot-pink-poison-green-electric-yellow clash-fests were so overpriced they were status symbols. Ilana thought she'd played it safe by showing up to her interviews wearing basic black. The problem was her ensemble included a black T-shirt that said *ORC: THE OTHER GREEN MEAT*.

Which brought her right back to That Attitude Thing.

Alone in the emptiness of the hall, Ilana gave the doorknob one more fierce rattle, then turned and started to walk back to the elevators. Great. No one had heard her lose her temper, but that meant no one was there. D. R. Temps had blown off the interview without so much as a courtesy phone call to let her know not to bother coming in. Pretty weird, especially after the confirming call yesterday, but—

What was that?

Ilana stopped dead in her tracks and tilted her head toward the locked door. She was willing to believe that she'd only imagined the first giggle; the vast halls in this old building did have some pretty bizarre echoes. She was willing to accept that the second giggle came from Mrs. Atatosk's as-yet-unseen secretary, a nervous reaction to being left alone.

But as for *this* one—!

There it was: plain as plain, louder, longer, shriller, and much, much snottier than the ones before, the in-your-face, thumb-to-nose mother of all neener-neener-neeners. She hadn't imagined it. She couldn't excuse it. No mistaking it for anything else and no mistaking where it was coming from. Someone *was* at D. R. Temps, and that someone was getting their kicks by messing with Ilana.

Not acceptable. Summer job or no summer job, *not* acceptable at all.

Ilana marched back to the door. *There are times,* she told herself, *when* bad *attitude is the only* right *attitude.*

She pounded on the door with a fist and made no attempt to be soft-spoken or polite. "Okay, jerk, I hear you, so don't pretend you're not in there! You don't want to hire me, fine, but don't you *dare* play games with me! I don't know where you got the idea that I'm wrong for your stupid job without even giving me a chance, and I don't care. Maybe *I* don't want to work for *you,* but at least I'd have the guts to tell you to your face! I wouldn't hide behind a locked door, giggling like a freakin' squirrel. Now, are you going to open up, or am I going to—?"

No response, not even that obnoxious giggle. Ilana seethed. Now she was determined to get into that office if only to give the giggler a piece of her mind. For one split second she flirted with the idea of kicking down the door, then dropped it just as quickly. She'd come to New Haven to get a job, not a police record.

Suddenly she smiled: Eureka. The same action-adventure-movie-addicted part of her brain that had suggested kicking down the door came up with another, better, more practical idea. Ilana reached into the pocket of her borrowed khaki skirt and pulled out her debit card. She crouched in front of the locked door and peered through the crack, eyes level with the double lock. She wasn't about to try anything if the bolt were engaged; she wanted to jimmy the latch, not snap her card.

Oh good: no bolt. Now, how did they do this in the movies? She steadied herself by holding on to the doorknob with one hand while with the other she pushed her debit card into the crack and carefully probed for the latch. She couldn't keep from grinning like an idiot when she felt plastic connecting with metal, then metal giving way. There was a soft click; the doorknob turned easily under her hand and—

"Brava, dear child! Brava, I say! Nobly done!" The door flew open, and Ilana pitched forward onto shag carpeting so thick and white it was like running headfirst into a polar bear's rump. As she sat up, a bit dazed, and looked around the small, simple office with its celery-green walls and dark oak woodwork, her ears filled with the sound of a crisp, jolly, woman's voice heaping praises on her.

"How do you do? I'm Mrs. Atatosk; Roberta." A small, plump older woman loomed over Ilana. Her hair was an odd shade of woodsy brown liberally sprinkled with gray, and her dark eyes twinkled. She had a charming smile, even with a bucktoothed overbite that was every orthodontist's get-rich-quick dream come true, and she turned the full force of it onto her caller. "That's *Mrs.*, not Ms.," she said. "Don't call me Ms., please, I am much too old to change my ways. Don't call me Roberta, either; familiarity is the last refuge of the used-car salesman. Actually, I believe I made my preferences in such matters clear when we spoke on the telephone the other day. I must say, you are *much* more impressive in person. I'm afraid your telephone manner was—how can I put this kindly?—rather pathetic. Namby-pamby. Wishy-washy. Wimpish. That's why I decided to test you this way. *Much* better in person, yes, much. Never have I seen such a splendid demonstration of fortitude since your sister, Dyllin, first came to us three years ago. To be honest, that's the only reason I decided to give you a chance, despite how . . . mediocre you sounded on the phone."

Ilana's face darkened. Dyllin again. Dyllin always. Was there nowhere she could escape from her older sister's overwhelming aura of can-do-no-wrong? At home, at school, everywhere Ilana went it was Dyllin, Dyllin, Dyllin, the golden girl, the ideal student, the perfect daughter. Only not quite so perfect these days, though neither Mom nor Dad was about to admit it. Just remembering the latest family dinnertime blowup—how tightly Mom had gritted her teeth, how close Dad had come to actually *yelling* at Dyllin-the-flawless—was enough to lighten Ilana's mood a little bit.

A *very* little bit.

"Fortitude?" Ilana smiled. "Is that anything like, oh, I don't know . . . *stubborn*?"

Mrs. Atatosk peered at her as if she'd grown a propeller. "Don't be silly, dear child, it's exactly the same thing; it just sounds prettier. Now, let me see, let me see . . ."

She began to scribble madly on the Lucite clipboard she held close to her chest, and to pace back and forth between the two doors on the back wall of the office. Unlike the front door, these were solid wood, with no fancy frosted-glass panels. "That will give you twenty points for initiative, twenty for persistence, twenty for courage, another twenty for creativity, and finally— Goodness, is that a khaki skirt you're wearing?"

"Uh . . . yes?" Ilana slowly stood up, using the lone desk to help her get to her feet. Resting one hand on the green leather blotter that was the only thing on the desktop, she brushed fluffy bits of white lint from her borrowed outfit. She'd been so frantic about getting this job that she'd let her friend, Heather, dress her for the interview. Heather immediately sidelined all of Ilana's gloomy, funky, functional black clothing before raiding her own closet in favor of a bland ensemble in shades of pink and beige.

"Oh dear. Khaki. That's so . . . inoffensive." The woman tapped the end of her fountain pen to her lower lip and made disapproving noises with her tongue.

"Inoffensive?" Ilana repeated, nervously tucking her hair behind her ears. "Inoffensive is *bad*?" She could hardly believe this, coming from a woman who was herself the picture of middle-aged, motherly, mousy normalcy. In her simple brown skirt and button-down blouse, Mrs. Atatosk looked like the world's oldest Brownie Scout.

"Goodness, of course it's bad! If you try too hard to please the world, it means you want everyone's acceptance except your own. We don't have much use for sheep in this line of work, dear. They're pretty, biddable creatures, but they do have a tendency to end up as someone else's dinner. I'm afraid that your display of such deplorable herd-instinct in connection with your wardrobe is going to mean I can't possibly— Wait a moment. Is that a *skull* on your cheek?"

Ilana's hand flew up automatically to cover the morbid design that lay just below the outer corner of her right eye, like a gruesome teardrop. Yes, it was a skull, a bit of freelance artwork no bigger than the nail on her littlest finger. She'd inflicted it on herself on the next-to-last day of school, a time for teachers and students alike to slump through the final, humid, useless hours of the semester and pray for the dismissal bell to ring. For lack of anything better to do, she'd decided to see if she could draw something on her own face, using the top of a silver lip gloss tube for a mirror. She gave herself extra points for not poking herself in the eye and was very pleased with the results.

She was *not* pleased when she realized she'd accidentally used a permanent marker instead of an ordinary pen for her little experiment.

To say her parents were also "not pleased" with Ilana's artwork was like saying Napoleon was not pleased with the final score at Waterloo.

The skull stayed hidden only if she brushed her blunt-cut black hair just right, then moussed, gelled, pomaded, and sprayed it into place as a modified pageboy and didn't touch it. Unfortunately, she had naturally curly hair that fought the assault of grooming products tooth and nail. She also kept forgetting to just let her hair *alone,* plastered down to hide the dismal doodle. Very hard to do that if you are a born fidgeter.

A still-unemployed fidgeter. It was the skull that had cost her every child care–related job in Porlock's Landing. The town offered plenty of openings for munchkin wranglers—day camps, beach clubs, kiddie programs at the library, even individual parents desperate for an hour or two of peace and quiet—but one look at that skeletal scribble was the deal-breaker. Ilana was willing to bet that the *kids* would think it was cool, but the kids weren't doing the hiring.

The dowdy clipboard-toting woman gently pulled Ilana's hand away and peered closely at the little black skull. "Why, so it is!" she said, eyes sparkling. "A tattoo?"

"N-No," Ilana replied. "It's not. It'll come off in time, but I can't *do* anything about removing it right away because—" She stopped herself. She didn't want to explain why her skin couldn't stand the industrial-grade scrubdown necessary to remove the skull.

"Oh?" Apparently Mrs. Atatosk didn't care whether she got an explanation or not. "What a pity. It's simply darling. Still . . ." Her lips moved as she scribbled on her clipboard again before speaking up and saying, "Even if it's not as permanent as a tattoo, it *does* counteract that dreary skirt. And a pink polo shirt? Ugh. Where *do* you get your fashion tips? From the Sugarplum Fairy? Dear child, please tell me that you have *something* else in your wardrobe. Perhaps in a nice, ominous shade of black?"

For the first time, Ilana knew how her previous interviewers must have felt when she made that tongue-splitting comment. Weirdness was like vitamin C: There was only so much of it that your system could absorb before you started to feel sick. She found herself slowly backing toward the office door while she replied: "Um, I think I could find something black to wear, yes. But about this job—"

"Good, good." If Mrs. Atatosk noticed that Ilana was trying to ease herself into a quick exit, she didn't remark on it. "In that case, what with the skull and all, plus your excellent scores in all other aspects of employability, I think I can justify giving you *ten* points for appearance. Tsk. For a while there I thought we had a second Dyllin Newhouse on board."

"Oh goodie. Following in my sister's footsteps has always been my dream." *Like I needed another reason to get the heck out of here!*

"Yes, indeed." Mrs. Atatosk was apparently immune to sarcasm. "We assume that if you're worthy enough for Dyllin to have let you know the whereabouts of our happy little service bureau, you're worth considering as a potential employee."

Well, that was sort of true: Dyllin *had* let Ilana know about the existence of D. R. Temps, she just didn't know she'd done it. It happened by accident one evening when Ilana was playing a game of Hide-and-Don't-get-dragged-back-into-tonight's-dinnertime-battle. Wisely she'd hidden in the one place her sister would never dream of seeking her, in Dyllin's own room. While she skulked there, waiting for the nightly blowup to subside, she passed the time by poking through some of the stuff on top of Dyllin's chest of drawers. She wasn't a snoop by nature, but she was bored and there was nothing to read in Dyllin's room except about two hundred fifty-seven bridal magazines, give or take a dozen. She found the D. R. Temps business card when she idly opened a pink leatherette jewelry box, only to set off a tinkly plastic ballerina alarm.

"Who's messing around in my room!" Her sister's outraged roar startled Ilana so badly that she stuffed the card into her pocket without thinking. She raced out of Dyllin's room and dove into the Neutral Zone, a.k.a. the bathroom, just as her sister came tromping down the hall, breathing fire. When Ilana found the card later that same night, she made a spur-of-the-moment decision to give those people a call.

"So Dyllin's the reason you're giving me a chance. Lucky me."

"You certainly are. I had strong doubts about you. The acorn isn't supposed to fall far from the tree, but believe me, I've seen some of those little buggers bounce, rebound, roll, and fly better than high-priced golf balls. Come to think of it, we could have saved ourselves this entire meeting if I'd only thought to have you ask Dyllin to vouch for you personally."

"I'm glad you didn't."

"Really?" Mrs. Atatosk cocked her head to one side and looked almost as pleased as when she'd discovered the skull doodle. "You wanted to be judged and hired on your own merits? Admirable! That's more of the sort of independent thinking that we here at D. R. Temps simply *adore.* Why, you sly minx, I'll bet that Dyllin doesn't even know you're here."

Minx?

"You got that right." Dyllin had no idea that Ilana was visiting her former place of employment. These days, Dyllin had no idea about a *lot* of things, including the fact that her daily behavior as good as told the world: I am acting like a complete and total psycho bride-monster with a bug the size of Alaska up my butt. Now stand aside, it's time for me to destroy Tokyo.

"Um, I can't take credit for being independent," Ilana said. *Especially when I'm about to run like a rabbit just as soon as I can reach that door.* "Dyllin wouldn't have the time to put in a word for me even if I asked her. She's got too much to do right now. She's getting married at the end of the summer."

"Married? Our little Dyllin?" Mrs. Atatosk laid her clipboard-free hand on her bosom. "Oh my. And here you are, trying to earn extra money so that you can buy her a wedding gift!"

"Sure, why not, let's go with that." *Just a few more steps . . .*

"Better and better." Mrs. Atatosk scribbled madly on her clipboard, then announced: "You'll do."

"I'll do?" Ilana echoed, still inching her way toward the door. "*What* will I do? See, I've been having second thoughts about this whole temping thing. I can file okay, but the way I understand it, temps have to do a lot of typing, and my keyboard skills aren't very goo—"

Mrs. Atatosk laughed, her eyes glittering like mirrored disco balls at high noon. "Typing will be the least of your troubles! The skills you need when you work for D. R. Temps are imagination, innovation, motivation, and the ability to run away. Fast. Often. A lot."

Ilana's eyebrows rose. "From what?"

"You'll know it when you see it. Or you won't, and then it

will be *such* a pity. Oh, but don't you fret about it. It's all covered in the Waiver. Once you sign that, we're not responsible for anything at all." She consulted her clipboard, her eyes crinkling with good cheer that Ilana didn't share in the least. "Now your first assignment is in Porlock's Landing. Terribly dull little town, about as exciting as a dog's dinner—"

"It's *my* town," Ilana said, somewhat defensively. Although she agreed that it *was* deathly dull, it annoyed her to hear this strange woman say so.

"Really? How convenient for you! You'll be reporting to Tabby Fabricant Textiles in the Yankee Peddler Industrial Park. Dyllin worked there several times. Perhaps she can give you some pointers."

"I don't think so." By now Ilana had managed to edge herself all the way to the office door and was groping around behind her back for the knob. What was it about Mrs. Atatosk that made Ilana's brain scream *Get me out of here!* Could anyone be so blasted *perky* without being hooked up to a perpetual intravenous drip of double espresso?

"No?" Mrs. Atatosk sounded surprised. "But Dyllin was always such a *helpful* girl."

"She's busy." Ilana's frantically questing fingertips touched the smooth curve of the doorknob. "Remember? Getting married right before Labor Day?"

"Ah yes, so you said, though you never told me to whom."

"Some . . . some guy she met while she was working for you. Ras somebody."

For once, Mrs. Atatosk's expression darkened. "*Erastus? Our* Erastus? Erastus Ames? You don't mean to tell me she's going to marry *him?*"

Ilana nodded. "That's the name. Only he prefers to be called Ras." *And who could blame him?* she thought.

"Hmph! 'Prefers'? More like *demands,* if I know that boy!" Mrs. Atatosk clicked her tongue and scribbled line after line on her clipboard. "This is bad, this is very bad, this won't do at all. Marrying *him,* of all people! What *is* she thinking? Oh, Dyllin, Dyllin, I expected so much better of you!"

"He-He seems nice," Ilana volunteered. It wasn't exactly a lie. He was the nicest-*looking* man she'd ever seen, but he hadn't said much beyond "Hello" and "Name's Erastus-call-me-Ras." And he hadn't killed his crazed bride-to-be yet, not even when she went ballistic over whether to have their names *or* the wedding date printed on the souvenir matchbooks because there wasn't room for both.

"Yes, I'm sure he *seems* like he's an awful lot of things." Mrs. Atatosk made a face. "Well, let it go. I must keep reminding myself that Dyllin is a big girl; she can make her own mistakes, just like the rest of you. It's only when *her* mistakes become *our* mistakes that— But no, no, it does no good to think like that." Her mouth went from pursed to a too-sudden, too-shiny smile as she told Ilana, "I'm sure that *you* won't let us down like that, will you, dear?"

"Yeah, well, about that—about this whole interview, this job—" Ilana turned the knob at her back and slowly pulled the door open just a hair. "I don't think that it's going to be right for—"

Mrs. Atatosk was too busy pulling papers from her clipboard to pay attention to anything Ilana was saying. "Now here's a highly informative brochure that we give to all of our new employees, and the Employee Information Form you'll have to fill out and bring back to me a.s.a.p.—whatever you do, do *not* forget to fill in the sections covering emergency contact and next of kin. And here are the instructions and driving directions for your first assignment—you start tomorrow at seven o'clock in the morning; do *not* be late; they hate that! And here's the Waiver—be *very* sure to sign that for me right now, before you leave the premises or I wouldn't like to think of the consequences. And this is our standard contract, of course. And this—"

Ilana pulled the door open some more and began sliding one foot out into the hall, all the while fending off the ever-growing pile of forms Mrs. Atatosk was pushing at her. The older woman didn't seem to care that Ilana hadn't accepted a single one of them. Unclaimed, they fluttered and flew across the white shag rug like dead leaves in a windstorm.

"Look, Mrs. Atatosk, I'm sorry to have taken up so much of your time, but I've thought it over and I changed my mind. I'd *much* rather spend my summer doing something with a whole lot less emphasis on the running-away-from-things, more on the you-want-fries-with-that. Thank you for everything, but—"

"And here is your first week's pay."

This time it was not a sheet of paper Mrs. Atatosk tossed at Ilana, but a thick, unsealed white envelope. Ilana didn't let it fall to the floor, but grabbed it in midair just before the wad of twenty-dollar bills inside could spill out and scatter. Her eyes went wide, then wider still as she counted out twenty-five of them.

"There's five hundred dollars in here!" she exclaimed.

"Oh, good!" Mrs. Atatosk made another note on her clipboard. "Math skills. Not a requirement for tomorrow's assignment, but it might come in handy later."

"Why are you paying me now? I haven't done anything yet. I haven't even filled out any of those forms. I haven't signed the Waiver! And in *cash*?" Ilana shook her head. "This isn't—"

"Enough?" Mrs. Atatosk cocked her head and looked troubled. "I'm afraid that's all I can manage for this week's work. By the way, you do understand that this first week is a trial assignment? We here at D. R. Temps have made mistakes about the capabilities of our employees in the past. Someone who sounds utterly perfect on paper is often a complete washout face-to-face, and sometimes a person who looks wonderful during the interview turns out to be a dreadful mistake under actual on-the-job conditions. However, if everything goes well during your trial week, perhaps we can keep you on board and increase your pay to six hundred dollars per—"

"No, what I mean is—"

"All right, all right, *seven* hundred! But that is my final offer. And if your employers decide to reward superior service with tips or gifts in addition to your salary, I *don't* want to know about it! Especially the gifts. Now, do you have everything, dear?"

"I-I—" Ilana clutched the envelope full of money with both hands and nodded helplessly at the scattered papers. She stuffed the envelope in her pocket and was about to get down on her hands and knees to gather the forms when Mrs. Atatosk gently touched her on the shoulder.

"Allow me, dear," she said. Scurrying busily here and there, she gathered the dispersed papers so quickly that it was almost like magic. "There we are, all together again!" she announced cheerfully, handing the reclaimed stack to Ilana. "Sign the top one before you go. That's the Waiver."

Ilana nodded, still amazed by how fast the older woman could move. Mrs. Atatosk passed her a pen, white and gold and shiny. It looked like plastic but felt like feathers in Ilana's hand. She tried to read the Waiver before signing it. This proved to be impossible. The print was tiny and set in a font that made it look like a chicken had walked across the paper with muddy feet. The only perfectly legible lines were midpage, block letters an inch high that said:

D. R. TEMPS, INCORPORATED, ACCEPTS ABSOLUTELY NO RESPONSIBILITY WHATSOEVER FOR EMPLOYEES' LOSS OF LIFE, LIMB, LUCIDITY, LAWYERS, OR LEMURS. SO DON'T GET SMART WITH US.

She looked up, puzzled. "Lemurs?"

Mrs. Atatosk smiled. Mrs. Atatosk smiled a lot. "It's a long story. It's got more to do with the lawyers than the lemurs, but I wouldn't worry about it if I were you. Dear child, don't tell me you're actually *reading* that dry old thing when all you really need to do is *sign* it?"

"My father said—"

"I'm sure I know *exactly* what your father said: 'Always read every document before you sign it.' Fathers are eternally saying silly things like that, but do they do it themselves?"

"Yes, but—" Ilana began to object, then realized that Mrs. Atatosk was right: Her father *didn't* read every word of any document placed before him. He warned Ilana to be alert, pay attention, take nothing on blind trust, but she knew for a fact that there were plenty of things he took for granted. Important things. Things that turned out to be a matter of life or death.

Oh don't worry if Ilana can't have the vaccine before we leave, he'd said to her and her mother on that day four years ago. *It's not like it's something she's got to have; it's not even required! Smallpox is a* dead *disease; everyone knows it. Mr. Billings told me so himself. I never had a boss I trusted so much. He wouldn't say it if it weren't so.*

Ilana's mouth tightened. Grimly she signed the Waiver.

"That's my girl," said Mrs. Atatosk, patting her hand. "Welcome aboard."

A loud, uncanny noise came from behind one of the two wooden doors at the back of the sparsely furnished office. Ilana's brows drew together.

"What was that?" she asked. It sounded like something between a roar and a howl, with a few notes of garbage-can-full-of-rocks-rolling-downhill thrown in for good measure.

"Mice!" Mrs. Atatosk cried, her lips pulled back in a smile that was too wide to be real. She dropped her clipboard and seized Ilana by the shoulders, twirling her around and propelling her toward the office door. "Yes, yes, mice, definitely mice, nothing more. Dreadful problem. Quite bold-faced, the little rascals. Well, mustn't keep you waiting. Calls to make. Superintendent. Exterminators. Police. The Authorities. Busy, busy, busy, that's the D. R. Temps motto! Good-bye!" She shoved the girl out into the hall and slammed the door after her.

Ilana was halfway home, head still spinning, before she realized that she hadn't handed the Waiver back to Mrs. Atatosk.

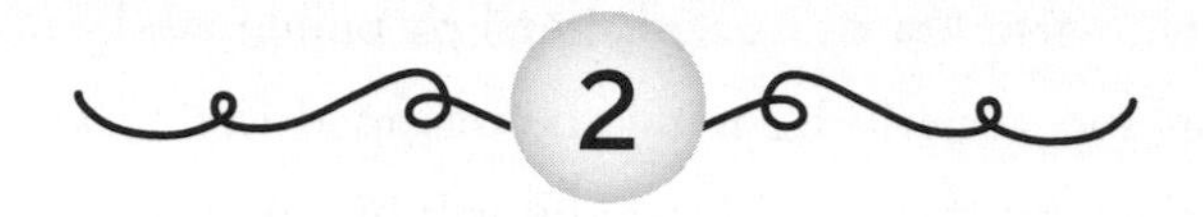

IMPRESSING YOUR NEW EMPLOYER

The Yankee Peddler Industrial Park looked like three loaves of sandwich bread set down in a broken U by some gigantic child on a picnic. Each dull brown building sported five glass-paneled aluminum doors, five corrugated steel garage entrances, and a pair of pale tan cement trash receptacles at either end. Cigarette butts littered the narrow sidewalks. Out in the rectangular splodge of a parking lot, the white lines divvying up individual car spaces needed repainting badly.

Ilana drove in at about 6:45 A.M. on Friday. The late June morning had dawned hazy and warm, with the promise of a hot, humid day to come: perfect beach weather. Porlock's Landing was famous for its beaches, which drew the Summer People like ants to a fallen ice-cream cone. Ilana sighed. No beaches for her this summer, except maybe on the weekends.

On the other hand, at least she wouldn't have to spend her *entire* summer trapped in a place as dreary and deadly as this seemed to be. Mrs. Atatosk had said this first job was only for a weeklong trial period. Even if she passed muster and these people wanted her to stay on beyond her trial run, she didn't have to go along with it. She could change her mind anytime she liked, go back to the D. R. Temps office, tell that weird Mrs. Atatosk she wanted a different assignment. And if that was unacceptable, she'd quit, contract or no contract. That was the beauty of temp work: She could always back out. Even if she hung in there, she still knew she'd be free sooner instead of later. She didn't have to stay for the next assignment.

Not like the poor souls trapped forever (or at least until retirement) behind the glass door with the TABBY FABRICANT TEXTILES sign. It looked like something you'd get made-to-order at the local photocopy/printing place: a blue plastic plaque with plain white letters etched into the glossy surface. The only interesting thing about it was the company logo, a golden spinning wheel flanked by a silver tape measure and a pair of black scissors.

Ilana opened the door, letting the sweet, air-conditioned coolness wash over her. Bliss! Then she looked around.

No one was there. Ilana made a face.

"Why am *I* suddenly the only responsible person on the planet?" she muttered. "Does no one else believe in owning a *watch*? You can get them for under fifteen bucks a pop at Wal-Mart!" She slouched up to the chest-high counter, rested one arm on the green plastic top, and slapped her hand down hard on the round RING FOR SERVICE bell.

Instead of the bright, crisp ring she'd expected, Ilana was assaulted by a deep, somber, brazen tolling that had somehow escaped from the tower of Notre Dame and hidden in that puny little desktop bell. Clapping both hands over her ears didn't help; she could hear that rolling, ponderous wave of sound with her *teeth*.

Her head was still throbbing when the door at the back of the office opened and a young woman dressed in sky blue silk came sweeping in. She didn't look much older than twenty-something, slender and graceful, so perfectly, unnaturally pretty that the total effect was just a little bit . . . eerie. Her pale blond hair streamed down to her hips, riding a breeze that blew for her alone.

"Oh my goodness, you must be our darling little temp, mustn't you?" she chirruped at Ilana. "I'm Tabby; *so* good to meet you! How lovely of you to have come early. I *do* hope it didn't inconvenience you too much? You *have* had your breakfast? A good one? Healthy? Plenty of fiber? You can never have too much fiber, that's what I always say." As she chattered, she sailed around the counter, threw one arm across Ilana's shoulders, and half steered, half shoved her toward the back door.

"Now, don't you feel at all shy if you haven't eaten yet," Tabby went on. And on. "We're all one big happy family here, after all.

We're here to *help* one another. We're here to make a *difference* in this silly old world. Now, as long as you're working here, if you want anything, simply anything at all, you must speak up. Dimity baked some delectable raisin-walnut muffins this morning, and there's plenty of coffee."

I'll say there is, Ilana thought. *And plenty strong, too, judging from you. Did you just drink a whole pot of triple espresso or are you part ferret?* She forced a smile and said, "You know, that sounds really nice, the muffins, but I can't. I'm allergic to eggs. I go into anaphylactic shock. Fatal reaction. Sorry."

Tabby stopped in her tracks and gave Ilana the strangest, most penetrating look she'd ever endured. "Well, of course you're allergic to eggs, darling. We know. That's why Dimity got her muffin recipe out of a special cookbook, made them with no eggs at all, just for you. Wouldn't it be silly of us to try to kill our own precious little temp, and on your first day, too! Georgette would never consent to it—she's the one you'll be replacing—and besides, we simply *couldn't* manage if you died on us unexpectedly, ha-ha. This *is* the start of our busy season."

"How do you know I'm—?" Ilana tried to remember whether she'd filled out any medical forms for Mrs. Atatosk or mentioned her allergy at all. Automatically she glanced at her left wrist where she wore her medical ID tag. The silver oblong tag was a must-wear for anyone with a significant medical condition.

So Mrs. Atatosk must have seen the tag and phoned ahead to tell Tabby about it, except—

Except Ilana always wore her medical ID bracelet with the logo-side showing. Her egg allergy had set her apart from other people since the day she was born. Who wanted to be the girl who couldn't have a slice of cake at her best friend's birthday party? So unless Mrs. Atatosk had X-ray vision, there went *that* theory.

Before Ilana had the chance to try conjuring up another perfectly logical explanation for Tabby's inside info on her allergy, the woman in blue had herded her through the back door and into another office. Ilana glanced around and smiled with relief. It was all so ordinary-looking.

I could use a big dose of ordinary about now, she thought. *It's much too early in the morning for weird. Weird should have the courtesy to wait until after lunch, at least.*

As a matter of fact, the rear office at Tabby Fabricant Textiles had elevated ordinary to an art form. The three gray steel desks were made in the same tedious style as those used in high school guidance offices across the country. The file cabinets lining the side walls were the same drab color as the desks. Even the computers were same-old-same-old gray, and none of those cool, streamlined, newfangled plasma screens or ergonomic keyboards, no sir! The monitors, the CPUs, the whole cyber nine yards was boxy, boxy, boxy. The only fancy pieces of office equipment were the desk chairs. They looked so welcoming and comfortable that you almost wanted to spend eternity cradled in them.

Two of the dull desks were occupied by women who bore

a striking family resemblance to Tabby. She introduced them as her sisters, Georgette and Dimity. If Georgette wasn't the oldest of the three in fact, she looked like she ought to be. Her hair was a faded brown already streaked with strands of silver and there was a pair of deep creases between her eyebrows. As for Dimity, she was all crisp precision. Her hair was not merely black, but BLACK, as if obeying the dictates of a secret rule book that set the legal value for all colors. By the same standard, her skin was WHITE, her eyes BLUE, her lips RED, and her pin-striped pantsuit GRAY. Ilana had the feeling that if Dimity stepped onto a scale she would be exactly the American Medical Association's recommended weight for her height. *Exactly.*

Tabby's vacant desk boasted fresh daisies in a pearly pink vase and an array of figurines showing chubby mice in cute-but-not-too-cute poses. Dimity worked behind such a clutter of technogadgets that Ilana was reminded of the mad scientist's lair in old black-and-white horror movies.

Georgette's desk was bare except for that fossil of a computer, a black stapler, a matching pair of scissors, and a picture frame. No little fussy touches, personal or professional, no color, all business.

Georgette herself, on the other hand . . .

"Oh, thank heaven!" With an exclamation that was almost a sob, dark-clad Georgette fairly threw herself into Ilana's arms, hugging her fiercely. "You came! You really came! You took the job! Oh, thank you, thank you, thank you! You can't even begin to imagine what this means to me. I haven't had a day off in—"

"Now, Popo dear, control yourself." Tabby stepped in behind her sister and gently pulled Georgette away from Ilana. "You know you have no one to blame but yourself if you're overworked. You made your own choice; no one forced you. You're the one who said that it would be easy to combine a career and motherhood."

"You can't blame her for that," Dimity said in level, measured tones. "You know you'd choose to do the same thing, if you could. I still might. It *is* doable. I checked the statistics. *They* do it all the time, sometimes because they really don't have any other choice. Popo's problem is that she's been trying to do it too well. Isn't that right, Popo?"

Popo? Ilana thought, bewildered. Not exactly the sort of nickname that came naturally out of *Georgette.* Weird. Not half so weird as "Popo's" staggering attack of gratitude, but weird enough.

And it was still hours to go until lunch. *Not* fair.

"Is it a *crime* to want to be a good mother?" Georgette (a.k.a. Popo) wailed.

"No, just a crime to kill yourself trying to be one." Tabby folded her arms and gave her sister a stern look. "And wouldn't that be ironic? You've got to accept the fact that you can't do your work *and* be at Harris's Little League game *and* Loden's class play all at once. Something's got to give, sooner or later, and it can't be the business. I won't stand for it. Now, I want you to show this darling girl what she'll be doing here for us and then I want you to go straight home, run a hot bath, dump a quart of aromatherapy oil into it, and *relax.*"

"But the children—!"

As Georgette picked up the frame from her desk, Ilana caught sight of the family photo it held: a candid shot of a bucktoothed boy about nine years old and a girl who couldn't have been more than six. They were romping on the lawn in front of a big Colonial house, laughing, playing, running . . . with *scissors?*

"Let me see that!" The words were out of her mouth and the photo was in her hands before anyone in the office could prevent it. Ilana gaped at the picture. Her eyes had not deceived her. Both of the kids were brandishing big, sharp, glittering scissors, and not just some dinky little things taken from a manicure set, either. These were serious scissors, one step below garden shears.

Ilana's eyes flashed accusation at Georgette. "Are those *real?*"

Georgette gave her a blank look. "Of course. They're never too young to learn. I value my children's education above all things."

"Education? Running with scissors is *educational?* Do you know the harm they could do if they—?"

"Oh, goodness, stop." Tabby snatched the photo from Ilana and set it back on the desktop. "You're much too young to sound like such an old fussbudget. Georgette's a good mother, she knows what she's doing. Now, let's see if she can't teach you what *you'll* be doing, hmm? Dimity, why don't you and I go into the back room and look after a few loose ends while Georgette shows Ilana the ropes."

"The ropes," Dimity repeated. "That's a good one. Ha. Ha. Ha." She followed her younger sister through a pair of double doors directly under the big clock set on the rear wall of the inner office. Every syllable of her laughter was distinct, separate, and precisely equal in tone, volume, and duration. It gave Ilana the chills.

"Uh, okay," she said, turning to Georgette. "So, what do I do here? File? Type? Take care of the mail?"

"Have a seat and I'll show you," Georgette replied, indicating her own desk. While Ilana gingerly settled herself into the cushy black leather swivel chair, her employer vanished into a nearby supply closet. She emerged bearing a manual typewriter, a battered Royal, one of those hulking black metal monsters with round keys and spools of typewriter ribbon. It looked like a refugee from a 1930s movie about hard-hitting newspaper reporters.

Georgette dropped the antique onto the desk in front of Ilana.

"You're joking, right?" Ilana asked.

Georgette frowned at her.

"You're not joking." Ilana uttered a heavy sigh. "What's the problem? Are you afraid to let me use your computer because you think I'll crash the system, or is it for security reasons?"

Georgette's frown melted into laughter. "'*Security reasons*'? In *our* business?"

"Well, *I* don't know. Textiles *could* become weapons of mass destruction in the hands of the wrong fashion designer."

Georgette laughed louder. "You'll be perfectly free to use the computer for all of your other word processing duties," she informed Ilana. "But your main job here is strongly tied to tradition, and this is the traditional way we have been handling *this* part of the business for over a hundred years. You really ought to be grateful. It took me until well into the nineteenth century to get Tabby to phase out quill pens, and when I think of the old split-reed-and-parchment days—!" She made a *Don't ask* gesture.

Ilana *couldn't* ask. She was dumbfounded. She'd heard that having kids could be a mental strain, but she'd never met a woman who'd actually gone entirely nuts from motherhood. Was Georgette really talking about *centuries* past as casually as if she were discussing the final episode of *Friends*? She rested her hands on the desk, ready to push back and dash out the door, never to return.

The stack of black-and-gold-bordered certificates thumped down by her right hand. She hadn't seen Georgette fetch them from anywhere; they simply *appeared.* The manual typewriter began to hum like a dynamo. The top certificate rose up, slipped itself behind the roller, and fed itself through. A faint haze of crackling blue energy clung to the round keys. Meanwhile, before Ilana's astonished eyes, the computer screen burst into life, scrolling out a list of names in 26-point Courier New type.

"Lovely," said Georgette, first checking the screen, then her wristwatch. "Don't you just hate it when the appliances start nagging? This is their subtle way of telling me that we're already behind. Drat. I can't stay and help; I'm supposed to swing by the market to get orange slices for Loden's soccer game in fifteen minutes—don't tell Tabby! You'd better get to work right away. Just type the name on the top line, the cause of death on the second line, then sit back and let the machine fill in the details. Then you place the completed forms over here to your left and—"

"'Cause of *death*'?" Ilana never knew her voice could hit such a screechy high note. "What death? Whose death? What are you talking about? What kind of a textile business needs *death* certificates?"

"They're not death *certificates,* dear." Georgette smiled at her indulgently. "They're death *receipts.* We're the Fates. It's what we do."

LEARN TO KNOW YOUR BOSS

"No," said Ilana. She shook her head emphatically. "When I read the Waiver, I knew this job was going to be *different,* but I was expecting *The Addams Family,* not Stephen King. Death *receipts?* Who signs them? How? With what? Never mind; I don't want to think about it. I quit."

"Don't quit," said Dimity in that cold, deliberate, creepy voice of hers. What was even creepier was the way she was suddenly *there,* on the far side of the desk. Ilana gave a little cry of surprise and pushed herself away from the typewriter, the stack of certificates, and that weird, weird woman. The black leather chair rolled backward fast.

Her short trip came to a tooth-clattering halt when someone intercepted the chair from behind. "*Please* don't quit, Ilana, dear," said Tabby, leaning over the back of the chair. "We *do* so need you!"

"You *can't* quit!" Georgette wailed. "I won't *let* you quit! I swear by the river Styx, if I don't get some personal time off *right now*, heads will roll!"

Her hand darted for the desktop, but instead of grabbing anything that was already there, it vanished up to the elbow. It was as if Georgette had plunged her arm into another part of the universe. When she pulled it back into the real world, she was holding the biggest, blackest, ugliest, most dangerous-looking pair of scissors Ilana had ever seen. They were at least three times the size of the black scissors still on the desk, and they had tiny coils of purple lightning crawling up and down the blades.

Why did they also look so . . . familiar?

All at once, Ilana knew: *Either I just bought a ticket on the* Insanity Express *or else what I'm seeing is real. I'm face-to-face with the Fates; the genuine, actual Fates!*

"Oh my, when Georgette says heads will roll, she means it," Tabby said. Clicking her tongue, she approached Georgette slowly. "Sweetie, listen to me. Put *down* the scissors and step *away* from the mythic rift. Death threats are *not* the way to persuade people to cooperate with you. I thought you learned that when you ran the gift wrap sale at Loden's elementary school."

"Gift . . . wrap . . . sale . . ." Georgette repeated the words like a zombie. "Magazine . . . subscription . . . drive. Band . . .

uniforms . . . fund . . . raiser. Bake . . . sales. So many . . . many . . . bake . . . sales." She shuddered, then muttered something under her breath. The black scissors vanished.

"There. There." Dimity patted Georgette on the back, exactly one pat for every word she spoke. "It's going to be all right. Yes, it is."

Meanwhile, Tabby spun Ilana's chair around to face her. "Dear girl, I wasn't born yesterday. I can tell that you're a bit . . . concerned about your temping duties here."

"What was your first clue?" Ilana snapped.

Tabby ignored her. "You know, I'll bet the problem is that Mrs. Atatosk didn't tell you a *thing* about us before sending you here. She's usually so very thorough about briefing new workers. You *are* new with D. R. Temps, aren't you, dear?"

"Brand-new," Ilana replied. "And I'm going to stay that way." She tried to get out of the chair, but Tabby pushed her back into it almost as an afterthought.

"Oh, foo. I really don't know why Mrs. Atatosk slipped up so dreadfully. It's not like her at all. Something must have been preying on her mind." All at once Tabby thrust her face within an inch of Ilana's. "Did *you* notice anything odd about her when you met?"

"Are you kidding or do you want a list?" Ilana tried to push her chair away again, but Tabby had an iron grip on the armrests.

"Dear girl." It was no longer an endearment. Tabby's normally perky voice was gone. Her new tone was dead serious, with a lot of emphasis on the *dead* part. "Dear girl, I assure you, we are *never* kidding. We may retain a sense of humor about many things, but not when it comes to our work. We are the Fates. We spin and measure and cut the life-threads of every human being on this planet. We don't kid around."

Tabby raised one hand. A long, golden spindle suddenly glittered in her grasp. Some kids might have recognized it from the old *Sleeping Beauty* video, but Ilana had seen the real thing being put to practical use by the women in a dozen African villages, twisting raw fibers like wool or cotton into thread.

"I am Clotho," Tabby said as the spindle twirled and the office filled with the sound of millions of spinning wheels whirring away. "I make the thread of life."

Dimity stepped in view, holding a silver measuring stick. "I am Lachesis," she said, taking hold of one end of the thread that Tabby/Clotho spun. "I measure how long each life will be."

A pair of deathly black scissors flashed before Ilana's eyes, slashing through the thread that Dimity/Lachesis measured. Their keen, lightning-haunted blades closed with a hungry snap that sounded like the slamming shut of a coffin lid. The scissors vanished as Georgette gathered up the severed thread.

"I am Atropos," she declared, clutching the thread to her heart. "And I really, really, *really* need time off to get a pedicure!"

"Uh-*huh*." Ilana nodded, never taking her eyes off the slightly frazzled Fate. It didn't matter that she'd recognized them before they'd introduced themselves; their presence was still overwhelming. She could feel her heart beating rapidly, just this side of a panic attack, but her thoughts remained surprisingly calm:

So the Fates are real and they have an office in Porlock's Landing. How about that. I guess even they couldn't afford the taxes in New York City. They don't look anything like the picture in that Greek myths book Dyllin gave me when I was four. All that time she spent reading it to me, who knew we'd both wind up working for them some day?

Wait a minute, what am I thinking? I'm not *going to be working for them. This isn't real; it can't be!* This *is crazy, and I'm already getting my Minimum Daily Requirement of crazy at home, thanks to Dyllin's stupid wedding. Okay, Ilana, you can get out of this: feet, door, car, home, call for psychiatric help and tell the nice doctor that you caught insanity from your sister. Nothing easier. Except—*

Except what if all this is *for real? What if these* are *the Fates? More important, what if Georgette* is *Atropos, the Fate with the power to wipe out cities with just one snip of those big, ugly shears? Georgette, who's obviously ready to snap.*

As if to prove Ilana's point, Georgette began babbling to her sisters. "Just a simple, basic pedicure, that's all I want. Although I do love the ones where they soak your feet in milk first. Sometimes they add rose petals to the milk bath, too. Oh, and have you ever had the kind where they massage your legs with honey? Or put heated stones betweens your toes? Or use chocolate-scented lotion?"

"There, there, dear," Tabby said in a soothing voice. "Calm down. We'll make sure that you get *completely* dipped in milk and honey and chocolate."

"And rocks," Dimity added.

"I don't want to be dipped in rocks!" Georgette wailed.

She's definitely in a bad way, Ilana thought. *When the Fate in charge of death is at the end of her rope, it could leave a lot of people at the end of their threads* way *ahead of schedule. Not good.*

She took a deep breath and concluded: *To heck with it, there's only one thing for me to do.*

"Pedicure, yes, right," Ilana said eagerly. "Great idea, just what I was about to suggest myself. Why don't you go do that? Have a pedicure. Have two! Have a nice relaxing massage while you're at it. I'll stay for the week, I promise."

"Oh, *will* you?" Georgette cried. She dropped the thread she was holding and swept Ilana out of her chair, into a rib-crushing hug. "I'm *so* glad you changed your mind! How can I ever repay you?" she asked when she finally released Ilana.

"How about by not trampling *that,* okay?" Ilana replied, pointing at the abandoned thread. "I know it's just a symbol, but nobody's life should be covered with dust bunnies, even figuratively."

The Fates laughed.

"Figuratively. Ha," said Dimity.

Ilana raised one eyebrow. "You mean that thread isn't just a symbol? It actually *is* someone's life?" She stared at it uneasily.

"Oh, that's not one of our *real* projects," Tabby said.

"That's just a demo model." Georgette grinned.

"Now it's a floor sample. Ha. Ha. Ha." Dimity picked it up and the thread crumbled into a tiny shower of dust.

Ilana wasn't amused. "I thought you took your work seriously!"

"We most certainly do." Tabby threw her arms around her sisters' shoulders. "Why do you think we called D. R. Temps? To give darling Georgette some time off. No one wants to see *her* get a bad case of job burnout."

"Not while she's holding the scissors," Dimity added.

"We're not so different from you mortals, you know," Tabby told Ilana. "When you get tired on the job, you get careless and make all sorts of little mistakes."

"What's a 'little' mistake for you three? The Black Death?" Ilana asked. "I'm not going to pretend I understand everything that's going on here. I don't know why three of the most powerful beings in the universe chose a flyspeck town like Porlock's Landing to set up shop, and I don't care. All I wanted was a summer job. I got *this* one, and Mrs. Atatosk gave me my pay in advance, so I promise I'm going to earn it. But the *second* that the seven days are up, I'm going to run out of here so fast you'll have to start *last* week if you want to catch me. Clear?"

"Of course, dear." Tabby spoke in the supersoothing tone most people reserve for pacifying cranky children, angry senior citizens, and anyone with an accordion. She took hold of Ilana's chair and steered her back up to the desk like a mother pushing a baby stroller. "And if you do a good job for us *this* week, we'll see if Mrs. Atatosk can spare you for another. I wouldn't mind getting a nice pedicure myself." She straightened the stack of certificates next to the typewriter before following her sisters out of the room.

"Did you even *hear* me?" Ilana shouted after them. "Mrs. Atatosk only sent me here for a one-week trial run, but as far as I'm concerned, the verdict is already *in*. As soon as I finish the week, I'm gone! I quit! I am *history*! Just *one* week and—!"

Tabby paused in the doorway. "Darling, you mustn't make such a fuss about what I just said. I was simply being polite. I didn't really mean that we'd want you back for another week. As a matter of fact, I doubt you'll last past next Wednesday, but I didn't want to hurt your feelings by saying so. If you can hang on long enough to give Georgette just eight solid hours of rest and recreation, we'll be satisfied."

"But Mrs. Atatosk paid me to work here for a *week*," Ilana protested. "It was a lot of money."

Tabby rolled her eyes. "Eight hours, three days, a week, whatever; we don't care. Why should mortal time and money matter to us? Just try to keep up for as long as you can, dear. We really don't have very high expectations for you. As long as Georgette gets a break and you don't do anything too stupid, we'll be satisfied. Ta-ta!" With that, she shut the door.

Ilana sat at her desk, folded her arms, and fumed. Her new employers had managed to get her so mad that resentment had overwhelmed every other thought and emotion, including her initial panic on discovering the true nature of the work done behind the doors of Tabby Fabricant Textiles.

How dare *that Tabby or Clotho or whatever her name is talk to me like that!* she thought bitterly. *I* hate *being patronized. So I got a little freaked when I found out I'm working for the Fates; did that give her the right to assume I was going to* stay *freaked?*

Huh! I'd worry if I hadn't freaked out. 'Hi, we're the Fates! You've read the myths, now eat the raisin-walnut muffins we baked for you!' Who could accept something like that *without panicking just a little? The kind of person who'd tell them, 'Why, thank you, I'll share them with my special friend, Boo-Boo the magic pink unicorn,' that's who!*

I guess it all comes down to this: Either I'm really working for the actual, genuine, straight-out-of-Greek-mythology Fates, or I've lost my mind.

She slipped one hand into the pocket of her black skirt and touched the comfortably fat roll of twenties. She hadn't had the chance to get to the bank yet, so she'd decided to carry her first week's pay with her rather than risk Mom finding it and asking some awkward questions. Carrying so much cash locally was fairly low-risk. Aside from the occasional schoolyard bully stealing lunch money, Porlock's Landing wasn't exactly teeming with muggers.

Well, the money's real enough, she thought. *I used some of it to pay for gas last night, and the cashier didn't act like I'd handed her a fistful of dead leaves. So I suppose the Fates are at least as real as that, except—*

Except even if I'm not crazy and this is all real, it's still kind of creepy. Death receipts. Ugh. I don't like it.

But just because I don't like *it, doesn't mean I can't* do *it. For God's sake,* Dyllin *used to work here! If she could handle it, why should the Fates think* I *can't?*

"Like I can't do a simple job," she muttered, glowering at the typewriter. "Like this is *so* hard that I won't last a week!"

"Like you never heard of reverse psychology," said a small, thin voice from somewhere high overhead. "Sucker!"

Ilana darted her eyes all around the room. She was alone, as far as she could tell. Then she recalled her recent experience with the Fates and realized that she probably *couldn't* tell. Not for sure.

"Who's there?" she asked the air. "Tabby? Dimity? Georgette? Do you want me to get some work done for you or do you want to waste time playing stupid games? Fine, have it your way. I don't care; I got paid." She stretched her arms up high, then linked her fingers, put her hands behind her head, and tilted as far back as her chair would go.

A huge dusty-gray spider the size of a tennis ball dropped from the ceiling onto Ilana's stomach. She was still gasping from the impact when it scuttled straight up her chest and onto the end of her chin. Ilana gazed into multiple pairs of beady eyes like tiny rubies, too petrified to scream.

"Hey, girlfriend, working hard or hardly working?" The spider's face shifted shape, the bristly surface turning to smooth, ivory-colored skin, the clashing mouthparts becoming a human smile, the multiple red dots merging into two golden-brown eyes complete with brows and lashes. A sharp nose and a tumble of silky black curls completed the change.

This time, Ilana *did* scream.

"Whoa, whoa, whoa!" The spider scrambled off Ilana's chin to the center of her chest. "Don't hate me because I'm beautiful!"

"GetoffgetoffgetoffgetoffgetOFF!" Ilana leaped to her feet and jigged around the room, fluttering her hands wildly at her uninvited passenger.

The human-faced spider hung on. It was amazing that something so relatively small could fill an entire room with a single, weary sigh. "You know, I don't want to act bossy, but if you *really* want me to get off you, you'd have more luck if you actually *swatted* me."

Ilana screamed again, grabbed the hem of her shirt and flapped it while she wriggled and shook herself all over. It did no good.

"Girl, do you *want* to see what spider barf looks like? Because I can tell you right now, you're going to and it won't be pretty. How about you stand still for a minute and *ask* me to step off? Nicely."

Ilana froze. She looked down the front of her shirt to where the outlandish arachnid still clung and in a strained voice whispered, "Would you mind getting off me? Now? Please?"

The spider grinned. "That's more like it. Give me a lift over to Georgette's desk, okay? My home's all the way up there—" The creature pointed one hairy foreleg at a web-draped corner of the ceiling. "And the commute's a pain in the spinnerets. Anything for a shortcut."

Ilana moved slowly over to the desk and even made a kind of drawbridge by stretching with the bottom of her shirt so that the spider didn't have to jump the distance. As soon as the creature scampered off her, she breathed again.

Instead of crawling away, the spider hoisted itself onto the typewriter keys, settled back, and gave Ilana a thoughtful look. "Isn't *this* interesting. You bounce back in, like, two seconds when the Fates reveal themselves to you in all their world-altering power, you're willing to spend a week up to your elbows in death receipts, but the sight of one poor, innocent, ordinary little spider sends you over the edge? Wow. D. R. Temps sure is hiring wimps these days."

"'Ordinary'?" Ilana echoed, so incredulous she forgot to be afraid. "'Little'? Compared to what, a rhinoceros?"

"Hey! Watch it with the cheap shots about my size." The spider scowled. "I can't help it if I have a slow metabolism. And it's summer; I always retain water in the summer. Besides, I'm big-boned!"

"You're a spider," Ilana said. "You're no-boned."

"Well, well, I see *someone's* got an attitude problem." The spider tried to stay angry, but its scowl twisted into a smirk. "Get you mad enough and you forget about everything else. Attitude like that, maybe it'll help you do this job. On the other leg, it could blow up in your face. Maybe you should try to control it just a bit."

"Look, bug," Ilana said. "I've gotten That Attitude Thing lecture from my mother, my father, my sister, my best friend, and half the teachers at school. Why should I waste my time listening to it from an eight-legged nightmare like *you*?"

To her surprise, the human-faced spider took the attack quite calmly. "Why listen to me?" the creature asked casually. "Because I *invented* That Attitude Thing over four thousand years ago, and look where it got me! The name's Arachne, not 'bug.' And you must be Loudmouth. Pleased to meet you."

OFFICE FRIENDSHIPS MAKE WORK *FUN*

Half a stale cinnamon donut and three soda bottle caps full of mint tea later, Arachne accepted Ilana's apology.

"Forget about it," the spider said graciously, wiping specks of cinnamon-sugar off her mouth. "To tell you the truth, I'd rather see a girl with too much attitude instead of some spineless little blob of dandelion fluff with none at all."

"Wasn't having *too* much attitude the reason why you look like . . . became . . . resemble . . ." Ilana knew the myth; she just wasn't sure if it was polite to bring it up.

"If you're trying to find a tactful way to say 'It's your own fault you got turned into a spider, stupid,' don't bother," Arachne said cheerfully. "It's the truth, in a way. I was the best weaver in all of Greece, back in the day. You ever do any weaving?"

Ilana thought about it. "I wove a pot holder for my mother once, at summer camp. We used those stretchy loops and a square metal frame with prongs along the edges."

"Was it fun?"

"You mean boring?"

Arachne chuckled. "Welcome to my world. Back then, weaving was something every woman *had* to do, even queens. So I figured as long as I *had* to do it, I might as well make the best of it. Funny thing, pretty soon I got so good at that no-choice chore that I liked it. I didn't just make cloth, I created *art*, and I was proud of it." She took another sip of bottle-cap tea. "Okay, so maybe I got a little *too* proud. I bragged about what a great weaver I was. The trouble was, I didn't know when to *stop* bragging."

Ilana nodded. "You said you were a better weaver than the goddess Athena, so she challenged you to a tapestry-weaving contest."

"Athena," Arachne grumbled. "Don't get me started on Athena. What a snot. You'd think that the goddess of wisdom would be a little . . . oh, I don't know, *smarter*? She's a goddess, I was a mortal, why should she care if I went around claiming that I was a better weaver than she was? I was going to be *dead* in twenty, maybe thirty years, tops! She could have waited. But no, she decided I needed to have a 'learning experience.'"

The spider tried to make sarcastic air quotes with her forelegs, lost her balance, toppled off the desk, and landed in the empty donut box at Ilana's feet. She was covered in powdered sugar by the time she clambered out.

Ilana couldn't help laughing. "Ooh, ghost spider: spooooooky!"

"Ha, ha, ha. You're a regular exterminator, I'm dying laughing," Arachne deadpanned, then scooted straight up Ilana's leg, into her lap, and leaped back onto the desk.

"Hey!" Ilana jumped up, wiping at the smeary white sugar trail Arachne had left on her clothes. "Do I look like a ladder?"

"That depends," Arachne said, gracefully grooming the powdered sugar off her legs and body. "If I say 'Yes, all rung out,' will you hit me with a *big* book or a little one?"

Ilana made a disgusted sound. "I've got to get some damp paper towels for this. Thanks a *lot*." She stomped off toward a small blue door in the back of the room.

"Hey!" Arachne hollered after her. "Wait a minute, you're not allowed back there! That's not the toi—!" It was no use, Ilana had already turned the silvery doorknob and flung the door wide.

"Wow." She stood in the doorway, gazing open-mouthed into the room beyond. "What *is* this place?"

"Like I was trying to tell you, it's not the toilet." Arachne sounded annoyed, but nervous too. "Now close that door and get back here. Coffee break is over. You've got a job to do."

Ilana didn't move. "So many spindles," she said in an awestruck whisper. "And they're all *turning*."

"Good, that's what they're supposed to be doing. You don't want them to stop, trust me." The spider anchored one end of a webbing thread to the corner of the desk and slid safely to the floor, then pattered across the linoleum to stand at Ilana's feet in the doorway. "Move along, move along. Go back to your job.

Nothing more to see here. Authorized personnel only. Shoo, scat, vamoose, *go*!"

Ilana went, just not in the direction Arachne wanted her to go. Instead of obeying the bossy bug and returning docilely to her desk, she walked straight into the room beyond the blue door.

"This is impossible," she breathed, looking all around her. "Where are the *walls*?" She was standing between a double line of sturdy bookshelves that ran endlessly into the distance. More lines of identical bookshelves stretched away to left and right, and when she tilted her head back she saw them soaring up, up, up toward a ceiling that wasn't there, either.

There wasn't a single book to be seen.

Instead, on every shelf, each in its own neat little glass-fronted box, a golden spindle twirled. Some spun wildly, some slowly, some turned so gradually that they looked ready to stop altogether, but all of them moved and filled the endless room with their own peculiar music, the warm, comforting, constant hum of life.

There was no telling how long Ilana would have stood with her mouth hanging open if Arachne hadn't scaled up her back like a cliff.

"Helloooo, I'm talking to you," the spider said, miffed. "Do you at least want to *pretend* to listen, or do you have an earwax problem?" She stuck the tip of one prickly foreleg into Ilana's ear to make her point.

It worked. It worked a little *too* well. Ilana squealed like a gerbil and jumped so high that she bumped into the nearest shelf with her shoulder, making the wooden boxes clatter. A sudden silence fell, a silence so deep and great and terrible that Ilana thought her heart had stopped. It lasted only an instant, but that was more than enough. Then the humming began again.

"Oh gods, I think I webbed myself." Arachne's voice was shaking. "Now will you please be a good girl and *get the heck out of this room?"*

Ilana didn't need to be told again. She sprinted out of the spindle room so fast that Arachne tumbled off her shoulder and had to scurry after her. The hapless spider came within an inch of being squashed when Ilana slammed the small blue door.

Panting hard, Ilana flopped into her chair and shivered. "What *was* that place?"

"You're no Athena, but I'll bet you can figure it out," Arachne answered, making her way back up to the desktop via Ilana's leg once again. This time Ilana didn't even flinch at the spider's touch.

"Was that—? Were those *everyone's* life-threads? Everyone on earth?"

"Everyone except this bunch." The spider crawled over and tapped the stack of death receipts still awaiting processing. "And the ones in the other offices."

"What other offices?"

Arachne rolled her eyes. "Do you really think that the Fates do all their work from *Porlock's Landing*? In *Connecticut*? It's a great place to raise kids, but the croissants are better in Paris, the sushi's fresher in Tokyo, the barbecued lamb ribs rock in Kansas City, and you can't beat the coffee in Hawaii."

Ilana sat up and confronted the spider. "Are you telling me that the Fates work out of different offices around the world for the *food*?"

"Would you want to manage the lives of every human being in the world on an empty stomach?" Arachne countered. "Especially when you stop and think about some of the things that *happen* to those people?"

"You mean the way they make them die." Ilana's face became unreadable. She touched the little skull doodle on her cheek unconsciously.

Arachne did a good imitation of a quiz show's WRONG ANSWER buzzer sound. "The Fates only decide *when* people die. *How* isn't their department."

"Whose department is it?"

"Why, you feel like doing some temp work *there*? Trust me, it'll never happen. Everything about that department is strictly permanent."

Ilana took a deep breath and let it out slowly. "So I'm only working for one small, local manifestation of the Fates."

"No, what you're doing right now is *not* working," Arachne pointed out. "How about we fix that before the sisters come back? You know, before *I* get in trouble?"

"Why would you get in trouble for something I did—I mean, something I didn't do?"

"Oh please, I wasn't metamorphosed yesterday. I've been taking the heat for stuff that's not my fault ever since the big weave-off with Athena." Arachne gestured at her inhuman body and gave a wry smile. "You know, I *won* that contest. Some prize, huh? We were both going at it full tilt. Athena was weaving a tapestry showing what happens whenever we uppity little mortals challenge the gods: Bellerophon tries to fly all the way to Olympus on a winged horse, Zeus flattens him with a thunderbolt, stuff like that. So I wove a tapestry showing that maybe the gods aren't so perfect either, that they're more human than they want to believe. I put in pictures of all the silly things they did when they fell in love with mortals. Mostly I zinged Zeus. He turned himself into a swan, a bull, a shower of gold coins, you name it, all just so he could score with the ladies. Next thing I know, Athena's tearing my tapestry to shreds, busting up my loom, and I'm dangling from the ceiling thinking, 'Boy, I could really go for some moth à la mode right about now.'"

"You got turned into a spider for *that*?" Ilana shook her head in disbelief.

"Well, you've got to remember that Zeus is Athena's father. I guess she didn't like anyone trash-talking, er, trash-weaving Daddy." Arachne sighed. "Anyway, ever since then, all the gods have had it in for me just because they can't take constructive criticism. What a bunch of omnipotent babies! That's why I holed up with the Fates. They're usually so busy that they leave me alone. It's hard to carry a grudge when your hands are always full. But just let anything go wrong around here, and what happens? Blame the spider."

"Why do you stay near *any* of the gods?" Ilana asked. "It's a pretty big world out there."

"It's a pretty lonely one, too." Arachne's bulbous body sagged with gloom. "Be honest: How many people would be willing to have a conversation with a king-sized spider, with or without a human face? Run away screaming, sure, *that* they'll do. At least the Fates don't do that. Sometimes I just need someone—any-one—to talk to."

"I understand." Ilana extended her index finger and gently lifted Arachne's right foreleg. It was the closest she could come to taking the spider by the hand. "Will I do?"

NEVER BRING YOUR OFFICE PROBLEMS HOME

"How did you like your first day of work, dear?" Ilana's mother asked as she passed the pizza.

"Okay." Ilana dropped a slice onto her plate, then quickly took a huge bite, hoping that a full mouth would excuse her from going into details.

The Newhouses were gathered around the dining room table that Friday night, but it wasn't because they liked to kick off the weekend with an elegant family dinner. How elegant could anyone be, eating pizza off paper plates left over from the after-Easter sale at the local discount store? Cheerful chicks and happy rabbits danced wing-in-paw over a pastel landscape that was quickly sinking under the relentless drip-drip-drip of hot olive oil and melted cheese.

The only reason the Newhouses were eating all their meals in the dining room was because the kitchen table was buried two feet deep in invitations, seating charts, fabric swatches, calendars, catalogs, contracts, business cards, brochures, photographs, and an assorted avalanche of other rubbish connected with Dyllin's wedding.

"Where *did* you go to work, Ilana?" Her father reached for the Parmesan cheese. "You never told us."

"Mmf, mmf." Ilana pointed to her crammed cheeks and gave her father an apologetic smile. Still chewing, she put down her slice and wiggled her fingers over the plate, working an invisible typewriter.

"Oh, *office* work." Her father nodded his approval. "For a while your mother and I were afraid you'd wind up flipping burgers. Not that there's anything wrong with an honest job, but let's face it, some work experience does look more impressive when the time comes."

Ilana didn't have to ask *When the time comes for what?* She knew. It was merely the second-most-important thing in her parents' lives, after Dyllin's wedding: getting her into a "good" college. And by "good" they meant "prestigious," as in Ivy League/Seven Sisters, as in something else to brag about to their friends.

"We're *very* proud of you, dear," her mother said. "Getting a good summer job all by yourself is a major achievement. It shows initiative, independence, motivation, focus . . ."

Jeez, why doesn't she just write my college application essay for *me?* Ilana thought, trying to tune out.

". . . drive, ambition, inspiration . . ." Ilana's mother continued to drone on through the list of words that were sure to make any admissions board worth its ACCEPTED stamp sit up and beg like a bunch of trained dachshunds. ". . . enthusiasm, and— Ilana, this place where you're working, are they at all connected with some sort of charity? Something altruistic? Do they *give back to the community?*"

Ilana swallowed her overchewed bite of pizza, took a quick sip of cola from the can, and said, "Oh, absolutely. They're totally involved. Globally. You can't imagine how many people depend on them for real life-or-death stuff."

"Wonderful!" Mrs. Newhouse exclaimed. Ilana's parents exchanged beaming smiles.

"You know, Ilana," her father said. "If you do a good enough job for them, they just might be willing to write you a letter of recommendation when the time comes."

Ilana shrugged. "I doubt it. I'm only there until the end of next week. It's just a temp job."

"Temp?" For an instant, Dyllin took notice. Up to that point she'd spent dinnertime sunk in a bottomless puddle of misery and gloom.

Ilana could have kicked herself. That was all she needed, Dyllin taking an interest in her job. What if she started asking questions? Questions like *What's the name of the temp agency?* and *D. R. Temps?* My *old place? How did someone like* you *ever find out about them?* and inevitably, because Dyllin was *much* too good at putting two and two together, *What the hell were you doing, nosing around in my room, you little brat?*

Ilana poised her pizza slice close to her lips, ready to take another huge, answer-avoiding bite.

Please *don't let her tell Mom and Dad about the kind of clients D. R. Temps helps! Somehow I just don't think "Has experience typing death receipts" and "Welcome to Harvard" go together in their book.*

"Temp work's good," Dyllin said. "You can make your own schedule. That means there's no way you'll miss the fittings for your maid of honor gown, or any of the showers and rehearsals. Perfect. For a moment I was afraid you'd gotten yourself a summer job that was going to interfere with my wedding."

"Oh, of *course* not," Ilana said. "I'd never want to have any part of *my* unimportant little life run the slightest risk of interfering with *your* wedding! The only reason I'm doing summer work is so I can save up enough money to have my appendix taken out in advance, just so there'd be no chance of it flaring up and ruining *your* wedding."

"Ilana," her father said severely. "Ilana, are you being sarcastic?"

She laughed so hard that bits of mozzarella flew everywhere.

"Ugh! That is *so* typical!" Dyllin leaped up from her place at the table and tossed her head like an angry Thoroughbred. "This is only the most important day of my life that we're talking about here, but does it matter to her? No! She couldn't care less. Did you ever see anyone so selfish in your life?"

A hush fell over the Newhouse dinner table. The girls' parents looked at one another nervously, biting their lips. Ilana clamped both hands over her mouth, trying to suppress another attack of laughter.

Dyllin glared poison-tipped daggers at her family. "Oh, thank you all *so* very much for your support," she snarled. "If that's all that my happiness means to you, then fine, forget about it, I'll call Ras, we'll cancel the wedding and just elope!" With that, she burst into loud, stormy tears and ran out of the room.

"Great!" Ilana announced cheerfully. "Wedding canceled, problem solved, and I don't have to wear that puke-colored dress. Dreams *do* come true!"

Her parents didn't share her joy.

"I'll go talk to her," her mother said, pushing her chair back and trailing after her elder daughter.

Ilana's father looked grim. "You'd better hope that your mother manages to get Dyllin to change her mind, young lady," he said.

"Why?" Ilana demanded. "I *want* her to drop this whole stupid wedding thing before it's too late and she drives all of us to be as crazy as she is."

"Your sister is under a great deal of pressure right now," her father said.

Ilana rolled her eyes. Here it came, the Big Excuse: the stupid, flimsy justification for all of her sister's bossy behavior. Ever since May, when Dyllin had announced her engagement and started making everyone's life a rose-petals-candlelight-and-lace nightmare, Ilana had heard the Big Excuse from one or the other of her parents whenever there was a major family blowup like this.

"I know, Daddy, I know." Ilana could recite the Big Excuse

just as well as he could. "They have to have the wedding in a hurry—notbecauseshe'spregnantGrandma—because her fiancé got a wonderful job offer in Europe, starting right after Labor Day, and it has to be a big wedding because that's always been her dream ever since she was a little girl, and it's the least we can do for Dyllin after all she's done for this family." Ilana stopped her recitation, caught her breath, then added her own footnote to the Big Excuse: "Whatever the heck *that* was."

"Your sister has done plenty for this family. She's been unfailingly helpful and *supportive.*" He gave his younger daughter a meaningful look when he said that.

"You got sent to Africa and dragged Mom and me with you for three years; *she* got to stay here and house-sit on the weekends she was home from college. She watered the plants, cut the grass, shoveled snow, changed lightbulbs, and stopped the local kids from egging the house on Halloween. You make it sound like she paid off the mortgage, fought wolves with her bare hands, and saved the homestead from a plague of locusts! Look, I know you think she's perfect, but stop pretending she's a total saint. If you and Mom want to keep Dyllin from eloping because you've already put down a big bundle of nonrefundable deposits for wedding stuff, just say so!"

Her father clicked his tongue. "Envy is not an attractive quality, Ilana. I realize that your mother and I have been paying a great deal of attention to Dyllin lately, but if you'll be honest about it, you'll realize that you had our undivided attention for the past three years."

"That's not all I had," Ilana said coldly.

Her father looked as if she'd punched him the chest. He said nothing, but he too got up and left the dining room. Ilana rested her head in her hands and stared at the grease swirls and pizza crusts on her plate, hating herself to the heart.

Stupid, stupid, stupid! *As if he doesn't blame himself enough for what happened to me, did I have to rub it in like that?* Ilana's angry thoughts were invaded by memories of how her father's face had looked when she'd finally come out of the fever. *That was when I knew: You don't have to catch a disease to be one of its victims.*

When the phone rang, she rushed to answer it, desperate for anything to take her mind off what she'd just said to her father. If only she had more friends! Then it might be a call from one of them asking her to go for coffee or something, anything to get her out of the house. But in the year since the Newhouses had come back from Africa, Ilana had only managed to make one.

"Ilana?" Mrs. Atatosk's perky voice was unmistakable. "Dear child, I'm so glad I caught you. I'm dreadfully sorry, but I must ask you to do me a little favor. I need you to go into New Haven this evening and meet with some of our other temps. We have these Friday meetings so everyone can compare notes and take care of silly little bureaucratic details. It's also where you'll be picking up your pay in the future—I don't feel comfortable sending cash through the mail, and it's *much* less stuffy than having all of you come trooping into the office every week. Here's the address."

Ilana jotted down the directions Mrs. Atatosk dictated, all

the while struggling to get a word in edgewise. "Mrs.— Listen, Mrs. Atatosk, it's kind of— Mrs. Atatosk, isn't it a little late for a meeting?"

"Don't be silly, dear, it's the shank of the evening."

"The what?"

"It's *early*; not even seven o'clock. Have you had your dinner?"

"Yes, but I—"

"Do you need a ride into New Haven? Is that it? Is someone else using your car?"

"No, but—"

"Well, then, do hurry up and go. You don't want to keep your fellow employees waiting; that wouldn't be professional of you."

"Listen, Mrs. Atatosk, about these fellow employees. Anything you want to *tell* me about them? Any distinguishing marks? Wings? Horns? Vast cosmic powers? Freckles? Or do you just want it to be another surprise?"

"Surprise, dear?" Mrs. Atatosk repeated. She tried to sound innocent and failed.

"Yes, surprise," Ilana said firmly. "Like the one I got this morning when I found out who I'm *really* working for. Why didn't you *tell* me?"

"Why didn't you ask? Goodness, child, we at D. R. Temps have to find out *somehow* whether our new workers can think on their feet. I'm sure that when you meet your fellow employees this evening, they'll tell you similar stories about their first day on the job. Now off you go!"

"But Mrs. Atatosk, I don't even know if they'll *be* my fellow employees," Ilana protested. "You've only got me signed up for a one-week trial period, remember? I don't even know if I *want* this job to last any longer, and I still haven't turned in my—"

That was when she realized that she'd been talking to a dead line. Mrs. Atatosk had hung up the phone.

○ ○ ○

Less than an hour later, Ilana was sunk deep into an overstuffed purple armchair in the back of the strangest coffee shop she had ever seen. It occupied a hole-in-the-wall storefront on a New Haven street within spitting distance of the Yale University campus and was so crammed with furniture, decorations, and bric-a-brac that it seemed ready to erupt into a sidewalk sale at any moment. Burgundy-draped walls were hung with images of stars, crescent moons, bundles of wheat and barley, mermaids, cats, rabbits, and foxes. The air was thick with the smell of cake, coffee, and oranges, loud with the sound of one female singer's CD after another. Several small blackboards displayed a menu featuring drinks like Latte Liberation, Matriarchy Mocchachino, Sisterhood Chai, and Triple Hot Chocolate Inner Goddess with Whipped Cream. Curlicued letters in ruby and gold on the narrow window named it the WYMYN'S KOFFEE KOVEN, though there were several male customers scattered among the plush chairs and gleaming coffee tables. All of them looked jittery, and not just from the caffeine.

A pretty girl sat in the matching armchair across from Ilana's.

She'd already introduced herself as Joanna Harris and she'd been waiting at the door to greet Ilana, discreetly holding up a D. R. Temps brochure. "Mrs. Atatosk told me it was your first meeting," she said between sips of espresso.

Ilana smiled. "Yeah, I'm a total newbie." Even though it was a coffee shop, she'd opted for herbal tea. With the excitement of her first day's work already likely to keep her awake, she didn't want to guarantee a night's lost sleep by drinking anything caffeinated.

"Welcome, total newbie!" A tall, dark-haired young man vaulted over the back of the chair facing Ilana, never spilling a single speck of froth from the huge cup of cappuccino balanced on his left hand. He flung himself into the seat sideways, legs dangling over one armrest, took a long, loud slurp from the red-and-black-glazed cup, and flashed Ilana a blinding smile from beneath a temporary mustache of milky foam. "Max Kaufman, at your service. So, has Joanna told you the rule?"

"What rule?"

"Newbie buys the first round." He rattled his cup, making the pair of chocolate biscotti on the saucer dance.

"Max, sit up straight and step out of the spotlight for once in your life," Joanna said. "Give Ilana a chance to breathe."

"Ilana? Pretty name. Hey, don't get me wrong; I'm all in favor of breathing." Max raised his cup in a toast to respiration. "Even for newbies." But he did sit up straight. "Tell you what, Ilana, let's shelve the Newbie Rule until next Friday. I've been getting no-show phone calls from most of the others, and it looks like

Joanna and I may be it for tonight. No sense making you buy a first round for just two people."

"We usually have our meetings on Friday afternoons, not evenings," Joanna said. "Our employers have to let us attend, and then we're honor-bound to put in a couple of extra hours at work afterward. Today, though, the Koffee Koven's owner needed the place for another afternoon event, so Mrs. Atatosk rescheduled us."

"Yeah, too bad the other temps couldn't make it here this evening," Max added. "You'll just have to meet them next Friday."

"I thought you *had* to come to these meetings," Ilana said.

Max shook his head. "That's not always possible. Some of them are temping so far away from New Haven that we might not see them all summer."

"I thought all our work was local," Ilana said.

Max shook his head. "The hiring's local, the work can be anywhere your employer needs you. Right now we've got one kid up in Toronto, another in L.A., someone who had to go all the way to Paris this week—I know, what a sacrifice, huh?—and there's even a rumor about a job opening next week in Hawaii."

"Hawaii . . ." A yearning look came into Ilana's eyes. For the first time since she'd begun work for D. R. Temps, she didn't feel compelled to mention that she might be quitting the temp agency at the end of next week.

"I know what you're thinking. Don't get your hopes up," Max teased.

"What Max *means* is you've got to have at least one of these before Mrs. Atatosk will send you anywhere too far from home base," Joanna said. She pointed to three tiny silver acorns dangling from the gold pin on her T-shirt. "One for every year with D. R. Temps."

Ilana sighed. "Just as well. I don't know how I'd manage to hide a trip to Hawaii from my parents."

Max snapped his fingers. "You never have to. D. R. Temps handles the details."

"Being in Hawaii for a whole week is a pretty big detail."

"Come on, Ilana, we're temping for the *gods,* here," Max said. "They've got the cash *and* the power to do whatever it takes to buy themselves a little time off."

"He's right," Joanna said. "My mother thinks I've been working at the Crystal Mall out in Waterford for the past three summers. Mrs. Atatosk took care of the whole thing."

"I guess Mrs. Atatosk isn't half as squirrelly as she acts," Ilana said. "It was nice of her to make sure I didn't miss my first temps' meeting." *Unless she figured I wouldn't last until next Friday and this would be my* only *temps' meeting,* she thought. "I really appreciate getting to meet the two of you."

"To trade horror stories?" Max shrugged. "What can I say? I'm a giver. I remember how freaked out I was after my first day working for D. R. Temps. I was sure I was having the longest, most detailed hallucination in the history of the universe."

"Not that Max ever exaggerates, you understand," Joanna said drily.

"Come on, like you never thought you were going crazy your first day on the job?" Max challenged her.

Joanna conceded. "We all go through that. But after the first group meeting, everyone always feels better."

"So this is not so much a 'Welcome, Newbie' meeting as a 'Hooray, You're Not Crazy After All' party?" Ilana asked, smiling.

"You could say that." Max nibbled one of his biscotti. "So who are you working for?"

"The Fates."

Max let out a long, low whistle. "Wow. You're a newbie and Mrs. A. sent you to *them*? That's pretty heavy stuff." Joanna nodded agreement.

"I guess." Ilana shrugged. Max made it sound like she was getting hands-on experience with the life-threads of every man, woman, and child on earth instead of face time with a souped-up typewriter and a spider. As for Joanna, she was staring at her in awe. It made Ilana feel extremely uncomfortable.

I don't want them to think I'm more important than I really am, she thought. *But if I tell them the truth, they'll think I'm just a grunt. Maybe I should just change the subject.* "Anyway, it's just for a week. So, who do you two work for?"

"I temp for Demeter and Persephone," Joanna replied with a happy sigh. All at once the air around her smelled like ripe peaches, apples, pears, and sun-warmed grain. "It's a great job, very down-to-earth. All I have to do is walk through the fields and bless the crops. Oh, and sometimes I have to put in an appearance at farmers' markets and country fairs. Demeter loves her work, but spring and summer are the only times she gets to spend with her daughter ever since Persephone became the bride of Hades, lord of the Underworld."

Max leaned over and whispered in Ilana's ear, "Ask her why a goddess married a mob boss."

"Nice try," Ilana whispered back. "I know what 'Underworld' means. Persephone's the queen of the dead."

"You *knew* that?" Max raised an eyebrow. "How?"

"When I was little, my sister gave me a big book about the Greek myths. She used to read it to me until I got old enough to read it to myself." Ilana's voice turned wistful as she remembered those times when every conversation with Dyllin *didn't* end in a fight. "I liked the stories, so I kept reading more."

"Oh." Max looked disappointed that his attempted joke had fallen flat.

"Better luck next time." Joanna laughed. "He always pulls that one on the newbies. Unlike you, Max, some of us actually *read* mythology before coming to work for D. R. Temps."

"I read mythology!" Max objected. Then, sheepishly, he added, "Now."

"Well, that's an improvement," Joanna said. "I heard that when you were a newbie, everything you knew about the gods came from reruns of *Xena, Hercules,* and a bunch of old movies."

"Hey, what's wrong with sword-and-sandal flicks?" Ilana spoke up. "*Jason and the Argonauts* is a classic!"

Max solemnly took his unnibbled chocolate biscotto and presented it to Ilana. "You are a woman of taste and discernment. It's an honor to work with you, unlike *some* people." He gave Joanna a theatrically scornful look.

"Oh, for—" Joanna rolled her eyes and chose to pretend that the entire exchange with Max hadn't interrupted her. "*As I was saying,* I temp for Demeter and Persephone, but I do most of the actual *work* for Demeter. I look after the crops so she and Persephone are free to hit the beach, catch a Broadway show in the city, even get mother-daughter pedicures."

"What is it with goddesses and pedicures?" Ilana wondered out loud.

"Who cares, as long as it keeps them crazy about Joanna?" Max said with a grin. "It pays to have connections, especially with the gods. That's why Joanna's one of our favorite people when it's time for the end-of-summer party. Since she temps for the goddess of the harvest, guess who brings most of the food? The *free* food?"

"What do you bring, Max?" Ilana asked.

Max puffed up happily under any kind of attention. "Oh, we can't have a really good time without me. I'm a specialist: I temp for the party gods!"

Joanna leaned toward Ilana. "What he means is he usually temps for Dionysus, the god of wine. Which would be great *if* any of us were old enough to drink and *if* the gods themselves didn't show up to chaperone the party. Some of them are really strict about rules and laws."

"Yeah, she's right." Max slumped in his chair, deflated. "Hades is the worst. If you get carded by the king of the dead, you don't forget it."

"Sit up straight, Max," Joanna said again, automatically.

This time Max didn't move. "As long as I keep my feet off the furniture, I'm okay. It's not a posture issue with her."

"What? I didn't say a word!" Ilana protested. "About posture *or* feet on the furniture."

"He doesn't mean you, Ilana," Joanna said. "He means the owner of this place. She's kind of . . . strict about the whole feet-off-the-furniture thing. But she's really supportive and lets us have our Friday meetings here. So she's not so bad, really."

"Speak for yourself," Max said grumpily. "I'm just glad she's out for the evening. The lady who made my cappuccino said so."

"Oh, too bad." Joanna looked disappointed. "I guess you'll have to wait until next Friday to meet her, Ilana."

"Sure, I'd like that," Ilana said. To her surprise, she realized she meant it.

This is one bizarre summer job, she thought. *But now that I've met Max and Joanna it doesn't seem so bad. I like them, and I think—I hope—they like me. Is this a misery-loves-company situation or something more?*

I wish I could talk to Dyllin about all this, the way we used to. She temped for the Fates and she found a way to handle it.

If she could get through three summers with D. R. Temps, I can get through one.

If I make it through my trial run, that is.

Ilana raised her teacup to Max and Joanna. "Here's to next Friday." *I hope I'm still working for D. R. Temps by then,* she thought. And for the first time, the idea of quitting her just-begun summer job was replaced by the fear of losing it.

EMPLOYEES MUST WASH HANDS AFTER USING BATHROOM FACILITIES

"What was I *thinking*, Heather?" Ilana stabbed a straw through the top of her soda lid and took a long drink. It was lunchtime on Saturday, but Friday's dinner table scene with her father was still along for the ride. "Why did I even mention it? He's never forgiven himself for what happened to me, and if I keep reminding him about it he never will. I am such a *brat*."

Heather didn't even look up from the tower of French fries she was building on her tray. For one of the most popular girls in Ilana's high school and a cheerleader to boot she had an unexpectedly offbeat side.

Ilana and Heather had been in the same seventh-grade class

at Nutmeg Rise Middle School when Ilana and her parents left Porlock's Landing for Africa three years ago. All of the kids had promised to write, and they had . . . once or twice at most. Heather was the only one who kept up the correspondence for the full three years that Ilana was gone.

When her family returned, Ilana hesitated to contact her faithful pen pal. Heather's letters had been all full of the typical, ordinary school stuff she'd been doing, even if it was all drenched in the magic potion of popularity. It was a far cry from Ilana's own experiences.

People who live in fairy tales don't have anything in common with people who've lived in nightmares, Ilana thought. *I'll bet the only reason she kept writing was because she felt sorry for me, especially after I got sick. Now that I'm back—a real person instead of a piece of paper—she won't want to bother with someone like me.*

And that was what Ilana sincerely believed up until the moment that the two of them met by accident one late September evening while waiting to get into Toad's Place in New Haven for a "Weird Al" Yankovic concert. They didn't recognize each other—they'd never remembered to swap recent photos, and after her illness Ilana wanted to smash any camera that came near her because of her scars—so they simply started to talk and before long they formed a "Wow, Porlock's Landing? Sorry to hear that; me, too" bond. By the time they exchanged names, followed by delighted shrieks of "No *way*!" it was too late for Ilana to maintain her conviction that she and Heather could never be friends. They already were.

After a whole sophomore year, their friendship was rock-solid. Unfortunately, it was also the only friendship Ilana had managed to make since her family's return.

She often comforted herself for her lack of more friends by thinking: *So what? I'd rather have* one *good friend like Heather than a room full of hi-how-are-you-have-a-great-summer people. I don't have to put on an act with her. She knows me, she gets my twisted jokes and I get hers. When I called her a Stealth Geek to her face, she took it as a compliment! If that doesn't say it all, what does?*

Now Heather's long, blond hair fell in two glossy curtains on either side of her face, and her bright blue eyes narrowed in concentration as she reached the final stages of turning lunch into architecture. Slowly she lowered the last fry in place, then held two opened ketchup packets in her fists and gave them a mighty squeeze.

"Look, the last days of Pompeii!" Heather uttered a mad scientist laugh as tomato-flavored lava spurted from the packets and surged down the sides of the fry tower.

"I was *talking* to you," Ilana snapped. "Want to stop acting like you're three years old long enough to *pretend* you're paying attention?"

"How many three-year-olds know about Pompeii?" Heather stuck out her tongue. "You never let me have any fun. Is that any way to treat a friend?"

"You're not even listening to me. Is *that* any way to treat a friend?" Ilana countered.

"I'm a *great* friend," Heather declared. "I know you better than you know yourself, and I know better than to try talking to you when you're beating yourself up over nothing."

"Nothing?" Ilana echoed. "I almost *die* from a disease I wouldn't have caught in the first place if I'd stayed here and it's nothing?"

Heather started talking to Ilana ve-ry pa-tient-ly. "You know damn well that wasn't what I meant *or* what you were talking about. Stop trying to dodge the truth. You're mad at your father."

"I'm *not* mad at—"

"And you're mad at yourself for *being* mad at your father. Hey, you're entitled. He hauled you off to Africa for three years! You wanted to stay here, like Dyllin, only she had an excuse. She was in college. Great for her, lousy for you. She was too far away to look after you during the week, and your parents thought you were too young to stay home by yourself twenty-four/seven."

"I could have stayed with my aunt Rachel." Ilana shredded her straw wrapper into bits smaller than the sesame seeds on her hamburger bun. "I asked her and she said yes. She's got this humongous house in Westbrook that's been empty ever since her kids grew up and moved out. She had plenty of room and she was willing to *drive* me to school here. But they wouldn't let me do that either."

Heather knew enough about Ilana's home life to say, "Let me guess why not. Because living in Africa would be a 'wonderfully enriching and invaluable' experience for you."

"Translation: It'll look good on my college ap," Ilana said, and then both girls recited together, "'When the time comes.'"

After the giggles stopped, Ilana fell right back into her mopey mood. "Why does everything in my life have to be aimed at getting into college? If I'd lived with Aunt Rachel, I could've gone to school here. I could've stayed friends with Jenny and Emma and Madison and all the rest of the kids I used to hang with in middle school instead of coming back and having them treat me like a total stranger."

Heather finished off her fries. "You didn't miss a thing by not staying friends with them. They turned into *such* a bunch of skanks."

"Yeah, but if I'd started high school with everyone else, I could've made some other friends."

"What, I'm not good enough for you?" Heather cast greedy eyes over Ilana's tray. "You going to eat that?" She nabbed the half-empty cardboard pocket of fries without waiting for an answer.

"It'd be nice to have friends who don't steal my lunch." Ilana folded her empty burger wrapper into smaller and smaller triangles. "It's bad enough being a stranger in my own town, but why the hell did my parents have to make such a big deal about what happened to me in Africa?"

Heather gave her a skeptical look. "I don't believe this. You whine because I don't listen to you and then you don't even listen to yourself. Okay, instant-replay time." She struck a Scarlett O'Hara clutch-the-pearls pose and exclaimed, "Ah jes' 'bout *dah* and it's *nuthin'*?"

"Yes, fine, I said that. That still doesn't change the fact that my parents were the ones who made sure everyone at school found out about it. 'Ooh, our poor baby is deathly allergic to eggs, and vaccines are made *in* eggs, so she couldn't get her shots before we went to Africa and she got smallpox and nearly *died*! If she eats the eensy-weensiest bit of an egg she could *die*! If anyone within five hundred feet of her even *thinks* of an egg, she could *die*! So could you please make sure that all her teachers and the cafeteria ladies and the whole damn school hears about this? Preferably over the PA system? And while you're at it, keep her away from chickens. You can't be too careful. Oh, and did we mention she could *die*?'" Ilana flicked the folded-up burger wrapper off the table. "Nothing says 'popularity' like a big case of Death Cooties."

"Well, you *are* that allergic to eggs; you told me so yourself. Anyway, the school Goths thought your Death Cooties were cool, and you do wear a lot of black. Why didn't you hang with them?"

"I don't like the music. Speaking of wearing stuff, how about after this we go to my house and I give you back that preppie interview outfit you loaned me?"

"'Kay." Heather crammed the last of Ilana's fries into her mouth, chewed thoughtfully, then announced, "Bleah. Volcano fries *do* taste better."

Ilana stood up. "I don't know you, we never met, and all the witnesses are lying. I'll be in the car."

○ ○ ○

The drive to Ilana's house took them past the Yankee Peddler Industrial Park. Without thinking, Ilana remarked, "Hey, look; that's where I started work yesterday."

"Yeah? Where?"

"Tabby Fabricant Textiles. Man, is my sister ever getting worse about that stupid wedding." Ilana skillfully changed the subject before her friend could ask any follow-up questions about her summer job. "And there's no talking to her. Mom and Dad are just standing back and letting her do whatever she wants because they've already put too much cash into this to turn back. It's not a wedding, it's an investment."

"Huh. Too bad they didn't put more money into it," Heather said. "Then they wouldn't have been able to afford music camp."

Ilana shuddered. Music camp was her personal summertime boogeyman, and her friend Heather knew it. It was the implicit, default *something* in her mother's dire promise to come up with "something" for her to do until fall.

"Trust me, it wouldn't make a difference. If I hadn't gotten this temp job, they'd sell their clothes, the furniture, both cars, *and* take out a second mortgage on the house if that's what it took to ship me off."

"That must be some pricey camp."

"You know what I mean."

"So what do you play?"

"What I *own* is a violin," Ilana specified. "It's left over from four wasted years of lessons back in grade school. I hated it and it hated me."

"Then why would your folks waste money sending you to music camp?"

"Because music camp is artistic, creative, enriching, blah, blah, blah, and it sounds better on a college ap than 'Actually had *fun* all summer.'"

"But if you play badly—"

Ilana dismissed Heather's protest. "It's not like I'm going to be a music major. No colleges are going to ask me to audition; they'll just assume music camp means I'm 'well-rounded.' You know, like a bowling ball?" She gripped the steering wheel tighter and added: "Score another strike for Mom and Dad."

○ ○ ○

No one was home when Ilana and Heather arrived. The family answering machine next to the kitchen telephone was jammed with more than a dozen messages from Dyllin, all in the key of Advanced Hysteria because she'd been to every florist within a twenty-town radius of Porlock's Landing and none of them had exactly the right shade of ribbon for the bridal party flowers.

"And Mom, I've been trying to reach you on your cell phone *all day*!" the machine squawked. "Why do you have it turned off? Some of the florists say they can order the color we absolutely *have* to have, but I don't trust them. Oh my God, I can't take this, the pressure is unbearable, my whole world is falling apart and nobody *cares*. Why does everything happen to *me*?"

"Oh look, Heather," Ilana said with a sugary smile. "It's Mr. Delete Message Key. Mr. Delete Message Key is our *friend*."

With that, she zapped Dyllin's message into oblivion. "There. A job well done. Come on upstairs and I'll give you your stuff."

She took two steps, then stopped in her tracks. *Uh-oh. Did I leave any of the D. R. Temps papers out where Heather could see them? I* know *I tossed the brochure the day I got it, but where did I leave the Waiver?*

"You know, Heather," she said, turning to her friend. "On second thought, why don't you just wait here and I'll bring your clothes down. My room is a disaster."

"Nothing-fits-in-the-closet disaster?" Heather asked.

"Can't-*find*-the-closet disaster," Ilana replied.

Heather shrugged. "I've seen worse." She walked past Ilana, heading for the stairs.

"Heather, no!" Ilana called after her. "I *meant* it's a Can't-find-the-closet-but-I-know-it's-there-because-I-left-a-tuna-sandwich-in-it-last-week disaster."

Heather sat down on the kitchen chair closest to the answering machine. "Ew. You win."

Ilana bounded up the stairs and was back with the borrowed clothes in under a minute. Heather sniffed the blouse cautiously. "Mmm, my favorite perfume: *Eau de* No Tuna Sandwich," she announced. Suddenly, the bright red blink of the answering machine's message light caught her eye. "Hey, look, Ilana, you missed one."

"I didn't miss a thing. I've suffered enough of Dyllin's snit-fits for one day. *No más.* Mom or Dad can deal with it when they get home."

"But what if it's not from Dyllin?"

Ilana gave Heather an *Oh, puh-lease* look. "I'm not that lucky." She thought about it for a moment. "I guess it could be from Mom and Dad. If they're going to be late, I want to know so I won't be home alone with the Bride from the Black Lagoon. Can I hide out at your house?"

Heather looked sheepish. "Um . . . sure, if you want, only . . . later today I'm going out with Jeff Eylandt. You know him, right?"

"Oh." Ilana put on a stiff smile. "Sure, I do. He was in my English class." *The toad,* she thought.

Jeff was one of those human fever blisters who treated girls like accessories or not-too-bright pets. If a girl tried to make a point in class, he saw nothing wrong with interrupting and talking over her. Why was someone as smart as Heather wasting her time on that obnoxious goon?

The answer was as simple as it was stupid: poetry. Jeff wrote it, spewed it, was a bottomless, gurgling swamp of the dullest, clunkiest, most self-indulgent free verse ever to offend the English language. But just as some chocoholics would eat lawn clippings if you covered them with enough extra bittersweet, Heather would devour any kind of poetry you offered her, from the sublime to the Jeff Eylandt. It was the one truly dangerous aspect of her Stealth Geek nature, because it flipped the OFF switch in her brain. History was full of poets who wrote spiritually uplifting works, yet led lives wild enough to make a rock star blush. Unfortunately this led Heather to believe that anyone who wrote poetry was entitled to act like a jerk: It came prepackaged with their Creative Soul.

"Jeff Eylandt: Lord Byron, only without the talent or the good looks," Ilana muttered.

"What did you say?"

"I said yeah, right, you told me about all that at lunch, only I wasn't really listening; I was too wrapped up in thinking about that whole thing with my dad. You know, if you'd just buy into the complete gorgeous blond, hyperpopular, nerd-snubbing cheerleader package and stick to it, I could presume you've *always* got date plans and then I wouldn't need to listen to you at all."

Heather picked up one of the countless pieces of paper from the pile on the kitchen table, deftly folded it into an airplane, and launched it at Ilana. "Just play the last message before I hit you with the awesome power of my secret ninja nerd-snubbing skills."

Ilana ducked the paper airplane and hit the *play* button on the answering machine at the same time. The message sounded rough and slightly garbled, with a few minor blank spots, but what it had to say came through loud and clear.

"Hello, Ilana? Ilana? Is this thing on? Hi! It's Tabby, dear. I'm calling from the office. No rest for the wicked, ha, ha. Now Ilana, I realize it's Saturday and you're not scheduled to come back until Monday, but we were just wondering if you wouldn't mind doing us an *eensy* favor and give us about three or four hours of your time this afternoon? At two-ish, perhaps? We've just gotten word that there's going to be a bit of a— Well, we girls like to call them 'piñatas' because they're situations that just seem to *burst* over our heads and there's *so* much cleanup to handle afterward. So if you could come in, we'd be ever so grateful. Georgette's always the busiest one when it's piñata time, so the more of her leftover paperwork we can get out of the way, the better. Bye-bye." The message came to a dead stop.

Heather looked at Ilana, perplexed. "Did she say they were expecting a *piñata*?"

"They run a very festive fabric business." She spoke lightly, but her stomach was churning. If the Fates knew they'd have to deal with a sudden, massive cleanup, that must mean that very soon things were going to get very bad somewhere in the world. She couldn't help praying it wouldn't be anywhere near Porlock's Landing.

"So, you're going to go?"

"I might as well." Ilana shrugged. "It's not like I have anything else to do."

"You know, if you want to share in the wild roller-coaster ride of hedonism and debauchery that is my social life, you could maybe, oh, I don't know, say *yes* the next time I ask you over to my house when there's a party?"

"'Wild roller-coaster ride of hedonism and debauchery'? Where did *that* come from?"

"Brace yourself, I've been *reading books*. Don't worry, that can be our little secret. Wouldn't want to risk my dumb blond cheerleader street cred, right?" She put on a happy, empty-headed look and chirped, "I'm a *girl*; math is *icky*."

"Idiot," Ilana said with a smile. She deleted Tabby's message. "Okay, I'll drop you off at your place before I go to work."

They were well on their way when Heather said, "Shouldn't you call to let your boss know you're coming?"

"I don't think I can reach her on my cell phone," Ilana replied. "She's in a dead zone." She smiled to herself.

Heather's family lived down by the shore while the Newhouses lived in what Ilana liked to call the "poor section" of Porlock's Landing, a woodsy area dotted with clumps of mass-produced fake Colonial houses. The shortest route to Heather's home took the girls past the Yankee Peddler Industrial Park again.

"Hey, pull in!" Heather exclaimed as they approached the driveway.

Ilana obeyed without thinking, steering the car into the nearest parking space. The complex looked abandoned, all the individual offices dark, locked up for the weekend, not another car in sight. It felt creepy.

"What's wrong?" she asked her friend.

"Relax, I just need to use the bathroom. Yes, I'm totally sorry that I didn't think to go before we left your house and no, I *can't* hold it until I get home."

"Well, that covers everything except where do you think you're going to find an open bathroom? This place is deserted."

"Please don't make me say 'Duh,' Ilana. Your office, where else?"

"Oh."

"What's the problem? Look, your boss asked you to come in, so the office has to be open. You're just dropping by to let her know you'll be working for her later today, the way she asked. You're doing her a favor; the least she can do is let me use her bathroom."

It all made too much sense. *And what could I say, anyway? "You can't use the bathroom where I work because you might find out who I'm* really *working for, and if* they *don't like that, one snip from Georgette's big, black shears and you're history?* She took a long, slow breath and summoned up calming thoughts. *It'll be all right, it looks just like a regular office, there's nothing weird in plain sight. We'll just drop in, Heather can use the bathroom, then we'll be out of there and she won't suspect a thing.* Reassured, she moved the car to a closer spot, parked, and led the way to the office door.

It swung wide open before she could knock or even try the handle. A delighted Tabby greeted her. "*Here* you are! Of course we knew you wouldn't let us down, but—" She glanced at her wristwatch. "You're early. We weren't expecting that. How odd. Well, never mind, sometimes there's a snag in the line that even we don't—" She paused again, abruptly aware that Ilana was not alone. "Who is *this*?" Her usually perky voice rumbled like thunder as she leveled an accusatory finger at Heather.

"This is my friend, Heather Hazelden," Ilana said, flinching under Tabby's stern scowl. "Can she use the bathroom?" Her voice rose to an embarrassing squeak as she added, "Please?"

Tabby folded her arms. "I suppose so. This once." Stepping to one side so that the girls could enter, she added, "The first door on the left; the one with the unicorn calendar."

It was a door that hadn't been in the front office before, but Heather wouldn't know that. She raced through it too fast to notice that the unicorn calendar was illustrated with photographs, and that the creatures in the picture were a far cry from horses with fake horns glued to their foreheads. Ilana had the feeling that her friend's rush to reach the bathroom had less to do with actual urgency and more with the desire to get away from Tabby's ugly stare.

"You know, I didn't bring her here on purpose," Ilana ventured to say. "She's only using the bathroom."

"That doesn't matter." Tabby lost all her charm when she was being stuffy and self-righteous. "We have the security of our business to protect. That is why the only people allowed on the premises are ourselves and the occasional *trusted* employee from D. R. Temps." Her tone made it clear that she thought Ilana had come close to betraying that trust.

Ilana didn't mind accepting responsibility for her mistakes, but she had major issues with getting blamed for things she *hadn't* done wrong. Her dread of Tabby's wrath began to seep away. "Then why did you set up shop in an industrial park? With neighbors? Why didn't you buy a house back in the woods, somewhere totally isolated?"

"Don't be silly, dear," Tabby said. "We can't run a business this big out of a private dwelling. That would violate the zoning laws."

She spoke to Ilana in the same condescending way she'd done the previous day, with the same results: It goaded Ilana's deep loathing for being talked down to, calling up That Attitude Thing in all its defiant glory.

"If *I* were trying to keep my business such a big secret, I wouldn't make a big scene over someone using the bathroom," Ilana snapped. "The worst thing you can do when you've got something to hide is *act* like you do."

"Young lady, when I want to know your opinion, I will run your life-thread under the Scry-o-Tron 9000. Now the instant your friend is done in there, you are to take her directly home so that she can prepare for her date with that dreadful boy, Jeff Eylandt."

"How did you know who—?"

Tabby looked smug. "Much as we trust Mrs. Atatosk's good judgment in picking out just the right people to work for us, we still run our own background checks on all potential employees. That includes investigating those people closest to them. It's all in the threads. Heather and Jeff are going to the movies to see the latest Tarantino film. Heather hates Tarantino, but for the moment she's quite attracted to Jeff, so she's willing to sit through it to please him. Such dedication." Tabby sighed and brushed away an invisible tear. "Such a shame, how badly it's all going to end."

"Why? What's going to go wrong?"

"Sorry, dear, that's classified information. We can't run the risk of you warning her."

"Warning her about what?" Ilana wanted to grab Tabby and shake a straight answer out of her, but even with That Attitude Thing at full power, she knew better than to try something like *that* on a goddess. "Is something going to happen to Heather?"

"Well, I should hope so," Tabby said. "Life is all about what *happens* to you."

"You know what I mean! Anyway, what good would it do even if I did warn her? You and your sisters make all the real decisions. We can't change them; it's impossible for mortals to do that."

Tabby chuckled. "Nothing is impossible until the moment that Georgette takes out her scissors and . . . *snip*! After that, what's spun is spun, but before—" She spread her hands wide. "I spin life-threads, child. *Threads*, not steel cables."

She might have said more, but the sound of a flushing toilet brought her back to the business at hand. "Come back quickly. Here is your overtime pay." She handed Ilana a fat, white envelope. "Now, if you'll excuse me—" Tabby vanished.

Ilana opened the envelope. It was stuffed with two hundred dollars in twenties. She had just stuffed it into her pocket when Heather came out of the bathroom.

"Where's the dragon?" Heather asked, looking around nervously.

"She had to get back to work," Ilana said, hustling Heather out the door. "And so do I."

MAKING THE MOST OF ON-THE-JOB TRAINING

The Fates did not return to the office that Saturday. Ilana spent the afternoon typing death receipts and running the Fates' junk mail through the office shredder. *I wonder what would happen if Georgette used the black scissors on any of this stuff?* she thought idly as yet another YOU MAY ALREADY HAVE WON! envelope got the automatic slice-and-dice treatment. At five o'clock she received a phone call from Dimity, telling her she could go home. "Come back Monday. Nine o'clock."

"Are you sure?" Ilana asked. "I came in at seven yesterday."

"That was because it was your first day."

"Oh. Well, do you want me to lock up here when I leave?" Ilana offered. "I don't have a key, but if there's some way I can make the door latch automatically when it closes—"

"No. We have our own ways of controlling access by unauthorized person or persons when the office is unattended."

"You mean you taught Arachne how to dial 9-1-1 if someone breaks in?"

"You are funny," Dimity said. "Ha. I hope you will continue to temp for us. I have not laughed this much in ages. Ha. But seriously, no one can enter our place of business unless we permit it or they have a key. That is the order of things. Those who attempt to violate that order learn better. That's funny, too. Ha."

"Ha," Ilana repeated uncertainly.

° ° °

On Monday morning she reported to work at nine, as directed, and found the Fates still absent.

"Dealing with cosmic piñatas takes time," Arachne informed her. "And a really big stick or a lot of duct tape, depending on whether you want to smash it apart or keep it together."

"I vote for together," Ilana said.

"Every vote counts," Arachne said. "Just not yours."

To Ilana's surprise, her work for the day did not involve death receipts. Instead, Tabby had left word for her to do some office maintenance—pure gofer-level chores like dusting, sweeping, cleaning the coffeemaker, buying more filters, tea bags, sugar, powdered creamer, and so on. It wasn't very exciting, but because she wasn't exactly crazy about the whole death-receipt business, she didn't mind. Like a swarm of mice, all the little tasks and errands nibbled away most of the week. Ilana didn't get back to her typing until four thirty Thursday afternoon. She wanted to stay on past five o'clock and catch up, but a call from Tabby nixed that.

"We appreciate your dedication, dear," the youthful Fate told her. "But we prefer that you don't put in any overtime unless we request it. Five o'clock is your official quitting time. All work and no play makes Jack a threadbare boy."

By the time Ilana came in to work on Friday, she had a full week's work under her belt and felt like an old hand at Tabby Fabricant Textiles. It helped that the Fates hadn't been around that much. Phone calls and e-mail messages were one thing, but in person the Fates still had the power to unnerve her.

Probably because I might have gotten my first look at Georgette's big, black, last-word scissors long before I ever signed up with D. R. Temps, she thought, and the chilling memories of how near she'd come to dying in Africa set her teeth on edge.

The front office was empty, and when she headed for the back room, she found a square white envelope with her name on it taped to the door.

Uh-oh, she thought. *Things were going so smoothly I forgot all about being here on a trial basis. Now the week's over; it's decision time. I thought Mrs. Atatosk would call me if there was any problem, but instead . . . this.* She took the note off the door and stared at it. *The verdict.*

As she tore open the envelope and removed the folded sheet of gold-bordered paper she said a silent prayer: *Please let this be good news. I know it sounds weird, but I've gotten to* like *this job. I want to go back to the Koffee Koven this afternoon, and see Max and Joanna again, and meet some of the other temps. I want to go to the end-of-summer party. I won't even mind getting carded by Hades, I swear! Please, please,* please, *let this be good news and not good-bye.*

She took a deep breath and read the note.

○ ○ ○

When Ilana entered the inner office, Arachne was still the only one there. The transformed weaver was in complete spider form, dangling from a thread she'd anchored to the center of the ceiling fan. When she saw Ilana, she put her human face back on and waved.

"Hey, look what the Cyclops dragged in!"

"They're not back yet?" Ilana asked.

"Nope." Arachne grinned.

"Still because of the . . . piñata? Know anything about that?"

"Sure. When it comes to hearing all the office gossip, a spider on the ceiling beats a fly on the wall."

"'Beats' or 'eats'?"

"This just in: Shut up." Arachne tried to turn her back on Ilana, but instead wound up spinning from the ceiling fan like a played out yo-yo.

Ilana reached up and steadied the twirling spider. "Sorry. I didn't mean to insult you. When I get worried, I say stupid things."

"No hard feelings." Arachne smiled. "And you can stop worrying about the piñata thing; it's not going to happen anywhere near here."

"That doesn't make it all right," Ilana said hotly. "It's going to happen *somewhere.*"

The spider gave her a shrewd look. "Mmmm, sounds like someone's so relieved to be safe that she's feeling guilty about it. Listen, there's a big difference between being glad when bad things happen to other people and being glad when they *don't* happen to you. If a disaster misses you, it doesn't mean it's *got* to hit someone else. Catastrophe is not a limited commodity; there's more than enough to go around. Good thing the same goes for happiness."

"Wow, for someone who's got to eat bugs, you're a real optimist." Ilana headed for the desk with all the cute little mousie figurines.

"Ha, ha, so very ha," Arachne said sarcastically. "You're so bright, you blinded yourself. That's not your desk."

"It is now." Ilana flicked out the gold-bordered note and read it aloud: "'Because of your fine work in Death Receipts, Tabby Fabricant Textiles would like to retain your services. We would also like to transfer you to Spindle-Sitting. Good luck in your new position.'" She flaunted it triumphantly at the spider. "How do you like *that*?"

Arachne swung herself back and forth like a pendulum at the end of her thread until she got enough momentum going, then snapped free and flew through the air to land on top of Tabby's computer monitor. "Let me see that!"

The spider muttered to herself as she read the note. "Huh! It's real, signed by Boss Lady Number One and everything. Great. Clotho's gone crazy. There goes the universe."

"Giving me a promotion is *not* crazy, bug-breath."

"That's no promotion, it's just a different job, and not the kind I'd give to a newbie; a *temp* newbie who's only been working here for one lousy week. It's one thing to let you cover for Atropos. You can't do too much damage to the dead. But leaving you in charge of the *spinning* department—? What was she thinking?"

Ilana lifted her chin defiantly. "She was thinking that I'm a good worker and it's time to give me bigger responsibilities."

"Sweetie, that was a rhetorical question. I *know* what she was thinking; I was here when she thought it. It all went down right before they got the heads-up about the piñata incident last Saturday. Clotho stepped into the *back* back room, gave your spindle the once-over with the Scry-o-Tron 9000, and told her sisters that you hated dealing with death so much that unless they gave you a different job, the odds were that you'd quit. That was when Atropos had hysterics because her son's birthday party is coming up soon, she's got to take a bunch of nine-year-old maniacs to the Mystic Aquarium, and between that and the piñata she's really going to need some *major* help with her workload. Lachesis kept a level head—no surprise there—and put in an emergency call to D. R. Temps, but Mrs. Atatosk didn't have anyone available to replace you. That's when Clotho said she'd cover for Atropos while you took over spindle-sitting for her." The spider shook her head. "I thought she was joking."

"They called Mrs. Atatosk?" Ilana couldn't believe it. "They tried to *replace* me?"

"It's not like you're two days short of retirement. Face it, you're a temp. You know what *that's* short for."

"How could they be so sure I was going to quit?" Ilana protested. "I might've *thought* about it, at first, but things change. And even if I do hate working with death receipts, that's what I was paid to do. If you're going to take someone's money, you do the work. Do they think I'm some kind of baby who believes that if you don't love your job *all* the time, it's okay to run away?" Her indignation heated up as she spoke. "They could have *talked* to me before they called Mrs. Atatosk. They could have treated me like a human being, not a spare tire. Tabby's the one who told me that life-threads still being measured out can change. Why didn't she ask *me* if I wanted to quit instead of believing the . . . the . . . the Whatzit 9000?"

"Scry-o-Tron," said the spider. "And if you don't know what that is, you're definitely jumping the gun by sitting at Clotho's desk. You can't do any real spindle-sitting until you know how to use it. If you don't believe me, go back to Atropos' desk and see what happens."

Ilana gave Arachne a dirty look, but did what the spider told her to do. No sooner did she sit down in Georgette's chair than the ancient typewriter reappeared with a tall stack of blank death receipts beside it. The computer screen blinked on, displaying Tabby's cheerful face.

"Hello, Ilana," she said. "Thank you *so* much for holding down the fort until we can get back, you darling girl. If you're seeing this message, it means you're smart enough to understand that your *new* job doesn't start until next Monday. *Well* done! *Goooood* girl! Until then, mustn't touch the spindles, naughty-naughty, no-no. Now please do see if you can finish up all of those tiresome old death receipts for us before you have to go to your little temps' meeting this afternoon. Fresh brownies in the fridge—egg-free, of course, dear—and help yourself to coffee. Bye-eee!" The screen went blank.

Ilana sat back, arms folded, glowering. The typewriter hummed to life, the computer screen re-lit, displaying the list of names she'd need to type onto the death receipts. Even the pile of papers rustled urgently at her, but Ilana didn't move.

Arachne made her way to the top of the untouched paperwork pile. "Tick-tock, Little Mary Sunshine," she said. "Time to get started."

"No, it's not," Ilana said. "I don't care how much I like working with you or what the Fates pay me, I've got my limits. I'll give back the money and I'll give you my cell phone number so we can keep in touch, but otherwise . . . I *quit*."

"After that big speech about how neither rain nor sleet nor snow nor carpal tunnel syndrome would stop you from doing the job you were paid to do?"

"Yes, after that!" Ilana snapped. "Because dealing with death is part of my job, but being treated like an infant isn't! 'Mustn't touch, naughty-naughty, no-no'? What am I, *two*?"

"If the tantrum fits," Arachne said.

Ilana started for the door.

"Come back!" the spider shouted after her. "I was only kidding. If you walk out now, they'll find some way to blame me for it. If Clotho and the others treat you like a baby, it's nothing personal. To immortals like them, you *are* a baby."

Ilana turned around. "Immortality is no excuse for snottiness. And what was that '*Goooood* girl' stuff? That's how you talk to a dog!" Still steaming, she returned to her desk. "I'm only doing this for you, Arachne. The gods've given you enough grief; I won't let them have an excuse to give you more."

The spider's bulbous body sagged with relief. "Thanks, Ilana; I won't forget this. If there's ever anything I can do for you—"A thoughtful look crossed her face. "Maybe there is. Hold on a sec." She scuttled down one end of the paper stack, her legs working busily at some task Ilana couldn't quite see. Then she repeated the whole business as she clambered up the opposite side of the blank death receipts.

"There!" she announced from the summit. "Done."

"What is?"

"You'll see." The spider jumped off the pile of papers and took up a position on Ilana's shoulder. "Pick up the top form, feed it into the typewriter, and enter the first name from the computer list. Then watch."

Reluctantly, Ilana followed Arachne's directions. She made a small spelling error while transcribing the first name the computer displayed, but the typewriter corrected that automatically, as usual. Then she pulled the carriage return lever and watched the machine complete the form, also as usual. When it was done, she reached to remove it.

The completed death receipt whipped itself out of the

machine so sharply that it almost left a paper cut on Ilana's fingertips. Before she could draw a breath, the next blank in the pile slipped slickly into place, the keys chattering wildly as they filled in every empty space on the form, including the name.

This was definitely *not* as usual.

"Hey, *I'm* supposed to do that!" Ilana yelled at the machine. She stared as the unprocessed death receipts lined up and streamed through the typewriter, while on the computer screen, the list of names scrolled swiftly on.

Craning her neck to confront the spider on her shoulder, she demanded, "What did you do, Arachne?"

"*Moi*? Nothing much," Arachne said casually. "Just a little trick I worked up in my spare time, linking the individual pages with timed-release superfine webbing. It snaps free as soon as a receipt is through the machine. The rest of the program initiates when you enter the first name on the list and—presto!—death-receipt assembly line."

"But that was *my* job," Ilana protested weakly.

"Can you keep a secret?" The spider crept up to her ear and whispered, "It didn't have to be *anyone's* job. If Atropos knew about my little computer-typewriter interface, the Fates wouldn't have needed to hire you at all."

"Why didn't you tell them?"

"Why should I? You know how long I've been hanging around this place with nothing to do? The Fates have lives of their own, especially Atropos; they can go *home.* When was the last time I got to do that?"

"I thought this was your home." As soon as Ilana said that, she knew she was wrong.

"This is where I live. A home is more than that." Arachne's voice broke. "If I could just *visit* a home—a real home—it would be enough. But do the Fates ever think to invite me? Ha! They gave me a roof over my head and then they never gave me a second thought. Why should I do anything for them?"

"Fair enough." Ilana could hardly take her eyes off the smoothly clattering typewriter keys and the rapidly shrinking pile of blank death receipts. "So how did you learn to make the machines do that?"

"At Crushing Boredom U., which is where I went after I graduated from Way Too Much Spare Time Academy," Arachne replied. "Would it *kill* Clotho to bring me a magazine sometime? There's just so many webs a girl can weave, you know, so I started making my own fun, got online, surfed around, cruised some chat rooms, learned how to program, even taught myself how to hack with the best of 'em."

Ilana shook her head. "I don't think the world is ready for a computer-literate spider."

"It's *called* the World Wide *Web*!" Arachne scurried down from Ilana's shoulder to the floor and made tracks for the file cabinets. "Follow me, girlfriend!" she called. "It's payback time."

"I don't like the sound of that," Ilana said. "You're mad at the Fates for ignoring you, but if you try to get back at them—"

"Not *that* kind of payback." Arachne jumped onto the handle of the lowest file drawer. From there she cast a loop of webbing to snag the handle above, then pulled herself up, and repeated the process until she was on top of the cabinet. "Open this one," she told Ilana, tapping the top drawer.

"Why?" Ilana wasn't mistrustful by nature, but she was willing to learn. It didn't seem like the smartest thing in the world, blindly obeying someone whose recklessness had earned her an eternity as an eight-legged bug zapper.

Arachne made an impatient noise. "Because this is how I want to pay you back for being my friend and for *not* walking out on me earlier. I know you'd rather have a box of candy or a cheese log, but until I can get to the mall, this is the best I can do."

The spider stepped back as Ilana opened the file drawer and peered inside. The only thing in there was a wooden tray lined with finely woven white wool that reeked of incense. Resting on the fragrant wool was what looked like an oversized pair of gold-framed sunglasses with swirling blue and green lenses. Two tiny snakes made of dull black iron perched atop the frames, facing the miniature silver tripod and basin balanced above the nosepiece.

"What *is* this thing?" Ilana asked, lifting out the tray and setting it down carefully beside the spider.

"*That,*" said Arachne, "is the Scry-o-Tron 9000."

LEARNING THE ROPES

"Wow," Ilana said, gazing through the Scry-o-Tron 9000 at the strand of golden thread in her hands. The enchanted typewriter had finished clattering through the pile of death receipts some time ago, but she hadn't noticed. *Wow* said it all.

And yet, this wondrous moment had begun with one of the most humdrum, commonplace, mundane things in the world: a name.

Arachne told her what to do. "Hold out your hand and say someone's name. Better make it someone you know, for your first try. How about your sister?"

"Why do you want me to say her name?" Ilana asked.

"Because without a life-thread to read, the Scry-o-Tron 9000 is just another pair of really tacky-looking eyeglasses, and you get a person's life-thread to come to you by calling for it by name."

"Maybe it works that way for you or the Fates," Ilana argued. "But for me? I'm not a goddess; I don't have any powers."

"You might be surprised," the spider replied. "Powers are like powdered-sugar donuts: They rub off everywhere. Besides, you work for the Fates and you've been given official spindle-sitting authority. I'm betting that gives you the power to summon spindles."

"You heard Tabby. I don't start the new job until Monday."

"I know that and you know that, but do the spindles know that?" Arachne arched one eyebrow. "*Try*, Ilana. The worst that can happen is nothing."

"Yes, but what if it does work? Are you sure it's *okay* for me to try doing this? If the Fates come back and catch me—"

There was no knowing how long Ilana would have gone on voicing her doubts if Arachne hadn't looked her in the eye and, in a perfect imitation of Tabby at her most condescending, said, "Well, aren't you such a *gooooood* girl."

Ilana's eyes turned flinty. She stood up straight, stuck out her right hand, and called out, "Dyllin Newhouse!" loud and clear. The moment the name left her lips, a golden spindle appeared in her hand.

She was so startled by the apparition that she almost dropped it. Luckily, Arachne was there to holler, "Hey! Hold on to that thing!" Ilana's fist clenched automatically. The spider nodded, well pleased, and went on to tell Ilana what to do with the spindle and how to coax out the thread. Ilana was good at following directions, Arachne was a born teacher, and it didn't take a degree in rocket science to use the Scry-o-Tron 9000.

All of which very quickly led to *Wow.*

"Like it?" The spider lounged in the empty tray, idly paging through a small booklet with the title *So, You're Going to Control the Destiny of the World*. "Aren't you glad you stopped whining about 'Ooh, I wouldn't, I couldn't, I shouldn't, what if the Fates found out?' and just *tried* it? See? Nothing bad happened. In fact, I'd say you are definitely having a major educational experience here."

"This is just . . . awesome." Ilana wasn't really listening to the spider anymore. She was too fascinated by the wonders passing before her eyes to remind Arachne that she'd been the one who'd been so upset at the thought of a newbie temp being given spindle-sitting duty.

Now Ilana sat at the desk nearest the file cabinets, Dimity's realm of precision, measurement, and painstaking calculation. Her sister's spindle lay within easy reach of her left hand while she gently played out some of the thread wound around it. Meanwhile, more thread continued to appear out of nowhere, adding itself to the golden filament she held delicately between three fingers of her right hand. Every so often, the golden spindle would turn itself, taking up the slack. Here and there along the unspooled thread were what looked like bits of fluff, specks of lint, and sometimes another thread or two winding around the main one.

And while she sat at the ordinary-looking desk, staring at a simple strand of thread, she was also floating above a winding road, looking down through the sun-drenched trees at a little blue Toyota and the unmistakable black-and-white-with-flashing-lights bulk of a police cruiser. There was no need to tell the Scry-o-Tron 9000 to zoom in for a closer view; the magical device was fine-tuned to respond to the unspoken whim of its wearer.

"Oh my God, my sister is such an idiot!" Ilana exclaimed. "Look at that: She's yelling at the cop who pulled her over for speeding. She's telling him that she just found out there's a florist in Essex who might have the right color ribbon for the bridesmaids' bouquets and she's got to get there before he closes for the day. Oh yeah, *that's* going to save you from getting a ticket, Dyllin." She chuckled when the Scry-o-Tron allowed her to savor the expression on her sister's face as the policeman took his sweet time writing out the ticket.

"Try another one." Arachne put down the little booklet. "Think of it as training for when you start spindle-sitting on Monday. You know the drill: Just say the name of the next person you want to . . . monitor."

"Nice way to say 'spy on.'" Ilana looked up from her sister's life-thread. "But what the heck, this is fun, and you're right, no harm done. Just one thing: What happens if I say a name like 'John Smith'? I could drown in the avalanche of spindles."

"First of all, you don't drown in an avalanche. Second, if you say 'John Smith' you only get the life-thread of the John Smith you've got in mind. The spindle room data retrieval system is like the Scry-o-Tron: It runs on psych-sync power."

"Of course it does," said Ilana. "Everyone knows that."

"Sarcasm doesn't match your shoes, sweetie," the spider said. "*Psych-sync*'s just a techno term Lachesis came up with. She loves that kind of thing. All it means is that the spindle filing system automatically gets psychically synchronized with anyone in this office who's permitted to touch the life-threads." Arachne tapped the booklet. "It's all spelled out right here, if you don't believe me."

"Why wouldn't I?"

"I said *if*. As in: I suggested your sister's life-thread for the trial run so that *if* you didn't believe that the Scry-o-Tron really works, you could ask her what happened to her today, and see if what she says matches what you saw."

"You mean the speeding ticket?" Ilana shook her head. "Even if she were still speaking to me, she'd never tell me about that. It'd ruin her image. The Perfect Older-Sister-slash-Daughter whose accomplishments I am not worthy to approach, let alone equal, does not fess up to speeding tickets."

"She's not talking to you?" Arachne was confused.

"Just since last night. She's still mad about this." Ilana self-consciously cupped one hand over the little skull inked on her face. It was just starting to fade. "It was a dumb thing for me to do, but it was never a sinister plot against my sister and her almighty wedding. You should've heard her howl the first time she saw it. She made Mom drag me to the dermatologist's and insisted on coming along so she could make sure Dr. Corelli got it all off."

Arachne cocked her head, studying the drawing. "He missed a spot," she said.

Ilana made a face at her. "Dr. Corelli's the specialist I saw as soon as we came back from Africa. My face was covered with smallpox scars until he gave me a bunch of dermabrasion treatments. But he couldn't do anything about this doodle. He told us that all we could do was wait for the ink to fade away on its own—weeks of waiting, maybe months—and that was that, the last word."

"Why couldn't he erase it the same way he got rid of your pockmarks?" Arachne asked.

"That's what Dyllin wanted to know. At the top of her lungs." Ilana shook her head. "He said the scar-removal treatments had left my skin too delicate for another session. It would do more harm than good. Dyllin's been looking for a way to deal with this ever since.

"Her latest idea was this heavy-duty stage makeup she brought home yesterday. It'd cover the doodle for the wedding like a layer of plaster on a wall, but I can't wear it. I'm sensitive to about a zillion of the ingredients. They'd turn my face into a blowfish, spikes and all. Then she accused me of being allergic to makeup on purpose, just to spoil her wedding photographs, and *then* things got beyond-the-power-of-makeup ugly. So as far as talking to her to prove that the Scry-o-Tron's on the level, forget it. I'll take your word."

"Ow," Arachne said sympathetically. "Still, I'd like you to have some proof that the Scry-o-Tron really does work. Call up another spindle, one that belongs to someone you know who *is* speaking to you."

Ilana thought this over. "I guess I could take a look at Heather's." She struck a dramatic pose, hands extended, palms up. "O great powers that be!" she intoned. "Fetch unto me now the life-thread of—"

"Just say the name, you big diva!" Arachne cut in.

"Spoilsport." Ilana lowered her hands. "Okay, in that case, forget Heather; I'm going to have some *fun*. Bring me the life-thread of Johnny Depp, and make it snappy!"

Nothing happened. Ilana slid the Scry-o-Tron 9000 down her nose and peered at Arachne over the snake-crowned frames. "Well, *that* worked."

"Hold on, hold on. There's got to be a perfectly simple reason why it didn't." The spider riffled through the little instruction booklet. "Just let me see what it—ah-*ha*!" She jabbed the tip of one leg triumphantly at a clump of red type in the middle of the last page. "Here it is, under 'Results Not Guaranteed, Certain Restrictions Apply: Use of the Scry-o-Tron 9000 by beings, entities, creatures, and/or individuals with blood/ichor proportions of less than 15%/85% is strictly limited to the review, perusal, study, and observation of life-threads pertaining solely to those mortals residing within a hundred *diskaroi* radius of the user. This limitation likewise applies to any and all permissible adjustments the user may attempt to—'"

"What's ichor?" Ilana interrupted.

"It's what the gods have instead of blood," Arachne said. "Now can I just finish reading—"

"What's *diskaroi*?"

"It's a measure of distance that the gods use. It's meaningless for mortals."

"Meaning you don't know what it is either," Ilana guessed.

"Meaning I don't care and neither should you. Either a spindle's out of your reach or it's not; adjust, okay? So it says here—"

"Speaking of 'adjust,' what does that mean, 'permissible adjustments'?" Ilana asked, removing the goggles and polishing the green and blue lenses on the hem of her T-shirt.

"It means you can read the stupid user's manual yourself!" Arachne shouted, flinging the booklet across the room. She had a good arm for someone without any real arms. It struck the far wall and plunged down the back of another row of file cabinets.

"Oh, *that's* nice," Ilana said, sticking the Scry-o-Tron 9000 on top of her head. "If you wanted to make sure we couldn't use the instructions, why didn't you just set fire to them?"

"Why didn't you let me *finish*?" Arachne shot back. "Why did you keep interrupting me with one dumb question after another?"

"They were important questions."

"Yeah, well, I've got an *important* question for you: What are we going to do when the Fates find out we lost the Scry-o-Tron instructions?"

"What do you mean 'we,' Spinderella? Anyway, it's not like *they* need them. They've been using these bad boys for a long, long time." Ilana tilted the goggles forward so that they were back on her nose, ready for action.

"They don't need to *use* the instructions," Arachne said, every wiry hair on her body quivering with tension. "They need to *see* that the instructions are right where they've left them for the past three thousand years! The minute Clotho, Lachesis, or Atropos needs to double-check someone's life-thread, they'll pull out the tray, pick up the goggles, and know what's missing."

"Maybe whoever uses the Scry-o-Tron next will think that one of her other two sisters lost the manual." Ilana sounded weakly optimistic.

"Why would she think that? Like a certain know-it-all I could name once said, 'It's not like *they* need them.' And if the Fates don't *need* the instructions, the Fates wouldn't have any reason to *touch* the instructions, let alone *lose* the instructions, and the instructions would still be right where they belong, in the box with the Scry-o-Tron 9000, instead of stuck behind a file cabinet the size of the Minotaur's butt!"

"Calm down, Arachne!" Ilana made shushing motions at the hysterical spider. "When the Fates come back, I'll take the blame for dropping the booklet behind the file cabinet. I'm sure they can just levitate it out."

"And who's going to take the blame for *showing* you the Scry-o-Tron?" Instead of calming down, Arachne was working herself up into a full-scale conniption fit. "Because that is not something you would've found on your own, like a stapler."

"I've got permission to touch the life-threads but *not* the Scry-o-Tron? That's stupid."

"Here's a good rule to remember if you don't want to spend a couple thousand years eating at McDragonfly's," Arachne said. "Never call the gods *stupid*; not even if they are; *especially* if they are. And you don't have permission to touch anything until Monday. They'll know I'm the one who turned Clotho's 'naughty-naughty, no-no' into 'what the heck, yes-yes.' Why did I do it? What was I thinking? I'm doomed."

"Maybe they won't punish you," Ilana tried to offer her eight-legged friend a scrap of comfort. "Maybe they'll forgive you for—"

"They're *gods*," Arachne wailed. "The gods don't just punish, they take *overreact* to a whole new level. Actaeon was a hunter who accidentally got a look at the goddess Artemis while she was bathing. She turned him into a stag and sicced his own dogs on him. They tore him to pieces. I'm a spider already! I don't want to know what's the next step down!"

"Shhhh, come on, we can fix this." Ilana abandoned Dyllin's life-thread spindle, slid the Scry-o-Tron goggles up to rest atop her head, and scooped up the spider. She put Arachne on top of the file cabinet hiding the lost Scry-o-Tron instructions and said, "Okay, let's work with what we've got. You're a spider; spiders spin sticky stuff. Shoot a strand of webbing all the way down the back of this file and wiggle it around. I'll get on the floor so I can see where the booklet landed, and guide you until the webbing hits the paper. Then you can reel it up again. How's that?" She waited for the spider to applaud her brilliant idea.

She kept on waiting.

"'Wiggle it around'?" Arachne repeated coldly. If it accomplished nothing else, Ilana's plan had done a miraculous job of restoring the spider's self-possession. "'Reel it up again'? Girl, you have been watching too many cartoons. I'm a spider, not a fishing rod! If that's the best you can come up with—"

Ilana stomped across the room to where a homely broom and dustpan stood propped in a corner. She grabbed the broom, marched back to the file cabinet, and stuck the handle in Arachne's face. "Here. Cover this with webbing, *lots* of webbing. I'd do it myself with bubble gum, but I thought it'd be nice if you actually *did* something to save your own hide instead of just shooting down my ideas."

Grumbling, Arachne spun a hamster-sized glob of spider-silk around the end of the broom handle. Ilana examined the results, was satisfied, and got onto hands and knees to go fishing for the lost leaflet. Arachne peered over the back of the file cabinet to supervise. "Little to the left . . . right . . . up just a little bit annnnnd . . . got it! Good girl!"

Ilana stood up, the retrieved booklet stuck to the end of the broom handle. She pulled it off and waved it victoriously, like a captured flag. "A couple of dust bunnies and a little of your webbing on it, but I'll bet we can clean it off before— *Oh my God, what's that?*"

Ilana dropped both broom and booklet. She dove for Dimity's desk where the spindle holding her sister's life-thread had begun to twirl and jiggle wildly on end, with absolutely no warning. The slack loop of golden thread Ilana had viewed not five minutes ago now whipped itself tighter and tighter around the spindle's core, with no visible hand turning it. Even more alarming, a *second* strand had appeared out of nowhere and lashed itself tenaciously around Dyllin's golden life-thread.

The second strand was dull, depthless, dead black.

TOOLS OF THE TRADE

As she leaped for the dancing spindle and the Scry-o-Tron goggles slid back onto her face, the rumble of an oncoming truck flooded Ilana's ears. The roar of its engine filled the room and shook her to the bones. She blinked and squinted through the goggles, her eyes dazzled by the glare of onrushing headlights as the huge vehicle took a curve badly and skidded into the wrong lane of the narrow, winding road. Time stretched out as Ilana sank deeper into the vision surrounding her, all of her senses becoming one with Dyllin's. Her stomach lurched, sharing her sister's blind panic as Dyllin's hands froze to the steering wheel, unable to do anything but stare helplessly at the doom barreling down on her. Over the scream of air brakes, Ilana heard her sister's faint, final words of surrender, "I'm going to die because I couldn't match some ribbons. Oh, *that's* worth it."

The next instant, Ilana's left hand closed on the spindle. Her right hand seized the black thread and gave it one sharp, short yank. It was like pulling the cord on a top: The black thread came away in her hand and crumbled into dust; the spindle went flying. It plowed through the array of cute little mice on Tabby's desk, leaving behind a classic 7–10 split before hitting the floor in a shower of shattered porcelain. Ilana scrambled after it, frantically groping across the linoleum, indifferent to the shards of broken figurines she was driving into her palms and knees. She pounced on the spindle at last and sat back, hugging it to her chest and gasping.

"What happened?" Arachne cried. She rappelled off the file cabinet and scuttled to Ilana's side. "Your sister— Is she all right?"

"I don't know, I don't know, I don't know, I don't—" Ilana couldn't seem to stop repeating the same words helplessly. She was shaking, and her bleeding hands held Dyllin's spindle in a white-knuckled grip. Finally she made a great effort, took a deep breath, and regained control. "I-I just looked at the thread and saw— I saw something terrible about to happen to her, and so I just— I just—" She inhaled again and let it out for a count of five heartbeats as her fingers slowly uncurled from the spindle. "Oh look," she said with a strange calmness. "It's gone."

"What's gone?" Arachne asked.

"The thread. The black thread." Ilana removed the Scry-o-Tron 9000 and wiped the lenses on her shirt a second time. "That's got to mean something good, right?"

"Why don't you just put those back on and see for yourself?" The spider waved at the goggles, now neatly folded in Ilana's lap.

Ilana shook her head. "I don't think I can," she said. "I don't think I want to, ever again." She got up carefully and took great pains to replace the instruction booklet and the Scry-o-Tron in their storage tray. Then she stared at her sister's life-thread.

The gracefully turning spindle tickled her palm as more of the golden strand appeared out of nowhere and continued to wind itself around the core.

"She's okay," Ilana said, smiling. "The thread's still coming; she's still alive."

"Careful, there," Arachne cautioned her. "You've got some open cuts on your hands. You don't want to get any of the blood on her life-thread."

Ilana gasped and dropped the spindle. It bounced and rolled across the floor, coming to rest among the bits of shattered mousies.

"And so now it's got porcelain dust all over it instead. *Much* better," Arachne said in the key of Sarcasm Major. She rushed over to retrieve Dyllin's spindle and carry it to safety atop Tabby's desk. The spider made little tsk-tsk-tsk sounds as she examined the life-thread. "Well, I'm not exactly sure what effect this is going to have on her, if any. I know that bloodstains are a bad thing, but other than that . . ." She shook her head. "Maybe we'd better give this a quick cleanup before we reshelve it, just to be sure."

"Okay. Just let me wash my hands first." Ilana headed for the bathroom. "Do you know if they've got a first aid kit?" she called back over one shoulder.

"In the front office under the counter, down in the little stack of utility drawers on the lower right side, in the bottom one," Arachne replied. "While you're there, open up the top drawer and bring back the Oopsie."

Ilana stopped dead in her tracks. "The what?"

"The Oopsie," Arachne said. "You can't miss it. It's the only thing in that drawer."

"The Oopsie." Ilana turned around, one finger lifted as a fresh question rose to her lips. Then the finger curled back down like a slowly deflating balloon as she decided that some things weren't worth debating with a spider. "Never mind. One Oopsie is probably worth a thousand words."

It didn't take her long to get cleaned up, to treat and cover her cuts, and to return to the back office carrying what looked like a red plastic wand from a bottle of bubble-blowing solution.

"Bad news, Arachne. It looks like one of Georgette's kids took the Oopsie and stuck this in its place. Someone's going to get a spanking."

"That *is* the Oopsie," the spider informed her.

"You're kidding." Ilana turned the wand this way and that, studying it from every angle. "I guess it *looks* Oopsie enough—even a little Yikes-ish—but it's plastic. If this is one of the super-de-duper *mucho* magic thingies used by the Fates themselves, with untold power over mortal lives, why is it *plastic?*"

"Spoken like someone who's never had a platinum credit card."

Ilana twirled the wand between thumb and forefinger. "At least it's got a name that's dumb enough to fit it."

"I don't know if it's got a real name," Arachne said. "'Oopsie' is just what Clotho says every time she uses it."

"Clotho . . . Tabby? Why does she need to use it?"

"Same as you: to clean up after her mistakes."

"You mean getting Dyllin's life-thread dirty?" Ilana held the Oopsie up to her right eye like a monocle. "Why can't I just brush it off?"

"Try," said the spider.

Setting aside the Oopsie, Ilana picked up Dyllin's spindle and played out all the dust-and-debris-laden thread. At first she tried pinching the thread and pulling it through her fingers, like running a strand of hair between the teeth of a comb. Not one particle of dust came off.

Next she laid the thread flat on Dimity's desk, took a ruler and tried scraping it over the taut thread like a squeegee on a windshield. Nothing budged.

"What *is* it with this stuff?" she cried in frustration, waving the dangling thread in Arachne's face. "It doesn't feel sticky, and

I had no trouble ripping the black thread off, so why won't any of this other junk let go?"

"Haven't you heard?" the spider asked with a smirk. "Life is tenacious. The black thread . . . well, you know what *that* meant. Life will do everything in its power to keep *that* from latching on, but the other stuff? All the little bits of baggage, the dumb grudges, the frustrations and annoyances you bring on yourself, the too-quick decisions and bad choices and mistakes you make, the things that tangle you up and weigh you down? Those are easy for your life to pick up, not so simple to let go of. That's where the Oopsie comes in. Second chances on a stick, that's what I call it. Want to give it a try? *Finally?*"

A troubling thought made Ilana balk. "I'm afraid, Arachne," she said. "What if I do it wrong? This is my sister's *life*."

"What do you want, practice?"

"That's exactly what I want."

"Isn't that nice. You won't risk damaging your sister's life-thread, but you wouldn't think twice about endangering any-one else's."

"Not anyone's," Ilana said. "Mine." She called out her own name in a strong, clear voice. The last syllable had scarcely left her lips when a second spindle appeared on the desk next to Dyllin's and rolled up against it with a low, solid *clunk*. It was smaller than Dyllin's, with less thread wound around the core, but it was enveloped in a hazy radiance all the colors of a sum-mer sunrise.

"Why is my life doing that?" Ilana asked.

Arachne acted as if the glowing spindle were something she saw every day. "All the spindles for you D. R. Temps kids do that. It's a warning beacon so that the Fates don't accidentally kill you. That would be awful."

"Oh, maybe just a *little,*" Ilana drawled. "This 'accidental' killing stuff—happen a lot, does it?"

"Look, it's a big universe. *Everything* happens a lot. You know how it is: You've got a major workload, all pretty routine stuff but tons of it, you're processing it on autopilot because you've done the same thing since *forever,* and if something slips into the pile that wasn't supposed to be there—"

"Oopsie?" Ilana suggested.

"Oopsie is for Clotho," Arachne said. "Lachesis the Measurer never makes mistakes, and Atropos— Well, all of her mistakes are permanent. Nothing that the Oopsie can fix, once the black scissors cut a thread."

"Hmm." Ilana contemplated her glowing spindle. "So if I keep working for D. R. Temps, I can't be killed? That's one heck of an on-the-job perk."

"No, you can still be *killed,*" Arachne corrected her. "It'd just take more paperwork, and it'd annoy whichever god was scheduled to have you work for them next. Good temporary help is so hard to find these days."

"I am reassured beyond all measure," Ilana said, deadpan. She picked up her life-thread. "Now tell me what to do."

"Simple: It's thread. You thread it."

"Through this?" Ilana held out the open loop of the Oopsie for Arachne's approval.

"No, through your ear. Yes, through *that*. Just start feeding it through the loop until you're out of slack, then pull it back out again. The spindle will only unspool so far. There's always a point when mistakes are too far back in the past to be fixed; then all you can do is live with them. Oh, and learn from them, if you're smart."

"Okay." Ilana began feeling nervous all over again as she aimed the end of her life-thread at the loop. This was harder to do than it looked. The longer she waited, the more thread kept materializing. "It's so weird," she said half to herself. "I've literally got my life in my hands."

Without thinking, Ilana took the end of her life-thread and put it in her mouth, the way she'd wet an ordinary piece of thread before trying to get it through the eye of a needle.

A slab of clear liquid plunged down from the office ceiling as five identical slabs slammed in from the floor and walls. Drenched and sputtering, Arachne glared at Ilana.

"Uhhh . . . Oopsie?" Ilana said sheepishly. She jabbed the thread into the red plastic loop without further ado. No sooner did she pull the first half-inch through than the office and all in it was suddenly dry once more. Ilana looked all around in wonder. "What happened?"

"You made a mistake with a life-thread and the Oopsie cleaned it up," Arachne said. "That's what it does. Keep pulling."

Ilana obeyed. Her life-thread passed through the red plastic loop for about three feet before the spindle tightened up and refused to release any more slack. "Now what?" she asked Arachne.

"Now nothing. Oh, you can give the spindle a twist if you want to hurry things along, but it'll reel in the thread by itself if you don't. See? It's starting to already."

Ilana watched as her life twirled itself back into place. "I don't feel as if that made much of a difference," she told the spider. "Aside from being dry again, I mean. Maybe there just weren't a lot of really big mistakes in my life. None that I made, anyway."

"How wonderful to be you," said Arachne. "Tell you what, before Your Imperial Mistake-less Majesty condescends to clean up your sister's life, why don't you take a quick peek in the mirror?"

Ilana gave the spider a quizzical look, but headed back to the bathroom. A moment later she came barreling out, waving her hands and shouting, "It's gone! It's gone!" She pulled back her hair to show the spot on her cheek where the skull doodle had been. Her cheek was bare.

"Not bad, huh?" Arachne looked as pleased as if she'd invented the Oopsie herself.

"Great," Ilana agreed. "Only . . ."

The spider rolled her eyes. "You're one of those people who finds a diamond in their breakfast cereal and worries about what *might* have happened if you'd bitten it, aren't you? What's bothering you *now*?"

"The doodle. It was a mistake I made before I came to work for the Fates. I thought the Oopsie only worked for on-the-job mistakes."

"Apparently the Oopsie thought otherwise," Arachne told her. "It's got a mind of its own, like a lot of the office equipment in this joint. You don't have to worry about what it can and can't do. It'll let you know. You don't even have to *think*. Now that's what I call a real labor-saving device."

"What if I *like* to think?" Ilana said.

"Then don't watch TV sitcoms and stay out of politics," Arachne replied.

"What else did that thing do to my life?" Ilana demanded, pointing at the abandoned Oopsie.

"Well, you can either waste everyone's time by running your thread past the Scry-o-Tron, or you wait to find out on your own time. Oh, and you can also do something for somebody else, for a change, like taking care of Dyllin's thread before all that junk becomes a permanent part of it."

Ilana picked up her own life-thread again. "I think I should put this back first. How do I do that?"

"Gimme." The spider stretched out her two foremost legs and accepted the golden spindle from Ilana. "Beat it," she told it. It vanished. She winked at Ilana. "It's back in its box; just like a homing pigeon. Now, about Dyllin—"

It didn't take Ilana long to feed her sister's life-thread through the red plastic loop. There was a faint crackling sound as the bits of floor fluff, dust, dirt, and crumbled porcelain entered the Oopsie and clean thread came out the other side.

"I wonder if it got rid of the speeding ticket?" Ilana mused aloud as she watched Dyllin's spindle rewind itself.

"It wouldn't," Arachne said. "She made that mess herself. The Oopsie's only for cleaning up life-thread mistakes made by the Fates or their duly appointed representatives, even mistakes you made before you worked for the ladies." She tapped her own cheek and stared meaningfully at the now-skull-less spot on Ilana's face.

Ilana ignored the little reminder, too excited by future prospects to consider any other past mistakes. "I'm a duly appointed representative of the Fates? Cool."

"Whoa, don't get a swelled head. Like you said, you're just a temp. When Mrs. Atatosk sends you to your next assignment, you're a duly appointed representative of nothing."

Ilana's face fell. "My next—?" She suddenly realized that she'd forgotten about the nomadic life of the temp worker. "But-But I like working here. I know it's only been a week, but I do, and a big part of that is—" She managed a shy smile. "I like working with you."

"You do?" Arachne's usually hard-edged voice softened. For a moment she looked like nothing more than a lonely girl, even if she was a spider from the almost-invisible neck down. Then she shook it all off and was her old, cynical self. "Yeah, well, don't get too attached, okay?"

"What is this?" Ilana demanded. "First you tell me you're unhappy because you don't have anyone to talk to, then you tell me not to get attached? Get off the seesaw, Arachne; that's not how friends act in my world."

"Then *make* friends in your own world! They'll last longer!" the spider shouted. She jumped off Tabby's desk and darted under it. By the time Ilana got down to look for her, she was nowhere in sight.

"Arachne? Arachne!" she called into the shadows. The only sound she heard was the hum of the computer and the quiet clicking as Dyllin's spindle continued to turn on the desktop above her head. "Stupid spider," she muttered as she got back on her feet.

She picked up Dyllin's spindle and stared at it balefully. *I guess I'd better put you back before I do something else to you,* she thought. *Of course I* did *save your life, not that you'll ever know. Even if you did, you'd probably be happier about my getting rid of the skull. What's saving your life compared to saving your wedding photos? Too bad the Oopsie won't let me zap some sense back into you, Bride Brain.*

As she took a breath, ready to send her sister's life-thread back to its place on the infinite shelves of the *back* back office, the tolling of a great bell shook the room. Startled and staggering, she dropped Dyllin's spindle for the second time. She made a wild grab for it and gasped with relief as she caught it before it could hit the floor. Her heart was still beating like a hummingbird's wings when the door from the front office opened just a crack and a long, skinny nose peeked in, followed by the long, skinny person attached to it.

"Uh, hi," he said. "I rang the bell out front but no one

answered so I let myself in. I'm Barry. Mrs. Atatosk sent me."

Ilana muttered a quick "Scram" under her breath, banishing Dyllin's spindle in time for her to shake the bony hand Barry extended. "Hi, Barry," she said, sizing him up. Aside from his overall scrawniness, there wasn't much out of the ordinary about him. In fact, the unexpected visitor was so *into* the ordinary it was amazing that he didn't turn invisible while you looked at him.

I didn't know people could be beige, Ilana thought. Aloud she said, "What does Mrs. Atatosk want? Did I do something wrong?"

She tried to make it sound like a joke, but she was worried. *What if Mrs. Atatosk* does *know what I just did with Dyllin's spindle?* she thought. *What if she's got some kind of on-site spy cam set up everywhere her temps work, just to keep an eye on us? No, no, stop being so paranoid. Arachne knows this office like the back of her hand, if she* had *a hand. She's my friend; she wouldn't let me do anything that would get me into trouble. At least nothing that would get me into trouble* too *easily.*

Barry shook his head. "You didn't do anything wrong. If you did, Mrs. Atatosk would contact you directly. That's how it works. So you're okay."

"Uh . . . that was just a joke." Ilana looked at Barry's blank expression and realized, *Oh great, this guy's one of those people who can't recognize a joke unless you tell them "Hey, listen, I am about to tell you a* J-O-K-E. *When I stop talking, you laugh."*

"Oh. Funny," he said drily. "Mrs. Atatosk wanted me to remind you about the temps' meeting this afternoon."

"Why didn't she just call me?"

He shrugged, a gesture that made him look like a flamingo trying to get comfortable. "It's Friday. Mrs. Atatosk always takes long weekends. She doesn't like to do any business Friday through Sunday unless she has to. But she knew I'd be working around here today, so yesterday she asked me to drop by and remind you about the meeting. Today."

"Uh-huh." Ilana pursed her lips in thought. *That has got to be some of the weirdest reasoning I've ever heard. On the other hand, weird goes with D. R. Temps like cute goes with kittens. Yes, it sounds just weird enough to be standard operating procedure for Mrs. Atatosk.*

"We should probably get going," Barry said. "The meeting starts in an hour, but you never know what the traffic to New Haven will be like."

"Okay, good idea. I'll see you there, Barry, and thanks for—"

"CanIhavearidewithyou?" The words tumbled awkwardly out of Barry's mouth, but Ilana heard the message loud and clear. A bit more slowly, he added: "I live in Hamden, just north of New Haven on the bus. I don't have a car."

Ilana tensed. Giving a more-or-less total stranger a ride was *not* on her list of Things Smart Girls Do. "If you don't have a car, how did you get here?"

"Someone from work dropped me off. Look, Mrs. Atatosk said you might feel uneasy about this. In fact, she said she'd be pretty disappointed if you didn't. Call the D. R. Temps number."

"You said she takes long weekends."

"Oh, she won't be there. But you should call anyway."

Never taking her eyes off Barry, Ilana went to the nearest phone where—to her utter lack of surprise—D. R. Temps was 3 on speed dial, after a local pizza place and Tip-Top Scissors Sharpeners. The phone rang five times before the answering machine picked up.

"Thank you for calling D. R. Temps," Mrs. Atatosk's chipper voice greeted the caller. "No one is here to take your call at this time. Please call back during business hours, Monday through Thursday, unless this is Ilana, in which case, please give Barry a ride to the temps' meeting in New Haven. He's been with us for years. I know his, er, personality takes some getting used to, but he's perfectly harmless and he *is* another one of your coworkers. You never know when a job might call for you dear little temps to work together, so it's best to try to get along. Besides, I have some hopes that socializing with him, even just for the ride into New Haven, will be a good experience for both of you. Trust me. I'm never wrong about these things, you know.

"If this is *not* Ilana, please record your message after the beep. Thank you."

Ilana hung up the phone before the beep and turned to Barry. "Sorry for not believing you."

He waved away her apology. "You can't be too careful. No hard feelings."

"Can we start over?" she suggested. "You know, go through the whole silly song and dance of formal introductions?" Whether or not Barry was the kind of person who'd appreciate it, Ilana tried to lighten things up by dropping an exaggerated curtsy, then extended her hand with a flourish and said, "So pleased to meet you, sir. I'm Ilana Newhouse, and you must be—"

"I know who you are." He uttered a faint, pathetic, whipped-puppy-dog whimper that was so eerie Ilana felt icy claws run down her spine. "You're *her* sister."

COFFEE BREAK!

The Friday afternoon scene at the Wymyn's Koffee Koven wasn't much different from the previous Friday night, just better lit. Ilana walked in to see that the section where she'd first met Max and Joanna was almost entirely empty, even though those purple plush chairs were the most comfortable seats in the house.

Correction: One chair was occupied by a slim, sweet-faced girl about Ilana's age. She had dark blond hair pulled back into a ponytail and was plainly dressed in a white short-sleeved blouse and modest black skirt. Over her heart, the little pin with its four silver acorns told the story: another member of the D. R. Temps team.

The only one here, Ilana thought. *Except for me, unless Barry gets over himself and shows up. He didn't say one word to me in the car, and then he ran away the minute I parked. Why is he so upset that I'm Dyllin's sister? It's not like it was a surprise; he knew it, he said so himself. Eh, maybe he's just too cheap to chip in for the parking meter. Troll.*

So where is *everybody else? Did something happen? Did they cancel the meeting and no one bothered to let me know? Or is everyone else too busy to be here? Don't tell me that girl and I are* it. *I do* not *do well one-on-one with total strangers. Unlike Heather, who's got the power to start a conversation with a stuffed fish.*

She stalled by going up to the counter to place her order. The woman at the cash register urged her to try the unadvertised special, something called a Double Espresso Mocha Empowerment. She described it in such persuasive, tempting terms that Ilana nearly ordered two. Then, mug in hand, she looked back at the table. No one new had arrived.

Damn! Where's Max or Joanna? Ilana thought. She took a deep drink from her mug. It was delicious: hot and strong and sweet, with a strange but wonderful kick to it. *Wow! Where have* you *been all my life?* Ilana felt a tingling sensation run over her skin. Suddenly she felt ready to take over the world, or at least the introductions. She walked right up to the lone temp as if she'd known her for years.

"Hi! Boy, am I happy to see you. For a second I was afraid I was *way* too early. It's my first *official* meeting. Ilana Newhouse." She offered her hand.

The girl hesitated, shy, then shook hands and said, "Sophie

Tilden. And you're right on time. Everyone else tries to be, but you know how it is if something unexpected comes up at work." She spread her hands in a helpless gesture. "How do you like your job so far?"

"It's different, but I like it." Ilana sat down in the chair next to Sophie's. "Of course just when I think I've adjusted to things— Well, let me put it this way, getting here today was *not* half the fun." She proceeded to tell Sophie about her encounter with Barry, up to and including the whimper and the emotional "You're *her* sister."

"Normal people don't make sounds like that," Ilana said. "Do you think he's a werewolf or something? A really *confused* werewolf?"

"Barry?" Sophie replied. "Oh, no. Mrs. Atatosk never hires werewolves. They're unreliable." She spoke with utter sincerity.

"Uh, I was kidding," Ilana said, giving Sophie an uneasy look. She regretted it immediately. The girl turned bright red and pushed herself deeper into her chair, as if hoping that the cushions would swallow her up.

Wonderful, Ilana thought grimly. *We've only just met and already I'm making her squirm. Maybe it's not just That Attitude Thing or the Death Cooties standing between me and universal popularity after all. I'd better try fixing this stat.*

"Hey, forget I said anything." Ilana set her mug down on the table and looked apologetic. "My fault, bad joke. I put my foot in my mouth so much, everything tastes like toenails. Considering who we're all working for, a werewolf on the payroll wouldn't be *that* odd. He could temp for Artemis, goddess of the hunt!"

Sophie managed a timid smile. "No, you're funny; I just take stuff too seriously. I wish I didn't. Dyllin was trying to help me with that. Even if you hadn't mentioned it, I'd have known: The two of you have the same sense of humor."

Ilana opened her eyes wide. "My sister has a sense of humor? Oh. Right, right, you knew her *last* year, back when that was still true."

"I've known her longer than that," Sophie said. "Three years. She told me all about her family, how they'd gone to Africa, how much she missed them." Sophie sipped her drink, a simple cup of coffee. "Especially you."

You'd never guess that from the way she treats me lately, Ilana thought bitterly. "We missed her too," she said automatically. To her surprise, the words came out sounding real, the way a sincere wish for someone else's happiness sounded different than a mechanical "Have a nice day."

"Lots of us temps lose touch during the school year, mostly the ones who are away at college. This is our reunion time. It's too bad that Dyllin couldn't come back to D. R. Temps this summer," Sophie concluded.

"She's otherwise engaged." Ilana steered the subject away from her sister. "So how long do we wait before we quit hoping anyone else will show up?"

Sophie glanced at the door. "Barry will be here. He's always been a very reliable, committed worker. Maybe he just had to . . . had to get a grip on himself. He's probably just walking around the block until he feels better. From what you told me, meeting you was kind of traumatic for him."

"It was Mrs. Atatosk's idea, but I do have that effect on a lot of people. So, why was meeting me rough on Barry, specifically?"

Sophie looked uneasy. "I don't know if I should be telling you this—" she began.

"In that case, let me!" Max Kaufman had come into the Koffee Koven so silently that Ilana didn't know he was there until he did a repeat performance of his chair-back hurdle from the previous Friday. This time his beverage of choice was a large latte, and once again he didn't spill a drop.

"Do you *always* pop into the middle of other people's conversations?" Ilana demanded.

"Like a champagne cork," Max replied with absolutely no sign of repentance. "Very appropriate when you work for the god of wine. So do you want the word on Barry or not?"

"I could stop you?"

Max sprawled across the chair sideways, as if it were a hammock. "Barry had the world's worst crush on Dyllin. You couldn't blame him. Your sister's hot."

"Oh, *do* go on," Ilana said, with a glare that a gargoyle would envy. "*Every* girl alive wants to hear that her sister is hot."

"But that wasn't the only thing about her." Clearly Max had a strong natural immunity to sarcasm. "She was *nice*, you know? She was always doing things to help the other temps. And she had this way of making you feel like you were important, just by the way she listened to you when you talked. The only trouble was, Barry decided that her being nice to him meant more than it actually did; a *lot* more. Oh man, you should've seen him! All last summer he kept begging Mrs. A. for assignments he knew would put him in Dyllin's path, and when that didn't happen, he'd call in sick some days just to be able to run into her 'accidentally.' It was sad. He's a good guy, but she just wasn't interested. She tried to tell him, but she wanted to spare his feelings. There's such a thing as letting a guy down too easily, you know? Particularly when he doesn't want to believe it's happening. I don't think he got the message." Max sighed and stretched his legs toward the ceiling, flexing his feet.

"Max, sit up straight!" Sophie squeaked. "Don't let *her* catch you sprawling all over the furniture again. You know what happened the last time."

"Oooooh, yeah, she said it was my *final warning*. Booga-booga, I'm so scared." He laughed, but it was a nervous laugh. For all his devil-may-care attitude, Ilana saw how quickly he snapped himself upright in the chair, just like last week when it was Joanna who'd reminded him. She also noticed that when he set his cup down on the low, round table in their midst he made very sure to slide a couple of paper napkins under the saucer, so that it wouldn't leave a ring.

Her own drink, however . . .

She picked it up, revealing a telltale white circle on the dark wood. To make matters worse, the Double Espresso Mocha

Empowerment came in a mug, not a cup. No saucer had shielded the table from the full, damaging effect of one very hot beverage. She sucked in a breath through clenched teeth. *Uh-oh,* she thought, taking an anxious sip. *And they told me the owner of this place is fussy about the furniture. This isn't good.*

She looked up at the other temps, indicated the ring, and asked, "Is this going to be a problem?"

Max made a face. "Not for you. You're a girl; you're *special.* According to her, girls can do no wrong. You could carve your initials in the wall and she'd give you a cookie for being *creative.*"

"Don't listen to Max," Sophie said. "He's just annoyed because he's on his last warning."

"Well, I'm not the only one. Corey's in the same boat. It's not fair, the way she picks on us." Max stuck out his lower lip, folded his arms, and sulked.

Wow, Ilana thought as she drank again, studying Max over the rim of her mug. *Does this guy ever make a move that doesn't look like he's posing for a hidden camera? Okay, so he's one of the handsomest guys I've ever seen—real male model material—but I'll bet that when he flies, he's got to buy an extra seat for his ego.*

A mischievous smile lifted the corners of her mouth. *All right, Pretty Boy; time for some fun.*

"You know what, Max?" she said, punctuating the question with another big gulp of her drink. "I haven't even met this furniture-fanatic yet, but if she's treating you badly, that's enough for me! For all of her unjust crimes against you, she is now my mortal enemy!" Here Ilana leaped out of her chair and took a heroic stance, one foot up on the coffee table. "If she wants to harm you in any way, she'll have to go through me to do it!"

The stunning silence that followed Ilana's dramatic outburst filled the little coffee shop and seemed to drip like custard from the blades of the ceiling fans. Max and Sophie stared at her in slack-jawed wonder.

"Don't everyone applaud at once," Ilana said, resuming her seat and taking another long slurp from her mug. She felt surge after surge of power rush through her body as she drank, an electric force that shot straight up her spine. Putting down the mug, she leaned forward until her face was about an inch away from Max's.

"What's the matter, sweetie?" she drawled. "Don't you *like* being in the spotlight? Or does it always have to be on *your* terms? Well, boo-hoo, for once a woman's the one in charge, like it or lump it. Why don't you say something? Why don't you start whining about how unfair it is that this is the one place on earth where women get treated better than men? Why don't you quit D. R. Temps and go out into the real world where you know everyone's going to knock themselves out giving you all the breaks, all the advantages, and all the best jobs because you're a good-looking white male? Why don't you—?"

"Right." A hand came out of nowhere, shooting past Ilana's face, making her jerk back involuntarily. It pounced on her drink, snatching it away. A young man with an awe-inspiring headful of dreds stuck his nose into the depths of the mug and took a deep sniff. "Just as I thought," he said. "This is a *triple*. No wonder you went meltdown on poor Max. That does it: You're cut off." He upended the mug into a plastic basin of dirty dishes under a BUS YOUR OWN TABLES sign.

"Who do you think you are?" Ilana was on her feet, shouting in the newcomer's face. "That was *mine*!"

"Unlike your mind, once you drank more than half of it," the boy said, holding his ground. "Or are you temping for the Furies?"

"Oh, you don't *want* to know who I'm temping for, you little twerp," Ilana shot back. "Because if you knew, your life could get reeeeeeeeally itchy, reeeeeeeeally fast."

"Oh, reeeeeeeeally?" His grin was twice as bright as Max's and about a hundred times as aggravating. Ilana couldn't let him get away with it.

"Is working for the Fates real enough for you, boys?" She bared her teeth and made snipping motions with her fingers.

"As if the Fates would let a raw newbie like you anywhere near the threads. I'll bet all they let you do is type death receipts. *If* that. You're probably just babysitting for Georgette's kids."

"I'll have you know that I not only get to *touch* the threads, I've even—!"

"Corey, Ilana, *please* sit down and shush. This isn't wise. People are staring." Sophie popped up between the two of them like a brave little blade of grass between two massive blocks of sidewalk concrete.

"I don't think that bothers Little Miss Drama Queen," Corey

said with a provoking laugh. "She's probably eating up all the attention with a spoon. *Dyllin* never had to grandstand for people to notice her."

Ilana felt her face getting hot. Was everyone from D. R. Temps part of her sister's secret fan club? "Dyllin's not working with you anymore, loser," she gritted. "She's getting *married.*"

She used the word like a weapon. For the first time in her life, she realized that she actually *hated* someone. The longer she stared at him, the more items added themselves to the Why I Hate Corey list in her head. She hated how smart he was for guessing that she temped for the Fates, she hated the way he'd dismissed her as a newbie, she hated the high-handed way he'd dumped her mug, she hated how casually he seemed to take whatever she dished out—scenes, threats, anger, everything. And she *really* hated the fact that he was probably comparing her to Dyllin. No need to ask who'd win *that* little contest. She hoped he liked Dyllin. No, she hoped he *loved* Dyllin. She prayed he was just like poor Barry, carrying a hopeless crush on her big sister, guaranteed to take the news of Dyllin's upcoming wedding hard.

"Married?" The little silver ring through Corey's left eyebrow rose. He smiled. "Who's the lucky guy? Ras, right?" Ilana pressed her lips together, refusing to answer. "Sure, it's gotta be Ras. Like we couldn't see *that* coming after what happened last summer. Mrs. A. only brought Ras in after Patrick had that family emergency the last week in August and had to quit all of a sudden, but he didn't waste time. He took one look at Dyllin and managed to connect with her more in seven days than poor old Barry did in months. Hey, Max, remember the fun we all had at that end-of-season party? The one at Six Flags?"

He sat down in the chair Ilana had deserted when she'd leaped to her feet, chatting about old times with Max, acting as if she'd suddenly turned invisible. Ilana fumed, speechless with rage. Her fingers curled and clenched, aching to reach down and yank that insufferable boy out of her chair by the neck or, even more satisfying, by the dreds. She imagined how wonderful it would be to grab the big plastic bin where he'd dumped her drink and dump *that* on his head.

Why stop there? Words buzzed like wasps inside her head. *Look at him sitting there, Mr. Big Important Man, acting like he's so much better than you are, pushing you aside, making sure that everyone keeps talking about things from the past, a past that doesn't include you. You should teach him a lesson. You should show him how dangerous it is to treat you like this. Yes, yes, make him sorry! Go get another coffee, nice and fresh and* boiling *hot.* You'll *know what to do with it, won't you?*

Ilana's mind filled with a vision of herself pouring a huge cup of scalding coffee into Corey's lap. It was such a vivid image that she could almost hear his scream. That was bad enough, but worse, the vision let her see the look on her own face, her reaction to causing so much pain: She was enjoying it. She was grinning like a jackal.

The ugliness of it all hit her like a physical blow. This was worse than her grandstanding in front of Max earlier, and the fierce, intense hatred she'd felt toward Corey. *Where did* that *come from?* she thought, bewildered. *I just met him! He didn't do anything that should have made me so angry, let alone want to* hurt *him like that. This isn't me. I mean, I* hope *it's not me. Why am I turning into such a monster? I've got to get away before I do something terrible.* She staggered away from Corey and the others, bumping into someone behind her. "Sorry, sorry," she muttered, turning around.

"Not a problem." A tall, unbelievably beautiful woman stood holding out a large, steaming cup of coffee. "Here's your order, dear. You'll know what to do with it, won't you?"

"No!" Ilana reacted as if the woman had said, "Here's your cobra." She jumped backward so fast and so far that she hit the back of one of the overstuffed purple chairs and went flipping over the top, right into Corey's lap.

"Wow, and I've got to *work* for that," Max said.

Ilana groaned and covered her face with her hands. "What's the matter with me?" she wailed. She cringed at the twisted, ugly thoughts she'd had. The worst part was how they'd all seemed to make horrible *sense* to her, as if they were things she should be doing, when in reality they were things she'd never want to do in a million years. "What *happened* to me?"

The woman crouched beside the chair and patted Ilana's arm gently. The cup of hot coffee she'd been holding had vanished like a popped soap bubble. "A *Triple* Espresso Mocha Empowerment happened to you, dear," she said. "It was an accident. I tell my girls never, ever give one of those to a new customer. First give her a double and see how she handles that. Apparently there was a slipup somewhere along the line." The woman made a compact, graceful gesture with her right hand and a glass goblet filled with bubbling golden liquid appeared cradled in her palm. She handed it to Ilana. "Drink this."

Ilana eyed the goblet suspiciously and made no move to take it from the woman's hand.

"What's the matter?" Corey asked. "You promise your mommy you wouldn't take candy or magic potions from strangers? Go ahead, drink it. It's ginger ale. It'll get the other stuff out of your system faster."

"How do you know?" Ilana said, giving him the same look she'd been aiming at the goblet.

"Corey knew enough to make you mad on purpose so that your rage would burn off most of the effects of your first drink," the woman said. "He's learned many useful things over the years." Her mouth quirked up at one corner as she added, "Including, apparently, how to be an armchair."

"Oh!" Ilana realized she was still sitting on Corey's lap. Red-faced, she jumped up and slipped into a seat across the coffee table from him where she sat curled up into a small, tight ball of embarrassment.

The woman glided over to perch on the arm of Ilana's chair, and handed her the goblet. This time Ilana accepted it without objection, took a tiny sip, discovered it was indeed ginger ale, and drained the glass before asking, "How much caffeine *do* I have in me?"

A ceramic mug shaped like a jolly piglet appeared in the woman's hand. She shook her head as if she were Ilana's favorite grandma instead of someone gorgeous enough to stop a charging herd of soap opera casting directors in their tracks. "It's not the caffeine that affects you, dear," she said. "It's the power. *My* power."

"Yours?"

"Why yes," she said, sipping a fragrant brew of lemon, honey, and sage. "I have enough to share, especially with those who might not have enough of their own."

"Girls?" Ilana asked, remembering what Max had said. *You're a girl, you're* special.

"Mostly. No one tells boys that math is hard. No one tells them that they probably won't enjoy science. Boys' athletic teams don't have to fight *too* hard for funding. And no one looks at them funny when they want to play electric bass in a rock band instead of piano at a recital. So, yes, sometimes I do give out a little taste of my power to those who need it most. Is it my fault if they're girls? And other times I like to use it as a test, above all with you dear D. R. Temps children."

"Ilana, this is Circe," Sophie said. "She's the owner of the Koffee Koven. She knows all about us, and she uses her magic to shield us from the other customers. Usually they don't even realize we're here."

"Unless *someone* makes a big scene," Corey put in with a wink. "Drama Queens trump shielding spells two to one."

"Corey, the triple is out of Ilana's system," Circe said frostily. "There is no further need for you to annoy her."

"Not even if it makes her look at me again?" he asked, all innocence. Ilana raised her eyes just in time to catch the full warmth of his most charming smile. She couldn't help smiling back.

"Whether or not you make scenes here does not matter, in the long run," Circe went on. "Even when other people do notice you, my spells stop them from remembering anything afterward. That's why you can have your meetings here in complete safety."

"Are you really *the* Circe?" Ilana asked. "The one from the *Odyssey*? The sorceress who turned Odysseus's crewmen into . . . into . . . ?" She eyed the piglet mug tentatively.

"That's right, dear: pigs. Every last one of them," said Circe. She gave the ceramic piglet a kiss on the tip of its snout. "And I prefer to be called an 'enchantress,' if you don't mind. 'Sorceress' sounds just too, too black-cauldron-and-brimstone for me. Besides, sorceresses have to *work* to obtain their powers. My daddy's Helios, the sun god, Mom's an ocean nymph, and they both agreed: Magic makes a *much* better birthday gift than new socks and underwear."

"So when you say that you like to test the D. R. Temps people—" Ilana paused and nibbled her lower lip. She didn't want to risk offending the enchantress by asking the wrong questions, yet she *had* to know: "What happens if we fail?"

"Oh, don't worry about that, dear." Circe dipped one finger in her mug and painted a glowing *A* on the air. "You passed, even though you were working under a disadvantage. A Triple Espresso Mocha Empowerment is a lot to handle."

"So if I'd failed the test, you'd give me a Get Out of Being Turned Into a Pig, Free card?"

"Don't treat this as a joke." Circe's perfect mouth contracted into a frown. "If you'd failed, I would have reported the results to Mrs. Atatosk. She would not be pleased, and you would be out of a job."

"I don't understand," Ilana said. "I mean, I'm happy I passed, but I still don't know how. I didn't *do* anything."

"Exactly." Circe's scowl began to fade. "I wanted to see what would happen if you had the power to hurt someone who'd offended you. You chose *not* to take advantage of that."

"Well, it's not like I've got that kind of power all the time," Ilana said.

"Yes, but as one of our temps, you might have access to it, sometime. *Unsanctioned* access. There's no such thing as petty theft when you work for the gods."

Ilana remembered the spindles and the Oopsie. *That wasn't exactly* illegal *access,* she thought. *Just a little . . .* early *access, that's all.* Still, she prayed that Circe couldn't read minds.

"It's not like we *never* get to borrow some of the gods' powers," Max put in. "It'd be kind of hard to do our jobs without it. We've just got to know our limits, and they"—he nodded at Circe—"have to know they can trust us not to get carried away with all the mythic mojo."

The enchantress gave him a look of grudging approval. "Giving too much power to anyone can be a dreadful thing, but it is most dangerous when power falls into the hands of a person who's never had any at all."

"We knew someone like that in Africa," Ilana said. "He was the youngest and poorest of five brothers until the others died in a smallpox epidemic. By local law, he was the only heir. His brothers had wives and kids, but he threw them out with nothing, just the clothes on their backs. He thought they hadn't respected him when he was poor, so now that he was rich, all he wanted to do was teach them a lesson."

"Now you know why I like to test the temps," Circe said. "If one of you might use your job to *mis*use our powers, best for us to know that now and stop it dead."

Ilana held her hands up as if warding off the very thought. "No, nuh-uh, not me, no way, trust me, honest." She looked at Corey. "Hey," she said in a quiet voice. "You did me a favor, dumping that cup. If I'd gotten the full force of a triple, maybe I wouldn't have passed Circe's test at all. Thanks. Sorry if I snapped at you. Or roared."

"Forget about it," he replied. "It's what I do."

"Corey's kind of a specialist when it comes to saving people, Ilana," Sophie explained. "He temps for heroes."

"Not gods?" Ilana was confused.

"Most heroes are at least half-gods," Corey said. "Theseus was the son of the sea god, Poseidon; Achilles' mother was a minor sea goddess named Thetis. Zeus was the father of Perseus and Hercules and—" He paused and gave her a devastating smile. "Let's just say that Zeus really, really, *really* likes big families."

"Oh yeah, right!" Ilana slapped her forehead. *God, Corey must think I'm a real airhead.* "And Zeus made Hercules a full-fledged god after he died," she piped up.

"Talk about the perks of being the boss's son, huh?" Max put in.

"So what does a hero temp do?" Ilana asked. And because she was feeling like her old self again, she couldn't resist adding, "Type rescue receipts?"

Before he could reply, Barry, Joanna, and a few other kids came into the Koffee Koven and joined the group already around the table. While they moved more chairs into the circle, Circe drifted back into the kitchen.

Joanna had just finished the introductions when Max turned to Ilana, grinned, and said, "Remember that little rule I mentioned last week?"

Ilana took the reminder with good humor. "Newbie buys the first round? No problem. Who wants what?" she asked her assembled coworkers. Everyone cheered.

By the time she returned with a tray full of brimming cups, mugs, and glasses, the meeting was under way. One of the newcomers had taken her chair, but there was a vacant one next to Corey.

Aside from the newbie buys the first round rule, there were no formalities at the temps' weekly meeting, no chairman, no raised hands, no *Robert's Rules of Order.* The only two "official" events were introducing Ilana and handing out everyone's pay. Joanna took care of both duties, producing the stack of envelopes from the blue Lucite clipboard she carried. Ilana opened hers and looked inside immediately. She still couldn't get over the sight of so much cash.

"Boy, she's brave," Ilana muttered.

"Who is?" Corey asked.

"Joanna. I'd be scared out of my wits if I had to carry that much cash around with me every week."

"I hate to break it to you, but we all have to do it, sooner or later," Corey told her. "Mrs. Atatosk contacts a different one of us every Thursday for payroll duty. Wait, that's wrong, sometimes it's the same person for two, three, even four weeks in a row. The clipboard just poofs itself into your hands and Tag, You're It. It's totally random, but that's Mrs. A. all the way. Even if she is one of my favorite people, sometimes I think the wheel's still spinning but the squirrel is dead."

"Don't you mean hamster?"

"I'm a city guy; I know squirrels."

"What about when you're working?" Ilana asked. "Don't you ever get to go somewhere that's *not* a city?"

"There's just not that much call in the suburbs for the kind of work my bosses do. It's all rescues and high adventure and quests. What's the worst threat anyone ever has to face in Country Club Land? Crabgrass?"

"Not that you're prejudiced or anything," Ilana said wryly. "So what *have* you done, temping for those big-shot heroes? Besides bravely making fun of how you assume other people live?"

"Fought crabgrass," Corey replied.

A touch on her arm made Ilana turn before she responded. It was Max. "Hey, would you mind putting this on hold for just a sec and helping me get us all some munchies? My treat."

Ilana followed him to the Koffee Koven counter where he put in an order for a couple of plates of assorted cookies, cakes, and biscotti, then spoke to her about something definitely *not* pastry-related.

"Look, Ilana, you're never going to get a straight answer out of Corey about his work. He doesn't like to talk about it, but trust me, every summer there's suddenly a big crush of mysterious Good Samaritan stories in the papers: saving kids from getting hit by cars; getting medical help for homeless people; fixing things on a city block where the old people got mugged so much they were too scared to go outside, even in the daytime."

"But it can't be all Corey's doing," Ilana protested. "The heroes he works for must do some of it."

"You can tell the heroes' deeds from Corey's easily: They always get their names in the paper or on the air. Sure, they use aliases, but they still make damn sure they're spelled right in print.

"Corey works secretly, quick getaway, no name left behind, and if any reporters got too close, Circe smacks down one of her spells and they lose the trail. You know he's even stepped in to save the necks of some kids from his school, the same kids who hassle and bully him all year long? Boy, does that take a lot of cover-up spells afterward!"

"Why would he do anything for them?" Ilana asked.

"My question exactly," Max replied. "I asked him, Why did you waste your time and risk your neck for those jerks? Why didn't you just walk away and save someone worth saving? And he told me, 'Who gets to decide who's worthy and who's worthless, Max? Walking away isn't what you do.'"

Corey smirked at her when Ilana finally returned to her seat carrying the snacks. "You and Max have a nice time all by yourselves?" he asked lightly. "Pick out your china and silver patterns yet?"

"Shows what you know," Ilana countered. "First he's got to beat my father in a round of golf before he can win my hand in marriage. *That's* how we do things in Country Club Land."

"Hey girl, you've got *attitude,*" Corey said happily. He leaned back, linked his hands behind his head, and stretched his legs, letting his feet come to rest on the tabletop. "I think I like—"

"What did I tell you last time?"

Thunder shook the Koffee Koven. Cups rattled in saucers, tables did little jigs across the floor, clouds of steam worthy of Old Faithful billowed from behind the counter. The air smelled of bubbling lava, burning cities, and fresh-ground Kona coffee. Ordinary customers screamed and raced for the exit.

When the effects of the potion in their drinks kicked in, they'd think they'd simply overreacted to a car backfiring, but for now they panicked.

The floor heaved and rumbled. Fake-wood-patterned linoleum turned bloodred, then charred to black as Circe burst upward from below, a golden wand in one hand, a platter of chocolate biscotti in the other.

"You!" She leveled the biscotti at Corey, then realized her

error and switched hands. "What did I tell you the last time you put your feet on *my* table?"

Before Corey could get out a single word in his own defense, she forged on, "Just because you temp for heroes, you think that makes you one of them? Well, let me tell you, I have known heroes in my day, and I wouldn't let them put their feet up on my furniture, either! There are no special privileges for heroes under my roof, no reason for you to ignore the rules, and above all—"

She raised her wand. Blue and silver lightning writhed and sizzled and slid up and down the length of it until a gigantic fireball formed at the tip. It hummed and crackled as Circe aimed it straight at Corey's heart.

"No!" Ilana cried, rising from her chair, but she was too late.

As the blast engulfed Corey in a blinding flare, Circe's words rang in Ilana's ears: "—above all, *no third chances*!"

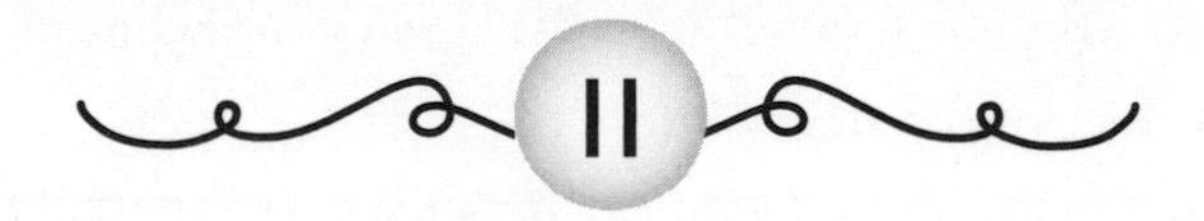

YOUR COWORKERS AND YOU

"Whoa." Ilana wiped smoky tears out of her eyes. "Overreact much, Circe?" But the enchantress had vanished.

"Oh man," said Max. "Oh man, this is really messed up." He stared at the scorched spot on the purple plush armchair where Corey had been sitting until a split second ago.

In the center of the blast zone a bewildered, half-grown, brown-and-white pig sat blinking at the other temps.

"She did warn him," Sophie said meekly. "Several times. He did get a third chance, and a fourth, and—"

"So that makes it okay for her to do *this* to him?" Max snapped at her. "For putting his freakin' feet up on the freakin' *furniture*?"

"She does seem to care about her furniture just . . . a little . . .

too much." Sophie's voice dwindled away to a whisper as she spoke. "Maybe if we asked her why—"

"So we can *understand* her? Oh yeah, that'll make it all better." Max threw up his hands in frustration. "Why don't you try to make *her* understand why Corey acts the way he does, instead? He lives with his grandma here in New Haven, on next to nothing except what he brings home from D. R. Temps. I went by their apartment last summer. It's tiny, and the furniture's so old that it doesn't matter *what* you do to it anymore. He didn't put his feet up on the coffee table to get in Circe's face, it's just a habit; he did it without thinking."

"Well, maybe he should try paying attention," Barry suggested. "His grandma's place isn't the world."

Ilana saw Max's hands become fists, but only for a moment. He rounded on Barry. "Whose side are you on anyway? Just because we're all still in high school and you're in—" He stopped and gave Barry a suspicious look. "Say, didn't you *graduate* from college already?"

"So what if I did?" Barry muttered.

"So why are you still working for D. R. Temps? Shouldn't you be off somewhere, being a grown-up? Couldn't you get a *permanent* job? Or did you stay because this is the only place you can feel like you're better than everyone else just because you're older?"

Barry's body stiffened. "I wasn't going to come back this summer." He spoke in a tight, controlled voice. "I only did it because . . . because you people need someone older to keep an eye on you."

"Bull," said Max. "You came back because you thought Dyllin would."

Barry turned bright red, but he continued as if Max hadn't said a word. "You're all like Corey: You think you know everything, but then you go and do something stupid. When you get punished for it, you whine about how the immortals are unfair. Did you ever think that they *are* fair and you just can't handle it?"

"Great. You sound like one of *them*."

"Hey, they're the ones who pay our salaries."

"Anyone ever tell you that there's a difference between getting paid and selling out? Or didn't you get to that chapter in the *How to Kiss Up to Immortals* book you've been memorizing?"

Barry swallowed hard. "I-I'm only saying that the gods . . . that they usually treat us okay, and if we don't like it, we-we're free to quit anytime we want."

"That's just the kind of answer I'd expect from you," Max sneered. "You wouldn't rock the boat even if it were sinking. Yep, good old Barry, just minding his own business, doing his job, and swallowing his pride. Not much of a mouthful, is it?"

Ilana dropped her head back and let out a half-strangled cry of exasperation that brought every eye in the Koffee Koven away from Max and Barry, and straight to her. "Stop that! Do we really want to waste time bickering or do we want to do something to help Corey?"

The youngest temp, a girl named Daniele Potter, hung her head. "Corey's beyond our help now," she said.

"No, he's not," Ilana countered. "He's right there." She pointed at the pig, who grunted mournfully.

"It doesn't matter where he *is*," Barry said. "We can't do anything to help him. Circe's the only one who can, and she won't."

"What makes you so sure?" Ilana demanded. "Do you know, or are you just too scared to ask her?"

Barry looked away. "There's a difference between being brave and being stupid."

"Oh wow, you *are* scared!" Ilana's hand flew to her mouth. "You're afraid that if you ask her to help Corey, she'll get mad and turn *you* into a pig."

"Wouldn't you be?" Barry's unexpected shout hit like a hurricane blast. "It could happen. Who could stop her? *You?*" He made a sweeping gesture that included all the temps. "Can anyone here be sure what the gods will do to us, even the ones we work for?"

"Exactly!" Ilana said. "We can't be sure *what* they'll do, so why assume it'll be the worst thing? If Circe turned *you* into a pig, would you want everyone to stand around paralyzed with fear, just talking about oh, it's sooooo hopeless and gosh, isn't it a shame, tsk-tsk, too bad?" She shook her head violently. "I won't do that, and I'll bet Corey wouldn't either. He temps for *heroes*."

"Heroes *try* stuff all the time, but they never win when they go up against the gods," Barry told her. "Bellerophon was a hero. He tried to fly the winged horse Pegasus all the way to the gods' home on Mount Olympus, but Zeus destroyed him with a thunderbolt."

"I know all about Bellerophon," Ilana said. "I read his story when I was seven or eight years old. He decided he deserved immortality, so he tried storming Olympus to *take* it. Sure, Zeus overdid it with that thunderbolt, but Bellerophon was still more like a bully than a hero."

"Well, how about Theseus, then?" Barry countered. "He tried to help his friend Pirithous steal Persephone from the Underworld, but Hades caught them and made them his captives."

"Since when is stealing someone else's wife heroic?" Ilana said. "It's just nasty. When Orpheus went into the Underworld to bring back his own wife, Eurydice, he didn't have swords or spears or even muscles to help him stand up to Hades; only his music. He knew that if he failed, he'd never see the sun again, but he took that chance anyway because he cared more about saving someone besides himself. *That's* being a hero."

"If you know so much about the gods and being a hero, why don't *you* show us how it's done?" Barry's challenge echoed through the suddenly silent Koffee Koven. Everyone looked at Ilana, including the pig.

Ilana folded her arms. "All right," she said. "I will. Where can I find Circe?"

No one answered.

"Oh, come *on*!" Ilana stamped her foot. "You don't have to be scared to tell me; she can't turn you *all* into pigs. It's against the New Haven zoning laws and she'd lose her lease."

"We're not afraid," Daniele said. "We just don't know."

"She got pretty mad," Max said. "I saw it happen once before, last summer."

"The book club ladies?" Joanna asked.

Max nodded. "We were trying to have a meeting here, and they were all at the next table, discussing some book that maybe *one* of them had actually read. The rest were arguing about it and yapping on their cell phones at the same time. Circe went over and asked them to pick a conversation and stick to it. That was when the woman in charge of the whole thing told her that *they* were her customers, *they* paid her bills, *they* were real women because they had husbands and families, which *she* obviously didn't—don't ask me why she assumed that—and if *they* wanted to talk on their cell phones, they would damn well do it." He sighed.

"Pigs?" Ilana asked.

"Parrots."

"It fit," said Daniele.

"And it lasted for a week," Sophie said in her mousy little voice. "Because when Circe gets mad enough to turn someone into an animal, she disappears right afterward to cool off. If she didn't do that, it might become a habit again."

"No one wants that," Max said. "Trust me."

"You don't want to know what poor Mrs. Atatosk had to go through to cover up *that* little incident," Joanna said.

"So Circe's gone?" Ilana swore under her breath. "Great. I

wanted to do something to help Corey, not sit on my butt and eat biscotti. Let's call Mrs. Atatosk."

Barry gave her a superior look. "I *told* you she always takes long weekends. No business calls; just emergencies."

Wow, this guy's got two personalities: in-the-background and in-your-face, Ilana thought, scowling at her sister's failed suitor. *I liked him better when he was beige. "This* isn't an emergency?" she demanded, waving a hand at Corey.

Joanna cocked her head and studied the pig. "He's not acting like it is. In fact, he seems pretty laid-back about it." She consulted the blue clipboard. "Let's wrap up the meeting, then try to reach Mrs. A. If she hears we took care of business first, maybe she'll help us."

"'Maybe'?" Ilana was surprised by how angry she was getting on Corey's behalf, even if he seemed to be taking his new shape quite calmly. Maybe he didn't mind spending a little downtime as a pig, or maybe it was a false calm, a side effect of Circe's spell. "What 'maybe'? She's *got* to help him."

"Mrs. Atatosk doesn't *have* to do anything," Barry said with a nasty tone in his voice. "This must be your first summer job, Ilana. You still haven't learned Lesson Number One: The boss has the power; the boss makes the rules and the decisions. That's true whether you work for gods *or* mortals."

Ilana opened her mouth, ready to tell Barry to shut up, ready to sting him with a barb about Dyllin's ongoing hate affair with kiss-ups, teacher's pets, and toadies. She stopped herself before the first spiteful syllable left her lips.

No, she thought. *Just because I* can *hurt him doesn't mean I* have *to.*

She sat back in her chair, arms crossed. "Fine. Let's do this."

"It won't take long," Joanna said, consulting the papers on the clipboard again. "Just a last-minute check to see if we've got any on-the-job problems or questions."

A low murmur ran around the circle of temps, punctuated by a few grunts and snorts from Corey. Apparently everything non-pig-related in the temps' worlds was going smoothly.

"I've got a question," Daniele said, raising her hand. "Anybody ever hear of a god called Pele?"

"God*dess*." Ilana corrected her without thinking. "But she's not Greek; she's Hawaiian. She's in charge of volcanoes."

"How did you know that?" Max asked, obviously impressed.

"Dyllin got me into the Greek myths when I was a kid," Ilana replied. "When I got old enough to hit the library on my own, I found out there were other mythologies in the world. Some of the Pele stories are pretty cool . . . for a volcano goddess."

"Ouch," said Max.

"Ohhhh, thanks, Ilana," Danielle said. "I start temping for her Tuesday. That could've been embarrassing, calling her a god."

"No problem. And did I mention how much I wish I were you? As in, you in *Hawaii*?"

Daniele smiled. "I'll bet Mrs. Atatosk will give you a more interesting job soon, too."

"I'm working for the Fates. We're talking the life-and-death-one-snip-of-the-scissors-and-you're-history Fates. I don't think I could stand something more interesting."

"How interesting can it be?" Max said. "It's in Connecticut." Corey squealed at him angrily. Max gave the pig a cynical look. "Oh, like you wouldn't rather temp for a Hawaiian hero-god like Maui? Or one from Japan or Kenya or India or somewhere *exciting?*"

"I think Corey's had enough excitement for today," Ilana said. "Is that it for the meeting? Because I'd like to call Mrs. Atatosk about finding Circe."

Joanna flipped through the papers on her clipboard, then paused and shook her head. "You're not going to find her, Ilana. She's gone. Circe appeared at the spa where Demeter and Persephone are staying. It's in Santa Fe, New Mexico. None of them will be coming back here for a week."

"How do you know that all of a sudden?" Ilana demanded.

"It's right here." Joanna passed her the clipboard.

Ilana riffled through the pages, her scowl deepening. "These pages are all blank!"

But as she spoke, a clear, firm strand of words materialized across the top sheet.

Dear Ilana,

Circe is taking a much-needed vacation, with my blessing, and promises to fix Corey as soon as she returns. I wouldn't dream of interfering with one of her spells. She's such a sensitive girl and she did promise to make everything all right. Do be patient.

And please be a good girl and send me your Waiver.

It must have slipped your mind, but I really can't be held responsible for anything that happens to you.
R. Atatosk

"You didn't sign the Waiver?" Barry sounded genuinely shocked. Ilana was suddenly aware that he'd been reading over her shoulder. She slammed her hand down on the paper, but it didn't matter. The writing had vanished.

"I *signed* it, if that's any of your business. I just never handed it back to her. Anyway, Mrs. Atatosk's got it wrong. Under the terms of the Waiver she's *not* responsible for anything that happens to me, including lemurs."

"Yeah," Max said. "Lemurs. I remember that one." He shuddered.

"Well, it's still not right." Barry was working himself into a full-fledged huff. "We all managed to sign the Waiver *and* hand it in. You think the rules don't apply to you?"

"That depends," Ilana said slowly. "Is there a rule against my kicking your—?"

"Out!" Both of the girls who worked behind the counter at the Koffee Koven suddenly appeared in the center of the circle of temps. They spoke with one voice and pointed firmly to the door.

"Hey, we're not done here yet," Max objected.

"Yes, you are," the blond one said. "Isaura and I may just be nymphs, but we're the ones in charge here whenever Circe leaves."

"Evadne's right," said Isaura, the brunette. "Hit the road. We're doing you a favor, throwing you out like this. Remember Circe's little . . . *demonstration* before?" She nodded at the charred chair where Corey still sat, grunting to himself. "How long do you think it'll be before the cops show up to investigate? Do you want to try explaining the explosion to them? Or the livestock?"

"Oh! I think I hear sirens!" Sophie began to shiver.

"So do we," Evadne said. "That's why we're giving you the boot. You know where the back door is. Use it. We'll handle the cops."

She began to weave strange signs on the air. Ilana stared as the Koffee Koven slowly filled with faint images of a crowd of pale, melancholy people, all of them dressed in black. One of them perched on a stool in the middle of the floor, a sheaf of badly scrawled papers in her hands.

Isaura strode back behind the counter and pulled out a set of bongo drums. "Don't be mean, Evadne; they can stay if they want to." She smiled at the temps. "I hope you enjoy poems about why life is *soooooo* unfair to poets. It'll be just like English class. Won't that be fun?"

Ilana was a pretty fast runner, but she was nearly bowled off her feet in the stampede for the back door.

SELF-MOTIVATION AND YOU

The traffic from New Haven to Porlock's Landing was ghastly, but making that rush hour drive with a pig in the car gave Ilana a whole new perspective on what "ghastly" really meant. The world's cleanest pig could still have just enough Eau de Barnyard smell to turn stop-and-go driving into stop-and-try-to-go-while-holding-your-nose-with-one-hand.

The after-work hush lay over the Yankee Peddler Industrial Park when she pulled into the vacant parking lot and hustled Corey through the front door of Tabby Fabricant Textiles. The outer office was empty.

Good, Ilana thought. *I just want to find Mrs. Atatosk's home phone number—if the Fates don't have it on file, who will?—and get out without having to go through a lot of explanations.*

At the inner office door, she turned and whispered, "Wait here," even though she felt a little silly, talking to a pig.

But he's not *a pig,* she told herself. *Even if Circe's spell has made him forget his human side, I'm not going to treat him like an animal. He's a nice guy. He helped me when I needed it, even when he didn't know who I was. Most people wouldn't bother going out of their way like that for a stranger, not even for a coworker. I like him, and I'm not going to let him down.*

"Psst! Arachne!" Ilana opened the inner office door just a crack and peeked into the darkness, her voice barely above a whisper. "Arachne, are you there?"

"No, I'm at Pismo Beach enjoying all the clams I can eat." The spider's peevish reply from on high came back so loud and clear that Ilana jumped. Several pairs of glowing red eyes glared down at Ilana from a web in the far corner of the ceiling. Arachne had her spider-face on. "Where the heck *would* I be?"

"Shhhh!" Ilana hissed like a boiling teakettle. "Don't yell like that. I don't want anyone else to know I'm back."

"Then this is your lucky day—there's no one here *to* know," Arachne grumped. She shifted into human-face mode just to be able to scowl. "No one but me. Oh, in case you're interested, the Fates called to say that they finished their off-site business."

"The piñata?"

"False alarm. It happens. The Fates don't control events like that, they just have to deal with the mess afterward. Believe me, they're as glad as you are when mortals dodge a world-class disaster. After all these years they actually *like* you people."

"How soon will they be back?" Ilana asked, still lingering just outside the inner office.

"Don't hold your breath. Since you're still supposed to be minding the store until seven, and Georgette's husband is minding the kids, they decided to take a little time off and go antiquing. Of course your mortal idea of antiques is their idea of season-end clearance."

Without another word to Arachne, Ilana switched on the office lights and came in, the small brown-and-white pig trotting at her heels. The spider stared.

"Let me guess: He put his feet up on Circe's furniture. Presto, change-o, ham-o?"

Ilana nodded, not at all surprised. Arachne had been around a long time. Even if she never left the Tabby Fabricant Textiles office, she still probably knew all sorts of things about the ways and whims of D. R. Temps clients.

"This is Corey," she told the spider. "Circe zapped him, then went to New Mexico for a weeklong spa vacation. Mrs. Atatosk is the only one who can help him, but she won't. I need to make her change her mind, but I need her home phone number to do that. I was kind of hoping that the Fates would have it."

"You were also hoping I'd know where they keep it," Arachne said, looking smug. "You don't want to ask them for it directly, do you?"

"Would they give it to me if I did?"

"No."

"So you see." Ilana squatted down beside Corey and scratched behind one of his ears. The pig made small, contented noises.

"If he's happy as a pig, why not wait for—?" Arachne began.

"Pigs don't live with Grandma in New Haven. Do you know how worried that poor woman's going to be if he doesn't come home tonight? Or worse, if he comes home looking like this? Mrs. Atatosk and Circe and the gods can do things to fool mortals, make us see what's not there, disguise what is, but I'll bet there's a limit to that power, and I *really* bet that something like this goes way beyond that limit."

Arachne dropped herself from the web to eye-level with the pig. "Why do I suddenly feel like I'm trapped in a children's classic?"

The pig snorted loudly in reply, sending her swinging on the damp, warm, miniature gale. "Oh, *yuck,* just what I wanted: a pig snot shower!" she exclaimed, busily using her forelegs to groom herself dry. "Does he do this when he's human?"

"I don't know," Ilana said. "We just met. He did me a big favor. I'd like to repay him, but without Mrs. Atatosk I don't know how I—"

Abruptly, Ilana stopped talking. A strange, thoughtful look came into her eyes. Slowly she smiled.

"You just thought of something, didn't you?" the spider said, cringing. Ilana nodded, still smiling. "And I'm not going to like it at all, am I?"

"Come on, Arachne, it'll be perfectly safe."

"That's what my mother said when she started me on weaving lessons and look where *that* got me!"

Ilana clicked her tongue. "You're making a fuss over nothing. Look, I can do this without your help. If you're that scared, go back up to your web and sleep. If anything does go wrong, or the Fates find out, you can honestly say that you didn't see a thing."

"Ohhhhh no you don't." Arachne said sternly, doing her best to cross her forelegs over her thorax. "I don't like the sound of '*If* anything does go wrong.' Because *if* it does—and by 'if' I mean *when*—it won't matter what I tell the Fates; you know what they'll do."

"Blame the spider?"

"Blame the spider." Arachne nodded. "So whatever it is you've got planned, don't. I'm not in the mood for dragging out the Oopsie for any more emergencies."

"Funny you should mention the Oopsie, Arachne dear."

○ ○ ○

"How did you do that?" Corey stood on Georgette's chair, patting his chest as if he were afraid it was going to fall off like a broken eggshell with his pig-self still inside. "Is this real? I mean, permanent?"

"Sure," Ilana said. "Unless you go putting your feet up on other people's furniture again."

Corey jumped off the chair so fast he sent it skidding halfway across the office. "I didn't do that!" he cried, pointing at the combination of hoof- and shoe-marks on the still-rolling seat. "You hauled me onto that chair just before you—!"

"Oh, relax; no one's going to find out. I'll get some paper towels and wipe off your footprints." Ilana headed for the bathroom as she spoke, but before she moved five steps, Corey grabbed her arm.

"Seriously, how did you do that?"

"Just a little something I picked up during on-the-job training." She held the Oopsie up for him to see, twirling it between her fingers. "Not bad for a newbie."

To her surprise, Corey gave her a hard look and said, "Ilana, did the Fates say you're allowed to be using that . . . whatever-it-is?"

"You're welcome," she said coldly. "My pleasure. Don't mention it. *De nada.* Oh, wait, wrong reaction. I was *expecting* to hear you say something like, I don't know, maybe 'Thank you, thank you, thank you *so* much, Ilana, for saving me from a fate worse than bacon. Thank you for risking Circe's wrath, thank you for actually *doing* something when everyone else was just sitting around talking, thank you for driving a pig all the way from New Haven to Porlock's Landing, even though it'll probably take weeks to get the smell out of your car, and most of all, thank you for figuring out a way to help me.' But that's okay. Yelling at me for breaking the rules is a good way to express your gratitude, too."

"I wasn't yelling, I was just—"

"You were just being the big, important, experienced D. R. Temps veteran. Big, important, experienced, and rescued by the newbie. Ow. Does it hurt worse because you're the one who temps for all of those Eek-help-save-me heroes or because you got rescued by a newbie *and* a girl?"

Corey eyed her narrowly. "Have you been drinking Triple Espresso Mocha Empowerments again?"

"I could be drinking water and you'd still tick me off." She turned her back on him and went into the bathroom. While tearing huge wads of paper towels off the roll, a glance at her scowling face in the mirror brought her up short. *Boy, when did I turn into* that *ugly thing?* she thought. *And why* does *Corey get under my skin so easily? He asked a sensible question, and I took it as an insult.* She shook her head. *Even if it was an insult, why should I care? Sure, he's cool, he's cute, and if Max is even half right he's a real hero, but the bottom line is he's nothing to me but a coworker. But is that all I want him to be?*

Corey tried to take the towels from her and clean the footprints off the chair himself, but Ilana angrily jerked away. She attacked the marks on the leather seat like they were her personal enemies.

"Look," he said while she worked. "You're right, I owe you. I should've thanked you first, then asked about that thing you used to help me."

"Or you could have just taken the help without questioning me," Ilana replied, raising her head sharply. He was looking at her so intently that it made her heart beat a little faster and her mouth go dry. *How does he* do *that to me?* she thought. She fought the awkward feeling by putting a little extra bite behind her words: "For your information, beginning Monday I will be spindle-sitting for the Fates, with full access to all the necessary tools for the job, including the one I used to de-pig you." She got up and slam-dunked the used towels into the nearest wastebasket.

"But today's not Mon— Uh, I mean, thanks. Thanks a *lot*. And I'm really sorry I upset you. Are we good?"

Ilana took a deep breath. "Yeah, we're good," she told him. "And we're even."

"I don't think so," Corey said. "I dump your coffee, you save me from being a pig for a week? I still owe you. Tell you what; anytime you need *my* on-the-job skills, call me." He flipped out his cell phone.

"Sure, why not?" Ilana took out her own phone so the two of them could swap contact info. "If I ever need to be rescued from a dragon, you'll be the second to know. After 9-1-1."

"Better stick to 9-1-1," Corey said. "You have to temp for the heroes for at least three years before they promote you to dragon rescues. So . . ." He scratched his head. "You want to get some coffee?"

"Didn't we just have a Learning Experience about too much coffee?" Ilana did her best to act casual, as if she got invitations like this all the time. "But I wouldn't mind some iced tea. Decaf. There's a couple of places in town we could try. Just let me stow this first." She gave the Oopsie a magic wand flourish before putting it away.

"Um, don't you have to put my spindle back too?" Corey sounded uncharacteristically anxious. "You know, so it's safe?"

"Done," Ilana told him. "I sent it back to the shelves as soon as you were fixed."

"How did you know which one was mine?"

"It was the only one that was oinking. So, tea?"

"Hold it right there, missy!" Arachne piped up. "No one said you could go off on some cute little coffee date."

"It is *not* a date," Ilana protested. "It's just coffee—I mean, non-empowering decaf iced tea."

"Call it what you want; you better not go. The Fates had to excuse you for the temps' meeting, but otherwise they expect to find you here." Arachne frowned at Corey and added, "And they *don't* expect *you*."

"I'm sorry, Corey; she's right," Ilana said. "Tabby went meltdown when my friend had to use the bathroom here, and Heather was only in the *outer* office."

"Okay, okay, I'm gone." Corey raised his hands in surrender. "How do I get back to New Haven?"

"Not without a car. Is there anyone you could call for a ride?"

Corey shook his head. "Even if we owned a car, Grandma doesn't drive."

"A friend?"

"I don't have a lot of those where I live."

"I know the feeling," Ilana said. "One of the other temps, then?"

Corey shook his head. "Max is the only one besides you who's got a car. He'd do it, but it's almost Friday night."

"So?"

"So he temps for the party gods, remember? You figure it out. Isn't there a bus or something?"

"Like you said, it's almost Friday night. All of the mass transit schedules between Porlock's Landing and New Haven follow the commuters: *to* New Haven on weekday mornings, *from* New Haven on weekday afternoons and evenings, and nothing to *or* from New Haven on the weekends. Welcome to the wonderful world of suburbia. I guess I'll have to give you a ride back after I get off work. At least you smell better now." She grinned at him.

"Hey! Unfair to pigs!"

"Meanwhile . . ." Ilana checked her watch. "Any idea what time the Fates are coming back, Arachne?"

"Probably not until seven, when they know you'll be leaving," the spider said. "When those sisters get some together-hours off, it's like me and houseflies: They suck 'em dry."

"Ew." Ilana shuddered. "Thank you for a mental image I did *not* need." She turned to Corey. "Do you know how to drive?"

"I have a license. No car, but a license."

"I'll loan you *my* car, you go hang out in town until I'm done here, then we meet up and I'll take you back to New Haven."

"You trust me with your car?"

"Why wouldn't I?"

"In case you didn't notice, I'm what the newspapers call an 'urban youth.'"

"I noticed. Want a medal? I'm what the newspapers call 'weird,' thanks to this." She pointed at her cheek.

"Thanks to what?" Corey squinted.

"Earth to Ilana," Arachne announced. "The skull is *gone*. It is *out* of your life. Get used to it or draw another."

"What skull?" Corey asked. Ilana sighed and told him the whole story. When she was done, he said, "Wow. Smallpox. I thought that was—"

"A dead disease? A lot of people thought that." She eyed him warily. "Well? Aren't you going to ask what it was like, almost dying?"

"Why?" he countered. "It's not exactly something superexotic for me; not in the neighborhood where I grew up. Want to talk *my* version of 3-D? Drugs, drive-bys, and dying. Maybe I never had your firsthand experience with death, but I know enough kids who did. Knew them." He almost made that sound like a challenge.

"Friends of yours?"

He shrugged. "I didn't make a lot of friends before I found D. R. Temps. Just as well; that way I never had to lose them."

"Yeah," Ilana said. She hugged herself as if the room had suddenly turned cold. "I did. My best friend, Atifa, back in Africa. She was one of the first people in that village to get sick. My parents were all set to throw me in the car and get us out of there when I caught it. I collapsed in the middle of writing Atifa a note apologizing for running away, saying I hoped my parents would bring me back to see her again after it was all over, telling her to get well soon." Ilana's laugh was empty. "Get well soon! As if she had a cold or something. When my fever broke, the first thing I did was ask Mom for that note, so I could finish it. That was when she told me."

Something tickled Ilana's cheek. She turned her head slightly and saw that while she'd been talking to Corey, Arachne had managed to climb onto her shoulder, unnoticed. The girl-faced spider's eyes were full of sympathy.

"They ever discover how that outbreak got started?" she asked Ilana.

"No one knew for sure. We heard a rumor that the last batch of smallpox vaccine they used in that village was no good. Someone in the government saw the chance to pocket some extra money and figured no one would ever find out. A dead disease . . ." She shook her head. "I guess the gods were on vacation for that one, too."

Corey's hand fell on her other shoulder. "Listen, you know as well as I do that bad stuff happens even when the gods are paying attention and taking notes."

"Oh *please* don't tell me 'That's just the way it is,'" Ilana said. "That one's right up there with 'Life is unfair' on my list of Things People Say That Make Me Want to Kick Their—"

"I've got a list like that," Corey said, interrupting her. "Know what's on it? 'Something bad happened to me; that proves the gods aren't there.' It comes right after 'Something great happened to me: Hooray, gods!' I guess doing what you can for yourself is a little harder than—" He stopped and looked self-conscious.

"Oh, go ahead and say it," Ilana told him. She wasn't angry.

"Instead of whining about it all the time, right?" This time her laugh was real. "Well, I guess you can't get any more hands-on about changing the world than temping for the gods. Especially when you work in this place." She threw her arms wide.

"Uh-uh," Arachne said sternly. "Ix-nay on the ange-the-world-chay. If you think there's too many nasty surprises in life as-is, you don't want to be fooling around with powers that do *not* belong to mortals. Not unless you *like* chaos."

"Grandma says I do," Corey told her. "Every time she comes into my room, anyway."

"That's not what I—"

"Arachne, do you like coffee?" Ilana broke in.

The unexpected question almost knocked the spider off Ilana's shoulder. "Me? I guess so. All I've ever had was a taste out of the bottom of any cups the Fates left lying around."

"Then it's time you had a cup of your own, and a day off to go with it. Or at least a couple of hours. And it's definitely past time for Corey to get out of here."

"Before the Fates get back?"

"Or before Corey and I get into a My Life's Been Harsher Than Yours contest."

"Yeah, let's not go there," Corey said.

Ilana offered Arachne the palm of her hand. The spider crawled onto it, and Ilana brought her to eye-level: "Go out, Arachne. Even going to a wannabe European bistro has got to be more interesting than being stuck in this office all the time. I've got a big, empty tote bag in the front seat of my car. If you don't mind hiding in that, I think you could have a pretty good time."

Arachne's eyes opened wide. "You want me to have a good time?"

"You've been doing nice things for me ever since I got here. It's my turn." Ilana handed Corey her car keys. "Look, we've got a local coffee shop called Wyndham's that's trying to be a sidewalk café, so they'll let you sit there for as long as you want. You okay having coffee with a spider, or does it creep you out?"

"Who do I look like, Little Miss Muffet?" He tossed the keys and snatched them back in midair. "It'll be cool. Come on, Arachne—" He imitated Ilana, offering the spider his own palm for a ride. "Let's go put the *beast* in *bis*tro."

Arachne hesitated. "Ilana, are you sure about this? If we go, you'll be all alone here."

"Alone? With the life-threads of every person on earth in the next room? Go, have fun, I'll be fine, I'll catch up to you later." She shooed Arachne onto Corey's palm. "If I get bored, I know where they keep the Scry-o-Tron."

"The What-o-Tron?" Corey asked as she shoved him from the inner office all the way out the front door.

She heard the sound of her car starting up and pulling away while she was turning the latch. Maybe it was a silly gesture—locking the door the mortal way after Dimity's dark hints about the Fates' own unspecified methods for keeping unwanted, unauthorized people out of their office—but it made her feel safe. She sighed happily. After most of a day spent dealing with enchantresses, pigs, smart-ass spiders, and way, *way* too much caffeine, it felt good to be alone.

The feeling lasted all of fifteen minutes.

"I'm bored," Ilana told the empty spiderweb in the corner of the ceiling. "I'm bored and I don't know what I'm supposed to be doing here." She turned on Georgette's terminal, but no list of names needing death receipts manifested. Arachne's cobbled-together processing-line had worked too well. For perhaps the first time in the history of the universe, someone had caught up with the paperwork of death.

For a moment, Ilana flirted with the idea of taking out the Scry-o-Tron and doing a little recreational life-thread reading.

"Reading? Ha!" she said aloud. "Spying. Might as well be honest about it. Just because I can do it doesn't mean I should. Gosh, thank you, Circe. You gave me a Learning Experience that actually made me *learn* something." She slumped in Georgette's chair, face on fist, and had a two-minute sulk before seeking out some way to earn her wages.

She was in the middle of doing a bit of thoroughly mundane dusting and tidying-up in the outer office when her cell phone rang. "Ilana?" It was Heather, and she sounded awful. "Ilana, where are you?"

"Still at work. Why? What's wrong?"

"He dumped me!" Heather's voice rose to a harsh wail, then shattered into tears. "Jeff and I were at the movies and he turned to me right in the middle of the film and he said it wasn't working out, he was seeing someone else, someone who wasn't a . . . a . . . a stereotype!"

"That rat! I'll bet he did it there so you wouldn't make a scene." Ilana smacked her hand down on the counter. *So this must be what Tabby meant when she said it was going to end badly for Heather and Scum-Boy,* she thought, seething.

Heather sniffled agreement. "And to make it worse, we'd gone to the movies in *his* car. I had to call Beth for a ride home because he refused to leave the theater until the show was over."

"Okay, he's just been promoted to *über*rat. And what does he mean, calling you a stereotype?"

"Oh, you know." Heather sobbed a little. "Just because I'm blond and a cheerleader and . . . and he said I was pretty and popular . . . that means I can't be anything else."

"He said something that stupid and you're *crying* because he dumped you?" As soon as she said that, Heather wailed louder. Ilana realized her mistake: She'd broken the first rule of discussing a friend's breakup, namely, *Never tell her it was a* good *thing.* That was a truth Heather would have to realize on her own.

"He said he was only dating me because it was so . . . so wonderfully *ironic.* Okay, I admit I wasn't that into him myself—not really—but how do you think I feel knowing that I wasn't a person to him, just some dumb piece of performance art? He used me! And now I bet he's going to turn it into a poem for English class next year, 'changing' the names. Probably by calling us Jeather and Heff or something, the little nose-goober. Oh, Ilana, I feel so *dumb*!"

Ilana let Heather vent for as long as she wanted to. She even suggested that her friend come by the office, but Heather turned down the offer.

"Your boss wasn't real happy to see me there the last time," she reminded Ilana.

"My boss is out of the office for a while. She won't be back until seven. You could still—"

"What if she comes back earlier? It could happen. I feel bad enough right now; if I got you in trouble I'd only feel worse. It's okay, we can talk face-to-face later; I'll be fine." A stray sob escaped into the phone as if to prove what a bad liar Heather was.

"No, really, you can come, it's safe. I'm the only one here."

"What?" Heather's self-pity dried up abruptly. "That means you're probably the only person in that whole industrial park. I don't think that's a good idea. What if some crazy drives by and sees just one car in the lot and decides to—?"

"Honestly, Heather, this is Porlock's Landing. We don't have any wandering crazies; we've got picturesque town eccentrics."

"Ilana, I'm not kidding. You shouldn't be alone out there. I'm coming to keep you company until— Oh, *damn*."

"What?"

"I just realized I can't. Remember how I called Beth for a ride? Well, I was so upset I had her bring me home instead of to where I left my car. Maybe I *am* a ditzy blond cheerleader stereotype."

"Oh, for God's sake, Heather!" Ilana made a disgusted sound.

"If you keep saying stuff like that, stay away from me because the next time I see you, I'm going to slap you. Now listen: I am fine. I don't need a babysitter. And I'm not stupid. I've got the door locked, okay?"

Very reluctantly, Heather said, "Okay. But call me in an hour or something, will you?"

"Yes, Mommy." Ilana snapped her phone shut. She drifted back into the inner office, flung herself into Atropos' chair and cast a longing look over the desktop. "Man, it's a good thing that I don't know where Georgette keeps those big, black scissors of hers, because right now I am *so* tempted to call for Jeff's spindle and—"

She stopped short. "And I can't. Not even if it *would* save the world from a whole lot of bad poetry." She sighed. "Oh well, at least I can dream." She rested her chin in her hand, closed her eyes, and let her mind drift through happy visions of Jeff trapped in a room with ravenous tigers, thorny vines, rotting garbage, and one very determined telemarketer.

13

IT'S NOT *WHAT* YOU KNOW . . .

It was just past six thirty and Ilana had grown bored with imagining more and more creative ways to punish Jeff Eylandt for dumping Heather. Now she was seated at Dimity's desk playing Tetris on the computer when a loud, insistent knocking rattled the locked front door. A wave of uneasiness hit her. Who could it be? The Fates would simply let themselves in. Could it be Corey and Arachne? Unlikely. The spider was probably enjoying her day out too much to come rushing back.

No one's supposed *to come here,* Ilana thought. *Maybe if I ignore whoever it is, they'll go away*. She slumped in her chair and kept playing.

The knocking intensified, backed up by the harsh, demanding buzz of the doorbell. Ilana turned off the game and noticed that her palms were damp.

Why am I so worried? The front door's locked, and Dimity told me that the Fates have their own way of dealing with trespassers. They've probably got all kinds of shielding spells set up, mystic booby traps, you name it. Still, suppose they forgot to turn them on or something? And who knows how long a trespasser has to be inside before anything happens to him?

She looked around for something she could use to defend herself. *Just in case,* she thought. Not only were Georgette's big, black, deadly scissors safely locked away, so was every other pair. The best she could come up with in the nasty-sharp-pointy-objects line was the spiky end of the compass from Dimity's desk. It made a pretty pathetic weapon, so she switched to the massive stapler.

If I hit someone with this hard enough, it'll do some *damage. Great. So this is how my life ends: figuring out how to protect myself with office supplies. What next, trying to strangle someone with a paper-clip chain?*

Wait a minute, what am I thinking? Instead of making a gallant, stupid last stand out here, why don't I just go hide with the spindles? I'll bet the Fates have the full-out, industrial-strength, heavy-duty shielding magic on that *door.* With that, she made a mad dash for the spindle room, slamming the door behind her.

The only trouble Ilana discovered with her chosen refuge was that once *in*side, it was impossible to tell what was happening *out*side. No sound could penetrate the little blue door. Even when she put her ear to the crack, she heard nothing.

I wonder if they gave up and went away? Then a fresh thought struck her: *What if it's someone I know out there? Someone who* knows *I'm here? Heather could've gotten her car back and driven over.*

She flipped open her phone to try calling her friend, but got a NO SERVICE message.

If that is *Heather, I'll bet she tried to call when I didn't answer the door,* she reasoned. *Only she didn't get through, and she'll get so worried she'll call 9-1-1, and then Mom and Dad will find out, and they'll stop me from working for D. R. Temps, and I'll be in music camp before you can say "arpeggio." Why did I think I'd be okay, staying here alone, if this is how I handle things? Why am I such a coward?*

She pressed her lips together in a determined expression. *That does it. I've got to go back and deal with whatever's out there. And if it is a wandering crazy, I'll . . . I'll . . . I'll give him the stapling of his life!*

With that, she opened the spindle room door just an inch and listened. Silence. When she peeked out, the back office looked deserted. Breathing easier, Ilana opened it all the way and headed for Dimity's desk.

"Boo!"

Ilana's scream was drowned out by a chorus of shrill giggles. In an instant she was surrounded by a trio of girls, all barely into their teens, as perky and bouncy as a basket full of puppies. They'd come out of nowhere. One was blond, one brunette, one redheaded, all of them dressed in shorts, T-shirts, and flip-flops that were identical except for color. The blond wore pink, the brunette chose green, and the redhead was all in blue.

I didn't think anyone dressed like that outside of hyper-cute animé *series*, Ilana thought, waiting for her heart to stop beating like a blender.

"You must be Ilana," the blond chirped in her face. "I'm Meg, and these are my sisters, Alec and Tissy." She nodded first at the brunette, then the redhead.

"Tissy?" Ilana repeated. "That's . . . really cute." Looking at those three, she got the feeling that *cute* was going to be the Word of the Day. "What's it short for?"

"Tisiphone the Blood Avenger," said the redhead, tossing her curls. She giggled, but not loudly enough to cover up a distinct hissing sound. A green and gold snake materialized around her neck, mouth gaping, fangs dripping black venom. The snake was most undeniably *not* cute. Ilana gasped and jumped back.

"Oh, Tissy, *honestly*!" Meg clicked her tongue and turned back to Ilana. "She's *such* a show-off; she just *has* to make sure everyone knows her full name. Not me, though. I think Meg is *much* cuter than Megaera the Jealous One."

"Yeah, plus that 'Jealous One' stuff *totally* scares off the really cute boys," dark-haired Alec chimed in. "Which is why I tell everyone, 'Call me Alecto-Unceasing-in-Pursuit and die.'" She wore a thick braid that trailed all the way down her spine. Without warning it rose up like a cobra ready to strike, and once again the sound of hissing filled the office. Shadows formed at her back, taking the shape of titanic bat's wings.

"Oh! Just because I take pride in my job, you two are always picking on me. You are *so* unfair!" Tissy pouted, then offered her hand to Ilana. "We're the Furies. Hi. We hunt down wrongdoers and oath-breakers, then we take a hideous vengeance when we catch them."

"And we *always* catch them," Alec put in.

"We have to," Tissy said. "If it weren't for us, people would get away with murder."

"That would be icky." Meg snapped her fingers and a many-lashed whip appeared in her hand. Ilana's heart lurched when she saw that the tips of the lashes were fiery scorpions. "We don't like icky things. We *take care* of them."

"*Nice* people don't call us the Furies," Alec said. "They call us the Kindly Ones." She looked at Ilana closely. "What about you? Do *you* think we're kindly?"

"I-I-I think it's very kindly of you to take care of the . . . icky stuff," Ilana managed to say. All the snakes and creepy-crawlies had shredded her nerves. "Was that you at the door before?" The Furies beamed and nodded like a row of bobble-head dolls. "If you could just poof yourselves inside, why did you bang on the door and ring the buzzer?"

"Because we *felt* like it, silly," Meg said, crinkling her nose.

"But . . . why are you here? Did I do something wrong?"

"Oh, *you*!" Tissy gave her a playful shove. "'Course not. We like you already. Let's be friends!" The venomous snake around her neck vanished in the same instant as Meg's scorpion-whip and Alec's bat wings and hissing hair. The three Furies circled Ilana, babbling about their favorite rock stars, fashions, TV shows, ways to drive murderers and oath-breakers insane with guilt, and why Johnny Depp was so *cute*.

"Oooookay," Ilana said, slowly recovering the ability to breathe normally. "I can always use more friends, and it was *very* friendly of you to get rid of the snakes and stuff, but still I don't understand why you're here. Did you need me to do some temp work for you? Because I think you have to arrange that through Mrs. Atatosk."

The Furies giggled. "We *know,* silly," Meg said.

"We *never* hire anyone from D. R. Temps," said Alec.

"We never hire anyone from *anywhere,*" Tissy clarified. "We never need to. Take time off from our jobs and miss all the *fun*? No way."

"You mortals would never be able to handle what we do," Meg told Ilana. "Most of you would have second thoughts about taking vengeance on someone."

"Yes, and any mortals who *don't* have second thoughts about bloody, nasty, no-holds-barred revenge are usually on our hit list already, so we wouldn't hire them," Tissy said.

"Do the Fates know you're here?" Ilana asked.

This time it seemed as if the Furies would collapse from laughing so hard. Meg was the first one able to speak. "It doesn't matter what the Fates know. They won't interfere."

"They wouldn't dare," said Alec. "We outrank them."

"It's a fear thing," Tissy explained. "More people are scared of what we can do to them than they are of the Fates' powers."

"But they control people's lives," Ilana objected. "And Georgette—I mean, Atropos—can *cut* a life-thread!"

Tissy gave a disdainful sniff. "That just means she can kill you. Snip, snip and it's all over; big whoop. *We* make you *wish* you were dead, and we can make it last a long, long time." She grinned, and for a moment Ilana thought she saw large, blood-stained, needle-sharp teeth filling Tissy's cute little strawberry-lip-glossed mouth.

"So if I haven't done anything wrong and you don't want me to temp for you, then . . . what *do* you want?"

The Furies smiled. All three of them took out matching coin purses decorated with pictures of cartoon hamsters. When they snapped them open, thunder shook Tabby Fabricant Textiles. Together, they turned the opened purses upside down over the nearest desk. It was like watching the ultimate magic-hat act: A flood of assorted objects poured out, an avalanche of things too many and too large ever to have fit into containers so small.

Yet there they were, in open defiance of the laws of physics: books, spoons, stuffed animals, flowers, soda bottles, mirrors, even a chicken riding a unicycle.

At least there aren't any more snakes, Ilana thought, just before the chicken pecked her arm.

"What am I supposed to *do* with all this stuff?" she asked, picking up a kaleidoscope and swinging it at the belligerent bird.

"Be creative," said Meg.

"Have fun," said Alec.

"Call up the life-thread of that icky boy who dumped your best girlfriend and teach him a lesson," said Tissy.

"What if I don't want to?" Ilana asked, throwing an orange at the chicken. It pedaled out of range and clucked at her nastily.

Alec gave a scornful little sniff. "Oh, please. You *know* you want to."

"*We* know you want to," Meg added gleefully.

"Okay, maybe I *do* want to," Ilana relented. "But I *won't*."

"If you don't, we will," Tissy told her. "Do you really want us to do that?"

Angry as she was at Jeff, Ilana had to admit that she didn't think he deserved to have a one-to-three confrontation with the Furies. Her shoulders slumped. "Okay," she said. "You win. I'll do it. But just tell me one thing: What made you show up here? It's not like Jeff hurt *me*."

"No, but he hurt your friend," said Meg. "She doesn't have the power to pay him back for that. *You* do."

"And once you deal with him, there's no reason you can't go on using the same power on other people's life-threads," Tissy suggested.

"But in the *good* way," Alec put in. "Nothing big, nothing global, just a few little . . . local details."

"Come on, just give it a teensy-weensy try." Tissy was a world-class wheedler. "It's not all about punishment. Okay, for us it is, but not for you. Jeff was a meanie, but don't you know other people, nice people, people who deserve something better than the lives they've got?"

"Don't you know that you can change life-threads for *good* reasons?" Meg asked.

Ilana remembered her sister's near miss on the road. "Well," she said. "I guess it'd be okay. If I only did it for *good* reasons, I mean. But first . . ." She spoke Jeff Eylandt's name aloud and held out her hand. Summoned, the spindle materialized at once. Ilana clutched it tightly and began rummaging through the pile of stuff overflowing the desk.

"Looking for something specific?" Alec asked. "Matches? Pliers? Water balloons?"

"I could lend you my scorpions," Meg offered.

"Have you got a book of poetry in here?" Ilana asked.

It took Tissy two seconds to find one. "What are you going to do?" she asked avidly, leaning in close.

"Jeff thinks he's God's gift to poetry," Ilana replied. "I thought it'd be fun if from now on, all he can *say* is poetry. Bad poetry."

The Furies giggled. "It's not as good as what you could do with the pliers, but if that's what you want—" Alec said. "Just slam his life-thread between the pages."

"That's all you have to do with any of these things," Meg added. "The magic works by touch." She waved a fashion magazine. "Know anyone who wants to lose a few pounds?"

Tissy picked up a CD. "How about giving somebody a talent for music?" The other Furies threw stuffed animals at her and the chicken ran the unicycle over her foot.

"That reminds me. Do you want to know what happens if you use the chicken and the unicycle?" Tissy asked eagerly.

"No. As in *never*." Ilana opened the poetry book, laid Jeff's life-thread across one page, and slammed the book shut, hard. Then she grinned and chanted:

"Roses love clouds,
Violets love sun,
Jeff Eylandt's a jerk,
This will be *fun*."

She didn't know if she needed to do that, but somehow it just felt right.

PERFORMANCE REVIEWS ARE YOUR FRIEND

And it *was* fun. Giving Jeff's spindle the full verse-immersion treatment was only the beginning. Once Ilana pulled his life-thread out of the book, she dug up the Scry-o-Tron 9000 and gleefully studied the results.

He was hanging out at a local McDonald's with a couple of other kids Ilana recognized from school. Like Jeff, they were convinced that no one could suffer as beautifully as they suffered and the only reason they couldn't get their too-too-brilliant poetry collections published was that no one understood their unique genius.

One of the underappreciated geniuses was objecting to eating in such a meat-for-the-mooing-masses place, which gave

Jeff the perfect opportunity to explain the delectable irony of it all. However, the words that came out of his mouth were:

"Nibble, nibble, little cow;
Listen and I'll tell you how
Acting like a pompous fool
Makes me think I'm wicked cool."

He was halfway through the second verse (even if he was a creep, Ilana had to admit she liked the way he rhymed "I'm a rat" with "fries with that") before he realized what was happening. He clapped his hands over his mouth so hard that his teeth clattered.

"Wow, he's not just spouting bad poetry, but bad poetry that tells the truth about him. I didn't expect that," she told the Furies.

"Why not?" Meg said. "Poetry's pretty. Pretty is truth; truth, pretty."

"I think you mean '*beauty* is truth,'" Ilana said.

"Whatever." Meg shrugged. "Beauty's pretty too."

Ilana gave up and moved on to the next life-thread. It was getting close to seven, and she wanted to try "improving" some others before the Fates returned.

First there was the one belonging to Mr. Renfrew, who'd turned her down for a summer job at La Mode du Monde, his Paris-wannabe boutique. It was because of the skull tattoo, of course, but she wasn't the only person he turned away solely on the basis of looks. Sure, he didn't want to scare off the country club–type customers by hiring a salesclerk with a steel-studded face, but he didn't stop at facial piercings and tattoos for his Do Not *Ever* Hire list. "Too full of holes" and "Too decorated" came right after "Too short," "Too fat," and "Too pimply." After a few years people noticed a definite pattern to his hiring practices. He could claim to be an equal opportunity employer until his face turned blue, but in a small town like Porlock's Landing, the truth got around.

Ilana tied his life-thread to one eyebrow ring, a tongue stud, and a box of chocolate cupcakes, all from the Furies' big pile-o'-props. Then she rubbed it against the tackiest black-velvet-Elvis painting she could find.

She couldn't wait to see what the display window at La Mode du Monde would look like tomorrow. She was betting on gold lamé, pink sequins, black spiked dog collars, and purple vinyl.

She didn't know if it would work, but she grabbed a plastic lei and a gold coin, and scrunched both of them around the life-thread of her favorite teacher, Mrs. Ghirardelli.

Come on, free trip to Hawaii! Ilana thought, concentrating intently on a vision of Mrs. G. amid palm trees, surfboarders, and luaus. *After putting up with Jeff's stupid poems all last term, the poor woman deserves something nice for a change!*

She twirled Heather's thread together with the one belonging to Luke Fowler, the editor of the school literary magazine. In Ilana's opinion, it was past time for her best friend to learn that *nice* guys wrote poetry, too. Professional bad boys like Lord Byron and Jeff were natural born spotlight-hogs; that was the problem. Luke had been in Ilana's English class last term, but unlike Jeff, he didn't need to make a big noise about what a misunderstood, suffering genius he was. He was simply a good writer.

He was also much too modest to believe that a girl like Heather could ever be interested in him.

Ilana grabbed a bottle of cologne, spritzed the tangled life-threads with a fine mist of lilac, and hoped it would add enough of a romantic atmosphere to do the trick.

Knowing Heather, I'd probably get better results if I made Luke's life-thread smell like French fries, she thought. *Oh well, if this doesn't work, I'll try something else Monday.*

She sent the two spindles back to their places and had just called for two more when the Fates walked in.

"Ilana! What on earth are you doing?" Tabby exclaimed, dropping her shopping bag. Something inside it made an expensive-sounding crash.

"Obvious," said Dimity. "Hello, girls." She nodded at the Furies. They giggled; big surprise.

"This is horrible!" Georgette wrung her hands. "Are those *spindles*? What have you done? Did you touch my scissors?"

"Just . . . just your stapler," Ilana said, hiding the spindles behind her back even though the Fates had already seen them. "And I didn't use it on any of the life-threads."

"'*Any* of the life-threads'?" Tabby echoed. "You weren't supposed to touch *any* of the life-threads until Monday!" She wagged a finger at the Furies. "This situation has your grubby paw prints all over it. Shame on you! I'll bet that none of this was Ilana's idea until she listened to you three little hooligans."

"Ooh, now we're *hooligans.*" Meg sneered and her sisters snickered. "I'm soooooo hurt. I was hoping she'd call us rapscallions, at least."

"Or scalawags," Alec put in.

Tissy shook an imaginary cane at her sisters. "You rotten kids get away from my spindles!" she hollered in a creaky old-lady voice.

"This is not funny," Georgette said sternly, stamping her foot. "You know what can happen if a mortal does too much . . . 'borrowing.'"

"Cool it, 'Snips.'" Alec yawned and waved away Georgette's fears. "Of course we do. We were only going to let her have three tries. That's way less than what it takes to set off the alarms in Mrs. A.'s office."

"Even so, Mrs. Atatosk will hear of this." As the only one of the Fates with children at home, Georgette naturally fell into lecture-for-your-own-good mode. "I wouldn't want to be in your shoes when she does."

"Tattletale." Tissy stuck out her tongue. It was forked. "Go ahead. See if we care. She'll know that none of this was our idea or Ilana's. Styx-y swear!"

The Fates gasped in chorus to hear Tisiphone swear on the Styx, the dark underground river between the worlds of the living and the dead. The Furies punished oath-breakers, and an oath sworn on the Styx was the most binding of all. She wasn't lying.

"Then who—?" Tabby began.

"None of your beeswax," said Tissy, and she disappeared in a cloud of smoke that smelled like blood and blueberries. Her sisters followed, pausing just long enough to make rude noises at the Fates before vanishing.

"Oh dear," said Tabby. "What *difficult* girls."

"Sloppy, too," said Ilana. "They left their stuff."

She made a sweeping gesture at the pile of things on the desktop. The chicken was still squawking as it lurched around the inner office on its unicycle, but it settled down when Dimity gave it a cold, appraising look and uttered the words "barbecue sauce."

Ilana stepped forward and handed Tabby the two spindles, then put the Scry-o-Tron 9000 back where it belonged. She felt the Fates watching every step she took, but they never said a word. It was like working under the threat of an impending thunderstorm. Ilana worked on. She tried to arrange the jumble of things the Furies had left behind into neat stacks, but failed. Then she found one of their hamster-decked coin purses.

What the heck, she thought, snapping it open. *The worst that can happen is nothing. I hope.* She aimed the open purse at the clutter. There was a gurgling roar, as if someone had pulled the drain plug at the bottom of the world's biggest bathtub, and all of the Furies' stuff rushed back into the little coin purse. As the last item disappeared inside, Ilana snapped the purse shut so quickly that she clipped off one of the unicycle-riding chicken's tail feathers.

Setting the purse aside, Ilana folded her hands and turned to the Fates. "I guess I'm fired," she said.

"Fired?" Tabby repeated, puzzled. "A good worker like you? Where did you ever get *that* idea?"

"There isn't a single death receipt left to process." Georgette beamed with delight. "You're the reason I'm not pulling my hair out by the fistful anymore."

"Very true," Dimity said. "At her former rate of self-induced hair-removal, calculations indicated that she would have been completely bald by August first."

"But . . . but I touched the spindles," Ilana protested. "'Naughty-naughty, no-no,' remember?" She knew she was probably shooting herself in the foot employment-wise, but she didn't see the point of trying to avoid responsibility. Facts were facts. "I touched them and I . . . I changed things."

"So you did." Tabby studied the spindles that Ilana had handed over. "Not these, though. Not yet. Ilana, dear, what *were* you going to do to your parents' life-threads?"

Ilana blushed and looked at the floor. "Try to find a way to make them stop nagging me about college applications all the time."

There was no audible response from the Fates, though Ilana heard Tabby and her sisters whispering among themselves. Finally, Dimity spoke up.

"You do good work. You did not harm the life-threads you touched. You are conscientious, reliable, responsible, and you cleaned up after the Furies. You will have access to the spindle room on Monday. Somewhere it is Monday already. It would be counterproductive to fire you at this juncture and have to train a new temp. You stay."

"I don't know where I'd be if you hadn't come to work for us," Georgette said, gently lifting Ilana's chin so that she could no longer avoid looking the Fates in the face. "Even if it's only for the summer, it's so good for me to have a little time off to think of something besides snip, snip, snip. I do hope you'll continue to work for us."

Tabby retrieved the Scry-o-Tron and made a quick visit to the spindle room before speaking. "Whatever you did to those life-threads hasn't upset the cosmic balance. Therefore I'd say that your 'alterations' were all things that could have happened in the natural course of events. In other words, no harm done."

"Are you sure?" Ilana asked anxiously. It was all sounding much too good to be true. "Even the part where I made Jeff Eylandt speak in bad poetry?"

"If I recall that young man's life-thread correctly, he was bound to make a fool of himself in public sooner or later. You just made it happen sooner, and rather creatively, too."

"We appreciate creativity," Georgette said. "When you've been in the business of minding life-threads as long as we have, it's a pleasure to see something different for a change."

"I promise I won't do it again," Ilana said.

"What fun would that be?" Tabby asked, smiling. "If the Furies thought you could handle life-threads, who are we to argue? They do outrank us."

"And if they gave you the green light to do it because someone who outranks *them* said it was all right, we'd never dream of interfering," Georgette added.

"Who outranks the Furies?" Ilana asked.

The Fates all raised their hands in a Don't-Ask-Us gesture.

"Of course you do realize that we'll have to have a few ground rules about this for the future," Tabby said, counting them off on her fingers. "First: You may not touch life-threads belonging to your immediate family or yourself. Second: You may not make any changes to the heart of a life-thread, merely to the surface. You are legally forbidden from turning a sow's ear into a silk purse or vice versa."

"That's more Circe's style, anyway," Georgette said, giggling like a Fury.

"Third: Until such time as the Furies come back to reclaim their belongings, I see no reason why you can't use their things to effect life-thread changes. Fourth and finally: You *must* limit how often you 'borrow' our powers to three times per working day, maximum. More would be dangerous."

"How?" Ilana asked. "What would happen?"

"Empires would fall. The world would end. Chaos would ensue," Dimity stated with as much passion as if she were announcing, "We're out of milk."

"Mrs. Atatosk would go squirrely," Georgette added. "Nobody wants to see that."

"Are we all agreed on the rules, then?" Tabby asked brightly.

"I guess so." Ilana was rather stunned to have been given so much, so easily. It made her a little wary and very apprehensive. "But I don't think it's going to matter, in the long run. I won't be touching the spindles ever again."

"Ha," said Dimity. "Ha. Ha. Ha."

"Aren't you the born comedian, Ilana!" Tabby exclaimed. "I haven't heard Dimity laugh like that since some silly Trojan said, 'Oh, come on, let's bring it into the city. What harm can a giant wooden horse do?'"

"Ha," Dimity said again. "Ha. Hahaha. Stop it. You are killing me."

"I'm not kidding." Ilana folded her arms. "I won't touch the spindles anymore, not for the rest of the summer. Cross my heart and hope to—"

Tabby's hand flew to cover Ilana's mouth before she could finish the sentence. "Ssh, dear; don't be hasty. Always think before you make the really *big* promises." She let her hand drop and added, "The summer is young."

"But it will be gone before we know it," Georgette said with a heartfelt sigh. "Leaves fall. Youth passes. Beauty fades. Towers crumble to dust. Soccer team sign-up is at our throats."

"Ilana's friends are waiting for her at Wyndham's," Tabby put in. She patted Ilana's cheek. "Don't look so surprised, dear. I checked *your* spindle while I was back there. Now, why don't we give you a ride to town? Oh, and when you see Arachne, tell her we hope she had fun."

"You're not mad that she went out?"

"We're just surprised she didn't do it years ago." Tabby

smiled. "I can understand her being a little suspicious of the gods after what Athena did to her, but trust me, we like her, we appreciate her, and no matter what she believes, we don't *always* blame the spider."

LOVING YOUR WORK

All of the outdoor tables at Wyndham's coffee shop were packed with customers when Georgette's big, black, fully loaded SUV lumbered up to the curb and let Ilana off. Rolling down her window, the motherly Fate called out, "Bring Arachne and Corey to me as soon as you find them, Ilana dear. I want to make sure everyone gets home all right."

"I'll bring them home," Ilana offered. "Just let me get my car."

"*Two* round-trip drives to New Haven in one day? I'd rather you didn't. Consider this a small token of thanks for all that you've done for me, staying on with us." Georgette smiled brightly and added, "I'm also going to see to it that you get a raise."

"You don't have to—" Ilana began.

"Girl, don't finish that sentence," Corey said. He'd been hidden away at a little sidewalk table just out of streetlight range until he caught sight of Ilana and came over, her car keys and the tote bag in hand. "When they say they want to give you more money, you don't say *no,* you say *thank you. Thank you* and *how much.*" He climbed into the SUV and tossed her the keys to her own car. "I parked it down the street over that way." He pointed with his free hand, then held the tote bag up. "Guess what I learned today? There's nothing cuter than a sleeping spider."

"Arachne's asleep in there? Didn't she have any coffee?"

"Three double espressos and she still went out like a light," Corey responded. "Spiders. Go figure."

After the SUV drove away, Ilana found her car and noticed that Corey had filled the gas tank. She smiled about that all the way home.

She stopped smiling when she walked in the front door and found Dyllin waiting for her, arms folded, the D. R. Temps brochure pinched between the fingers of one hand. She did not look happy.

Where did she find that? Ilana was taken aback by this very unwelcome welcoming committee of one. *I thought I tossed it in the trash the day Mrs. Atatosk gave it to me. Wait a minute, I did, only I used the little wastebasket down in the basement, the one next to the dryer, where we dump the lint trap. The one that nobody empties until it looks like the mother of all dust bunnies.* A closer look at the brochure in her sister's hand told all. Telltale bits of dryer fluff still clung to the glossy paper.

"Uhhhh, thanks for emptying the basement wastebasket?" She offered Dyllin a sickly smile.

Dyllin's stony expression did not change. Instead she pointed at the stairs. "My room. Now."

Ilana was too frazzled from the events of the day to protest. She no sooner flopped onto Dyllin's bed than her sister opened fire. "*You're* working for D. R. Temps?" she demanded. "*That's* your summer job?"

"Louder, Dyllin," Ilana replied. "I don't think Mom and Dad heard you."

"Mom and Dad are at the movies. Their car's gone, in case you didn't notice. Don't dodge the question."

"So what if I *am* temping for the gods?" Ilana shot back. "It was good enough for *you* for three years."

"Four," Dyllin corrected her automatically. "And it was different for me. I was in college."

"Meaning I'm too stupid to work for the gods because I'm still in high school? One of the other kids looks lots younger than me, and she's temping in *Hawaii* next week!"

Dyllin took a deep breath, as if she were about to blast Ilana into the next room, but then she let it out slowly, without a word. She sank onto the bed next to her sister.

"Did it really sound like I was saying you're stupid? Something *that* mean?" she said in a soft, small voice.

"Why, do you want to hear it on instant replay?" Ilana retorted.

"Maybe you didn't say it in so many words, but I got the message: You don't want me working for D. R. Temps because you think it's a job that only someone like *you* can handle; someone *perfect*. You think I'm too stupid to—"

"Oh, for God's sake, Ilana, not again!" Dyllin's eyes flashed at her sister. "I *know* you're not stupid. Will you listen to what I'm *actually* saying, for a change, instead of what you're *expecting* to hear?"

Ilana gave her sister an uncertain look. "You don't think I'm stupid?"

"*No*."

"So that's not why you're mad that I'm working for D. R. Temps?"

"I'm not mad, I'm *upset*," Dyllin said. "And the reason I don't like you working for D. R. Temps is—"

"You think it's going to mess up your wedding?"

Dyllin smacked her sister with one of the ruffled white throw pillows from the bed. "Where is Circe's wand when I need it?" she asked the ceiling. "I would turn you into a giraffe *so* fast—"

"Why a giraffe?"

"Because they're mostly *quiet*."

"Okay, so if D. R. Temps was good enough to be *your* summer job, why *don't* you want me working for the gods?"

"Because I'm afraid for you," Dyllin replied, dead serious. "Because I know that it's not all Koffee Koven meetings and lots of spending money and getting to do neat things when they let you borrow their powers. Temping for the gods can be dangerous. I don't want anything to happen to you. When you got sick last year, I wanted to fly right over, but Mom and Dad told me to stay put because I wouldn't be able to do anything for you. They didn't know how right they were. I was desperate to 'borrow' Apollo's power of healing for you or to beg the Fates to let me change your life-thread, but I couldn't, because they hadn't hired any temps that year. Not even Mrs. Atatosk knew how to reach them. Do you know how helpless I felt? You're my little sister; I'm supposed to protect you, and I couldn't. But now—" She held up the D. R. Temps brochure. "Now I can."

"How? By ratting me out to Mom and Dad so they make me quit?" Ilana grabbed the brochure from her sister's hand and waved it in her face. "You want to protect me now because you felt helpless about what happened to me in Africa. Did you ever think about what *I* want?"

Dyllin lowered her eyes. "I didn't mean for this to turn into a fight."

"Everything else does."

"I know. I have been pretty witchy lately, and most of the time I'm not even sure why. I'm sorry." Dyllin tried to give her a hug, but Ilana stiffened her shoulders and she gave up. "Part of it's the wedding, isn't it?"

"*Part* of it?" Ilana echoed, incredulous. "Try *all* of it. Try every single waking moment, plus in your dreams, I bet. What happened to you, Dyllin? You used to be so . . . so much more— Look, let me put it this way: If you'd been like this four years ago, I wouldn't have missed you so much the whole time we were apart."

"You missed me?" Dyllin looked pleased.

"That's what I said in my letters, didn't I?"

"Everyone says 'I miss you' in letters."

"Well, I meant it. You're my sister and I love you, even if you are this superhuman monument to perfection that I'm never going to be."

"Since when am I perfect?" Dyllin was genuinely surprised.

"Only since forever. Even before we went to Africa, every teacher I had always started off the school year saying, 'Oh, you're *Dyllin's* sister. It was *so* wonderful having a student like her in my class. I do hope you'll be just like her.'"

Dyllin groaned and covered her eyes. "Did your teachers actually say something *that* dumb?"

"Maybe they didn't *actually* say the last part, but they made it pretty clear they were thinking it. When I was in sixth grade, I once got an English paper back from Mrs. McCutcheon with a note at the bottom that said, 'Excellent work as usual, Dyllin.'"

"You're kidding!"

"Okay, she didn't write out 'Dyllin,' but she started to—I could see the D-Y-L she crossed out before she wrote 'Ilana.'"

"Wasn't Mrs. McCutcheon the woman who looked like that guy with the pointy ears from *Star Trek*?" Dyllin asked.

"Which one?"

"Mr. Spock."

"I meant which *Star Trek*: Classic Trek, diet Trek, caffeine-free Trek, Trek with lime—?"

Dyllin laughed. "Ilana, you are *such* a geek." She threw her arms around her, and this time Ilana hugged back.

They went back downstairs to the kitchen for sodas and took them out onto the back deck. Fireflies were dancing through the warm summer air. Dyllin turned off the deck lights so they could have a better view of the insects' twinkling display.

This feels good, Ilana thought, sipping her soda. *Better than good, this feels* right. *This is how I want it to be with my sister. So what if she's prettier and smarter and more talented and popular than I am? So's Heather, and we're still friends. So what if Mom and Dad expect me to be a younger version of Dyllin? That's their problem, not her fault.*

At that moment, Ilana's thoughts were interrupted by a soda-induced belch that rattled every window in the house and scattered the fireflies. Out of the darkness, Dyllin said, "Oops. 'Scuse me. So much for perfection, huh?"

"Untrue. That sounded like the perfect belch to me, one that I can never hope to equal or surpass. Dyllin, you've done it again."

"Fear my skills," Dyllin said, deadpan. "Be glad that I employ them for good and not for evil. Speaking of employment, who does Mrs. A. have you temping for?"

"The Fates."

"No kidding? One of my old jobs?" Dyllin's joy suddenly turned serious. She switched on the outside lights and looked steadily at her sister. "Was that you?"

"Was what me?"

"I didn't tell anyone, but I was almost in an accident, a bad one. I just missed hitting a truck, but at the last minute—" She shuddered. "So, the reason I'm still alive . . . was that you?"

Ilana nodded.

"Oh. Thanks."

"Hey, what choice did I have?" Ilana tried to shake off the unnerving memories as a joke. "If you got ki—stuck in the hospital, Dad'd lose all kinds of nonrefundable wedding-stuff deposits."

"*Now* who's obsessed with my wedding?" Dyllin chuckled.

Another voice came out of the shadows, "Me." Erastus Ames stepped into the light, leaped up the deck steps, and swept Dyllin into his arms for a kiss that soap opera stars would envy. Ilana squirmed and pretended to be fascinated with her empty soda can until the two of them broke that spectacular lip-lock.

The only problem was, they didn't.

Seconds ticked by. Ras and Dyllin showed no signs of coming up for air. *At least now I know why Dyllin's been acting so crazy: Ras keeps cutting off the oxygen supply to her brain,* Ilana thought.

"Dyllin?" she said, tentatively trying to reestablish contact with her sister. "Dyllin, you're cool with me working for D. R. Temps now, right?" Dyllin made a small sound of agreement and nodded her head, all while continuing to kiss Ras. "And you won't tell Mom and Dad? Promise? *Swear?*" Dyllin made a brief "okay" sign with her right hand. "Great. 'Night."

Ilana headed back into the house. Behind her, she finally

heard the kiss end in a gasp from her sister and Ras's voice saying, "Darling, I've got some wonderful news!" But by that time, Ilana was too tired to care about what Ras's wonderful news might be.

○ ○ ○

The following Monday at nine on the dot, Ilana swept into the back office of Tabby Fabricant Textiles like a hurricane. The Fates all glanced up from their desks and did a double take when they saw her, even the usually straight-faced thread-measurer, Dimity. Arachne took one look at Ilana's expression and retreated to her most inaccessible ceiling web, where she nibbled nervously on a mosquito.

"Gracious, dear, what's wrong?" Tabby asked.

"Oh, *please* don't say you changed your mind about working here!" Georgette exclaimed. "I was all set to take the children to the beach the *instant* you came in today."

"Don't worry," Ilana said. "I'm still working here, but before I get started, I just have one question for you." She held up her index finger to illustrate. "*One.* You've been around for thousands of years, so you'd better be able to answer it."

"Well, we'll certainly try. What is it?"

"Love." Ilana spat out the word like an olive pit. "Why does love make people so unbelievably, hopelessly, pathetically *stupid?*"

The Fates exchanged uncertain glances. "Love isn't exactly our field of—" Georgette began.

"Do you *know* what my sister did?" Ilana cut her off. "She moved the wedding date up, that's what! Now it's just three weeks away, instead of at the end of the summer. *Three weeks!* And do you know *why* she did it? Because her precious Rassy-Wassy said he had *wonderful* news, a *fabulous* opportunity to take her on an extra-long honeymoon to Paris for free—something to do with that job he's taking over there—but only if they get married sooner."

"Mmmm, Paris." Tabby stared off into space in a happy dream.

"Are you *listening?*" Ilana exclaimed. "Ras said 'Jump' and Dyllin asked 'How high?' I wouldn't mind if she moved up the wedding itself—get married by a judge or a justice of the peace or by some wedding chapel Elvis impersonator in Vegas—but she's moving up the whole wedding *circus.* All this weekend she begged and pleaded and nagged and cried until Mom and Dad agreed to do whatever they could so she'll still get the wedding of her twisted little dreams."

"I don't see how you can move a whole wedding," Georgette said. "The ceremony, yes, but everything else? Most reception halls have to be reserved at least a year in advance."

"Dyllin's having the ceremony and reception in our backyard." Ilana snorted. "Lucky us."

"Ah!" Georgette smiled. "A home wedding, how charming. Small, intimate, romantic—"

"You've never seen our backyard, have you?" Ilana said. "You could land small airplanes out there. Listen, if I promise to take a pay cut, will you let me work here on weekends, too? Just until after the wedding? I do *not* want to go home. Dyllin's got Mom and Dad with their cell phones glued to their heads, desperately calling the caterers, the florist, the woman who's altering the wedding gown and my revolting maid of honor dress. Oh, and the *guests*? A super-hyper-rush order for a bunch of Ignore Previous Wedding Date postcards, plus emergency e-mails, plus Mom and Dad calling everyone and practically *groveling* so they'll show up for Dyllin's big day."

"Oh my, how embarrassing," Tabby said.

"No, *embarrassing* is phoning Grandma about the new wedding date and then spending an hour trying to convince her that Dyllin's not pregnant. Again. Mom had the same conversation with her about the original wedding date, so this time she forced me to make the call. I finally gave up and told Grandma that the baby's due in September. Let *her* figure out why Dyllin's got a stomach like a pancake when she gets here."

"Ilana, dear, you can't stay in this office twenty-four/seven," Tabby said gently.

"Pleeeeease? Arachne does. I'll be good."

"But we *can* help make things a little easier for you."

She stood and motioned for Ilana to take her place at the desk. With one wave of her hand, Tabby made the Scry-o-Tron 9000 appear, along with a wedding card the size of a road atlas. The outside was a white-and-silver clutter of bells, doves, ribbons, rings, and big-eyed angels, the inside dripped with syrupy sentiments expressed in appalling verse. Ilana read two lines and said, "Barf."

"To you, it's barf," Tabby said. "To other people, it's a reminder of all the sweet, sentimental, romantic hopes and dreams you mortals attach to weddings. Close this card over someone's life-thread, ask them for any favor connected with your sister's wedding, and they'll crumble like a fistful of feta cheese. What do you say to that?"

Ilana put on the Scry-o-Tron 9000 goggles, stuck out her right hand, and pronounced the name of the wedding florist. A golden spindle appeared. It smelled like roses.

"I like feta," Ilana said. "Let's do this."

REWARDING WORKPLACE EXPERIENCES

It took Ilana most of that first week to compel the cooperation of all the businesspeople associated with Dyllin's fast-forwarded wedding date. The only thing that slowed her down was the Fates' three-a-day limit on altering life-threads. She bagged the last business on Thursday, then worked extra hard on Friday and all through the following week to catch up on the assignments she'd put on hold—using the Oopsie on a basketful of sluggish spindles that Tabby brought her for the Fates' version of defragging; keeping the Scry-o-Tron 9000 sparkling clean; patrolling the spindle room to report anything unusual, from odd noises to funky smells; correcting the computer files when Tabby accidentally converted all of Dimity's upcoming thread-measurement notes to the metric system; taking Georgette's kids to the dentist. (She got hazardous duty pay for that last one.)

And here it was, Friday again, and just a week to go until the wedding.

"I still say they should have counted everything I did to fix Dyllin's wedding stuff as *one* life-thread alteration," she told Arachne as they sat at Dimity's desk, assembling the wedding favors. It was early evening, after Ilana's return from the temps' weekly meeting in New Haven. The Fates had gone to a wine and cheese party Dionysus was hosting (cheese optional), so the two friends were alone in the office.

"I'll bet they love you on the nine-items-or-less checkout line at the supermarket," Arachne remarked. She batted her eyelashes and did a dreadful, baby-voiced impression of Ilana: "'I *know* I've got carrots, cereal, ice cream, spaghetti, apples, soy sauce, and fifteen different kinds of soup, but it's all food, so it should only count as *one* thing. Pleeeeease?'"

"This was different." Ilana dropped a handful of Jordan almonds into a net bag, pulled the ribbon drawstring, and tied it with a lopsided bow. "It was like working on a spindle assembly line. I didn't even have to think about how to get the effect I wanted. The minute I slammed someone's life-thread inside that giant card, they were ready to do anything to help the bride-to-be."

"What I want to know is why you slammed both of *our* life-threads into that card, too," Arachne said.

"I didn't."

"Then why am I wasting the best years of my eternal punishment doing *this*?" The spider scuttled over to Ilana's badly tied bow and redid it, then dropped the finished favor into the box on the floor.

"Because I promised to take you to the concert on the town green tonight if you helped me." Ilana laid out a fresh circle of netting and began threading ribbon through the slits around the edge.

"And coffee after?"

"Coffee after. And cake."

"Now you're talking!" Arachne helped herself to more mesh circles and deftly wove ribbons through five in the time it took Ilana to complete one. Having eight legs came in handy. "We can make this go faster. I'll lace, you fill, you close, I'll tie," she suggested.

"It sounds like Ping-Pong, but sure." They worked diligently in silence for a time, and the piles of supplies dwindled like snow in the sun while the box of finished favors filled up. When they were down to the last ten, Ilana announced, "Break time!" She stood up, stretched her hands high overhead, and wiggled her fingers. "Ow, ow, ow. I can't wait for this wedding to be over. If I never see another white dress, flower, ribbon, or cake, hooray! No more dress fittings, no more of Dyllin's hissy fits or Dad's muttering about how much it's all costing, no more having to put up with Barry's whining."

"Is he still doing that?" Arachne asked.

"Today he showed up at the temps' meeting just long enough to ask me if Dyllin's going through with the wedding. When I said yes, he stormed out again. At least he didn't do the whipped-puppy-dog thing. If he was so interested in her, he should've spoken up *last* summer. God, I hope he doesn't make some kind of scene at the wedding. Dyllin will slaughter him."

"He's invited?" Arachne asked.

"All the temps are. So are you."

Arachne was so taken aback by the news that she tied one of her legs into the bow she was working on and had to use three more to get it out. "*Me?*" she squeaked. "But I'm a spider!"

"I noticed." Ilana played it casual. "You're also my friend, like Heather, and she's invited, too."

"Need I remind you that some people have a little problem with big spiders?"

"*They* have the problem."

"No, *you* have it the minute they see me and turn your sister's wedding into a screaming stampede."

"For God's sake, Arachne, that's not going to happen! No one's going to see you unless they *look* for you. Corey's agreed to bring you in a bag again, okay?"

"Sorry if I'm being a pain." Arachne looked away. "You're so nice, including me like this. I don't want to ruin the wedding, that's all."

"Trust me, at this point the only person who's going to ruin Dyllin's wedding is Dyllin." Ilana rested her hands on her hips and did a back stretch, then checked her watch. "Fifteen minutes till quitting time. Perfect. There's something I want to do before we leave."

As the spider watched, Ilana reached under the desk and hauled up a plastic bag emblazoned with the name of a major discount chain store. When she turned it upside down, an assortment of CDs, candy bars, paperback romance novels, barrettes, and cosmetics tumbled out. There was also one packet of ketchup.

Ilana stretched out her right hand and declared, "Heather Hazelden!" No sooner did her best friend's spindle appear than Ilana opened her left hand and called out, "Luke Fowler!" She placed the two spindles on Dimity's desk, side by side, sat down, and began to unspool their life-threads with painstaking care.

"Again?" Arachne asked while Ilana clipped the threads together with one of her barrettes. "What is this, your fourth try?"

"Fifth," Ilana said.

She sandwiched the clipped-together threads between two CDs, then made one of the paperback romances into a tiny tent, balanced it on the upper CD, and flicked a few drops of scented after-bath body splash over the whole structure. Arachne watched the entire process solemnly, though once or twice Ilana was certain she'd heard the spider suppressing a giggle.

"What's so funny?"

"Nothing, nothing. Um, would you like to explain what you're trying to do there?"

"Okay." Ilana pointed at each component of the little construction as she mentioned it: "I clipped their threads together so they'll *get* together, I put them between two CDs because that symbolizes music and we're all meeting at a concert tonight, I put the romance novel on top because, duh, *romance* novel, and the cologne's for atmosphere."

"What about the ketchup and the candy?" Arachne asked.

Ilana smacked her forehead. "Thank you! How could I forget those?" She set a chocolate bar on top of the paperback's spine like a seesaw. "Love is *sweet,* right? And because Luke is creative, and Heather does insane—I mean, *creative* things with ketchup, the finishing touch!"

She placed the ketchup packet at the midpoint of the chocolate seesaw. "Tah-dah!" she declared.

Or rather, just "Tah." The whole motley arrangement collapsed before she got to "dah!" The pieces scattered across the desktop, the two life-threads broke free of the barrette and whipped themselves back around their spindles with a rattling sound like a suddenly released window shade. Arachne exploded with laughter. Ilana gave the spider a dirty look and sent the uncooperative spindles back to their proper places with a heartfelt "*Go!*"

"Hey, don't feel bad, Ilana," Arachne said, wiping tears of mirth from her eyes with one foreleg. "Your other projects worked out just fine."

She pointed to a display of postcards and newspaper clippings on the office bulletin board. Even though Ilana had been preoccupied with fixing things for Dyllin and making things happen for Heather and Luke, she'd still found the time to try her hand at altering a few other life-threads. One of the cards came from her former English teacher, Mrs. Ghirardelli, who was still enjoying the Hawaiian vacation she'd won in a contest she couldn't remember entering. One of the clippings recounted how local high school student, Jeff Eylandt, had been banned from a nearby cineplex for rushing to the front of the theater in the middle of a screening, tearing off his shirt, shining a high-powered flashlight to illuminate the huge lipsticked heart he'd drawn on his chest, and hollering "Quentin Tarantino, you're the *ginchiest*!"

Of course it had all been done with the Fates' tacit approval. Tabby and Dimity had assembled the bulletin board display themselves, honoring their temp's ever-improving on-the-job skills. (Even though she promised she wouldn't use *those* scissors, Georgette's offer to help clip newspaper articles was met with a resounding and horrified "No!")

"*Those* worked," Ilana said. "Why won't *this* one?"

"Simple," the spider replied. "There's one basic truth about life-threads, Ilana. Clotho spins, Lachesis measures, Atropos cuts, but there are some things even the Fates can't touch or change. They rule life, not love."

"But Heather and Luke would be *perfect* together," Ilana protested. "Maybe I'm just no good at making romance happen. If the power of the Fates can't bring two people together, it must be a job for the god of love. Or his temp."

"Eros has a temp?" Arachne asked.

Ilana nodded. "Max; as if he doesn't think he's irresistible enough already. He works weekends for Dionysus, but the rest of the time he's been temping for Eros. Max says it pays something like triple wages because he's got to do all the work. Eros is off somewhere for the season. Max gets an e-mail from him now and then, but that's all."

"Funny, a god taking the whole summer off," Arachne remarked. "Especially a hands-on god like Eros."

Ilana shrugged. "Maybe love takes care of itself in the summertime."

○ ○ ○

Summer concerts on the town green were one of the nicer traditions of Porlock's Landing. People sat on blankets or lawn chairs, brought picnics, and choked on competing clouds of insect repellent while enjoying the music. With Arachne tucked into her tote bag, Ilana had no trouble finding her friends.

"Hey, Ilana!" Heather waved at her from the blanket she was sharing with Luke Fowler. For a moment Ilana felt a surge of hope that her attempts to bring the two of them together had worked out after all. Then she saw Luke get up and unfurl a blanket of his own.

"Heather told me you've got a couple of friends from your summer job joining us. I figure we'll need room to stretch out." He smiled at her. "Have a seat?"

"No, thanks; not just yet." Ilana watched unhappily as he

lined up the two blankets but then settled down at the far edge, away from Heather. "I want to make sure my work friends see me when they get here."

And I don't *want to sit close to you or Heather,* Ilana thought. *Not while I've got to keep Arachne out of sight. It's one small step from 'What's in the bag?' to 'Aiee! Spider!' and I'd rather we didn't take it.*

"No problem." Luke opened the little cooler he'd brought and took out three bottles of iced tea. "Want one?"

Ilana's disappointment grew as she watched Luke pass Heather one of the bottles. *What was I expecting? He offers her some iced tea, their hands touch, their eyes meet, a spark is kindled, they kiss, the sky fills with fireworks, and afterward they recycle the empties?* She sighed and drank her tea. *Who knew that failed matchmaking tastes like artificial lemon flavor.*

"Yo, Ilana!" Max, Corey, and Sophie came strolling across the green together. They'd come prepared with a blanket and cooler of their own.

"Max, what are you doing here?" Ilana asked. "I thought you had to temp for Di— your boss on the weekends."

"He doesn't need me; he's hosting a party. You ought to know: Your boss ladies were on the guest list. Lucky for everyone he gave me the night off, 'cause Sophie doesn't drive, Joanna got a last-minute overtime call, and *that* means I'm the only one who could get us here." Max glanced down and got his first good look at Heather. "*Very* lucky," he added as a playful smile slowly spread across his face.

By the time the concert started, Max had positioned himself

so that he was the only one Heather could talk to unless she got up and moved. Apparently this wasn't going to be an issue: She looked perfectly content to give all of her attention to him.

"It's like watching a wolf pack cut a reindeer calf out of the herd," Ilana murmured. In spite of Luke's offer of a place on his blanket, she'd chosen to sit as far from the nontemps as possible, for Arachne's sake. That put her at the far edge of the blanket Corey had brought along.

"That's Max," Corey said. "A wolf pack of one. But your friend Heather looks like she can handle it."

"Max isn't her type," Ilana said sullenly. "She likes artsy guys."

"Maybe you should remind her about that, because she's definitely acting like he *is* her type, artsy or not. Why do you look so mad about it? Don't you like Max?"

"Of course I like Max."

"Hmmmm." Corey stroked his chin in thought. "Maybe it's envy. You don't just like Max, you *like* him."

"I do not!" Ilana objected so loudly that the people on the next blanket over hissed at her to quiet down.

"Great!" Corey exclaimed a little too eagerly. Then he caught himself and quickly added, in a more subdued tone, "I mean, okay."

"If I tell you why I'm annoyed about Max monopolizing Heather, will you promise not to laugh?" Ilana asked. Corey crossed his heart and laid a finger to his lips. "It's because I wanted to fix up Heather with someone else."

"Someone else?" Corey's eyebrows rose. Silently Ilana pointed at Luke; Corey nodded. "Good. For a second, I was afraid you meant me. I don't like fix-ups."

"Why not?"

He looked deep into her eyes. "Because I guess I'm just more of a do-it-yourself guy at heart."

He leaned closer. Ilana sensed her heart beating fast and her thoughts flashing through her mind even faster. *Oh my God, he's going to kiss me! Do I want this to happen? Now? With him? Do I want it* because *it's him or because if* any *guy kisses me it means I'm not a total reject? Oh God, the last time a boy kissed me was back in seventh grade! Where do the noses go? Argh! I think too much, that's my problem. Corey's nice and sweet and thoughtful and whoa-boy, is he ever* cute, *so who cares why I'm doing this or where the noses go, bring it on!*

She closed her eyes, puckered her lips, and leaned in to meet him.

"Hey! Watch it! I'm a spider, not a tuffet!" Arachne's strident cry broke the mood and the moment. Ilana jerked back, realizing that she'd accidentally rested her hand—and weight—on Arachne's tote bag when she'd moved in for the kiss-that-almost-was. By a stroke of bad luck, Corey had done the same. "You klutzes! You nearly squashed me."

Ilana and Corey mumbled a long string of apologies mixed with urgent whispers for Arachne to keep her voice down and stay hidden. Grumpy but appeased, the spider responded, "Fine. Apology accepted, but I'd better get a *darn* big slice of cake later. Okay, don't mind me, go back to what you were— Say, what *were* you doing?"

"Listening to the concert," Ilana said hastily. *"Shhhhh!"*

"Uh-*huh*." Arachne gave a skeptical snort, then retreated into the semi-crushed shelter of her tote bag, muttering, "Listening to the concert. And there's a lovely bridge in Brooklyn for sale on eBay."

MUST BE WILLING TO WORK WITH ANIMALS

The Saturday of the wedding dawned bright and clear and stinking hot, made worse by the fact that the Newhouses' central air-conditioning system had died the day before. Ilana dragged herself out of bed and stumbled to the window. The white open-sided tents in the backyard threw back the fierce sunlight with blinding intensity. The caterers were setting up the buffet table while the florist's deliverymen waited impatiently with the shipment of centerpieces. At the far end of the yard, where the actual ceremony would take place, two groups of folding chairs faced an arbor that a harried florist's assistant was trying to cover with white roses and greenery. The flowers were no sooner in place than they went limp from the heat. Even the fat bows of white silk ribbon on all the aisle-side chairs were drooping.

Ilana thought of the hideous maid of honor dress she would have to wear for most of the day and groaned. Then she remembered Dyllin's bridal gown with its long train, cumbersome skirt, smothering veil, and layers of scratchy tulle petticoats, and she smiled.

She was still smiling when her cell phone rang.

"Good morning, Ilana dear; it's Mrs. Atatosk. Would you mind attending a little temps' meeting?" Her perky tone sounded forced and brittle, as if she were down to her last nerve and a grizzly bear was using it for dental floss.

"*Now?*" Ilana was thunderstruck. "I couldn't make the regular one *yesterday* because of what's going on here! Don't you know it's my sister's wedding day?"

"Yes, dear, and I was *so* looking forward to it, but we *must* have this meeting or I'm afraid that there isn't going to be any—" The rest of what she had to say was drowned out by a surge of noise, a thunderous din that sounded as if someone were trying to cram a pride of lions into the world's biggest blender in the middle of a hurricane.

When the uproar subsided, Mrs. Atatosk said, "Oh drat. It's getting worse."

"What is?" Ilana asked apprehensively.

Mrs. Atatosk sidestepped the question. "I promise you, this meeting won't impede your wedding preparations."

"Driving round-trip to New Haven, plus the meeting itself? How could that *possibly* interfere with anything?"

"Ah, sarcasm," Mrs. Atatosk stated. "How original. You needn't bother coming to the meeting, Ilana. Why don't I just bring it to you." With that she hung up, but not before Ilana heard her employer make an unimaginably bizarre sound.

Was it her imagination or had Mrs. Atatosk actually *chittered?*

Uh-oh, she thought. *How mad does someone have to be to do* that? *And talk about sarcasm! I hope I didn't just kiss D. R. Temps good-bye, but honestly, what did she expect, today of all days?*

As if on cue, a commotion came from elsewhere in the house. Apparently, Dyllin was wailing because she'd carelessly put on black eyeliner instead of brown and the humidity was doing unspeakable things to her hair. Her anguish was loud enough for Ilana to hear every trivial word.

That does not *sound like someone who's going to be kind and understanding if I'm not ready on time,* she thought. She sprinted for the shower and a little while later emerged refreshed and ready for anything.

The upbeat feeling vanished like a stray shampoo bubble when she returned to her room and found Max, Corey, and Sophie sitting in a row on her bed.

"*What are you doing here?*" Ilana yelled, clutching her terry-cloth robe tightly around her.

"Didn't Mrs. A. tell you about the meeting?" Sophie asked meekly.

"Yes, but—"

"She didn't want to hold up the wedding," Max said. He looked at Ilana, standing there in her bathrobe, and his mouth twitched.

"Max, I swear to God, if you leer at me, I'll kill you where you sit," Ilana said fiercely. Her eyes swept over the three temps, all of them decked out in their wedding outfits. "Boy, do *I* feel underdressed."

Corey folded his hands around the little silver-and-white wedding gift bag on his lap. "We'll get out of your room as soon as we take care of business."

"What business?" Ilana asked.

"We don't know," Corey replied. "Mrs. A. said she'd tell us when she gets here."

"Mrs. Atatosk is coming?" Ilana was alarmed. "To my *room*? What are my parents going to say if they run into her in the hall?"

"I don't think that's gonna be a problem," Max said. "We were all heading here in my car when Sophie's cell phone rang. One minute she's telling me, 'It's Mrs. Atatosk and she doesn't think you're driving fast enough,' and the next minute, *poof*!" He patted the bed. "All I can say is, I hope I can find where she poofed my car."

"Good thing I had a grip on this," Corey added, holding up the gift bag.

"You're telling me," said a small voice from inside the bag. Arachne stuck her head out. She appeared with her human face, and had managed to tie a fancy bow in her hair with leftover ribbon from the favor bags. "What, can't a girl look pretty?" she demanded, primping.

"Hey, anybody home?"

Arachne ducked out of sight just in time as Heather Hazelden sailed into the bedroom. Ilana's friend did a double take when she saw the assembled temps. "Wow, Ilana, I came up here to see if you needed help, but it looks like you've got that covered."

"That's right, Heather, so feel free to just go outside and wait for the wedding to start," Ilana said, steering her friend back toward the hall. *I can* not *start explaining D. R. Temps to her right now,* she thought. *If I'm not ready on time, Dyllin will strangle me with her garter, then she'll complain to Mom that I ruined her wedding by being dead.* "We're kind of busy."

"You mean you've got to do that whole temping-for-the-gods thing *today*?" Heather was astonished, but not half as astonished as Ilana.

"How do you know about that?"

"D. R. Temps?" Heather shrugged, then smiled at Max.

"What?" Max said innocently. "I thought she'd fit right in."

"We all *know* what you thought, Max," Ilana said.

"Hey, don't bust my chops! There's no rule against recruiting. Ask Mrs. A. if you don't believe me."

"I'll be happy to, if she ever gets here." Ilana stalked to the open window. "Look out there. The guests are starting to arrive. Where the heck is she-*EEEEEEE*!"

Ilana let out a wild shriek as a coal-black squirrel, bigger than a full-grown tomcat, leaped in through the window. Eyes glowing like bloody flames, foot-long tail streaming, it raced around and around the room in wild circles and zigzags punctuated by sudden leaps and the occasional midair full somersault. Papers scattered under its feet, everything on top of Ilana's chest of drawers and night table went flying. The beast bounced off the walls and made the closet-door mirror scream as its claws slid down the glass. When it saw Ilana, it leaped for her face, chittering frantically. Ilana shrieked again, and threw her arms up to ward it off.

"Mrs. A.! Mrs. A.!" Max threw himself between Ilana and the mad squirrel. The beast thudded into his chest like a cannonball. He toppled backward, heels over head, rump in the air. The squirrel scrambled up his leg and perched on the seat of his pants, nose and whiskers twitching.

"Max, hold still, I'll smack that lunatic rodent into next week!" Heather grabbed a copy of *Rolling Stone* off the floor and rolled it into a makeshift bat.

"Heather, no! Don't touch that squirrel!" Corey grabbed her arms. "She's our boss!"

"She's what?" Heather and Ilana said in chorus. They stared at the squirrel. It climbed off of Max's rump, letting him sit up slowly while his fellow temps gathered around the creature.

Ilana knelt on the carpet. "Mrs. Atatosk, who did this to you? Was it Circe?"

The beast gave her a prim look. "Don't be silly, dear; Circe can't touch me. I outrank her, for I—" She laid one forepaw over her heart and flourished the other dramatically. "*I* am Ratatosk, the Dark Squirrel of Doom!"

"Gee, Doom is cute and eats peanuts," Ilana remarked. "Who knew?"

Ratatosk ignored her; "Eternally I gnaw at the roots of the great World Tree, Yggdrasil, which sustains the earth and all upon it! Some day I will weaken it enough so that it crashes down, destroying all! Fear my power!"

"Um, what power?" Heather asked. "You're not gnawing anything; you're here."

Ratatosk dropped the pose and sighed. "I'm *here* because it's no fun being a myth no one pays attention to anymore. You people still remember the Greek gods—you can't ignore beings with stars named after them. But Norse myths like me? No. A spear-waving woman in a winged helmet and a bronze bra yodeling *The Ride of the Valkyries,* and that's it."

"Not true. *I* know Thursday's really Thor's Day." Max looked ready to receive a gold star for being so smart.

The squirrel was too preoccupied feeling sorry for herself to be impressed. "Why stay in the game when all you get for your troubles is a mouthful of splinters? You humans don't need *my* help to bring on the end of the world, so when I was offered the chance to manage D. R. Temps, I jumped at it."

"You know, I just *love* tree stories," Ilana said, getting back onto her feet. "And I'm *so* glad you wrecked my room before you told it, but do you think you could've saved it for *after* the wedding?"

"My apologies," the squirrel said coldly. "I am under a lot of stress at the moment; stress always makes me . . . *revert.* Far be it from me to hinder Dyllin's marriage, whether or not I approve of it. I've called this meeting in the faint hope that if we work together there might *be* a wedding today."

"Why wouldn't there be?"

"Child, do you know what Chaos is?"

"Are you kidding?" Ilana replied.

"She's not talking about the wedding," Max said. "She's talking about what she keeps behind the office door."

"What office—?" Ilana began. Then she remembered her job interview, the wild sounds that had come from beyond one of the two doors at the back of the D. R. Temps office, and how Mrs. Atatosk had hustled her out so fast that she still held the signed Waiver.

"Mice," Ilana said, thinking aloud. She looked down at the black squirrel. "You insisted that creepy, loud racket behind the door was *mice*, and I was too weirded out to stick around and argue with you. So what *do* you keep behind the door?"

"Actually it was the unbridled forces of primal Chaos, the unchecked embodiment of madness, havoc, and devastation that can annihilate the world," Ratatosk admitted.

"An honest mistake," Arachne piped up, peeking out of the gift bag again. "It's *so* easy to confuse mice with Chaos."

"Oooh, talking spider!" Heather exclaimed. "Cool."

Ratatosk glowered at Arachne. "New employees can be skittish. I didn't want her to worry."

"Uh-huh." Ilana nodded. "Now this may seem like a silly question, but *why* do you keep a primal force of annihilation in your office? Couldn't afford a paper shredder?"

"I have no choice. This is what myths do. We stand guard over Chaos."

"I thought your main job was explaining things," Ilana said. "You know, like What makes the seasons change? or What causes lightning? or Why is the world a mess?"

"That's part of it," said Ratatosk. "Myths help keep the forces of the cosmos in balance; we let you see them in perspective. We are stories, and stories have *endings*. When you mortals face small tastes of Chaos, like floods or fires or epidemics or wars, just knowing that it all has to end *sometime* can save you from feeling completely helpless."

"How does *your* myth fit in?" Heather asked. "You're supposed to destroy the world; how does that make anyone feel better?"

"If you know *how* the world will end, you can start thinking about what you might do to prevent it," Ratatosk replied.

"Saving the world with peanut butter crackers and a live-catch squirrel trap?" Heather mused. "I like it."

"So what's that got to do with—?" Ilana asked.

"It's Barry," said the squirrel. "He wants to stop your sister's wedding."

"*Barry*? Puh-lease." Ilana rolled her eyes. "Everyone knows he's *always* wanted Dyllin, but all he does about it is whimper. If he tries to say one word when the minister asks if anyone objects to the wedding, Dyllin will stuff her bouquet in his mouth. It'll be embarrassing, but I wouldn't call it Chaos."

"Child, don't jest." The black squirrel was grim. "Barry has stolen the powers of a god."

"*Barry*? Wow. That's one giant step up from whimpering. Which god?"

"It could be any of his many former employers," Ratatosk responded. "I was informed anonymously; the victim was too ashamed to reveal his identity, and Barry left him just enough power to keep me from tracing the message."

"How do you rip off a *god*?" Heather asked.

"You know temp jobs," Ilana said. "The longer you do the work, the more skills you pick up. I guess Barry just happened to pick up the wrong ones."

"Maybe he didn't *steal* the god's power," Sophie said hopefully. "Maybe he only 'borrowed' it. That's allowed."

Ratatosk made a helpless gesture with her paws. "'Borrowed' means you're going to give it back. He won't. The moment he succeeds in claiming Dyllin, he'll realize he must hold on to his power in order to hold on to his prize. Mortals who use the power of gods too long forget they *are* mortal. If that happens with Barry—"

"It'll be like sticking too many appliance plugs into one socket," Max said. "*Bzzzt!*" He did a creditable imitation of an overloaded electrical outlet blowing sky-high. "And *bzzzt!* means bye-bye cosmic balance."

"In other words, Chaos," Ilana concluded. She looked at the squirrel. "Was that the noise I heard in the background when you called me?"

Ratatosk nodded. "The longer Barry wrongfully holds a god's power, the stronger it gets. If things are not set right, it will become mighty enough to break down the door to Chaos and overrun the world."

"So what's the plan to stop him, Mrs. A.?" Corey asked.

The squirrel drooped. "I . . . I was hoping *you* might have some ideas. I'm better at gnawing the World Tree's roots than devising strategies. You mortals are such clever little things!"

The squirrel's optimism was met with bleak silence. Then Ilana spoke up.

"Okay, people, I did *not* suffer through week after week of Dyllin's bridal insanity to have some lovelorn loon like Barry throw the wedding and the whole freaking universe into the Dumpster. I have a plan. Step One—"

Everyone leaned forward eagerly.

"Step One is you all clear out of my room and *let me get dressed!*"

HOME/WORK

Circe stood in the Newhouses' backyard—in the midst of a swirling sea of college-age servers bearing platters of assorted appetizers—and steamed. "This is *so* counterproductive to female empowerment, it hurts," she said.

"If you don't think this wedding was all about Dyllin being empowered to the *n*th degree, I'll fill you in later," Ilana hissed at her. "If there *is* a later."

"Oh, don't you worry," the enchantress said, licking her lips. "The instant Barry shows so much as one hair of his head around here, I'll zap it into a pig-bristle so fast that—"

"Hey, Circe-babe, can you get me a refill?" Dionysus, god of wine, stuck a plastic glass under the enchantress's nose.

"Anything'll do. I can always change it. I'm the original BYOB guy, y'know? Thanks, you're beautiful, love ya, *mmmmwah*!" He winked at her and blended back into the crowd of wedding guests.

"Gods," Circe spat, then crushed the plastic cup to splinters. "I'd like to give that overgrown frat boy a drink he'd never forget." She stomped off.

"Gods." Ilana pronounced the word far less ferociously than Circe. "If this is how well those two work together, maybe it's a good thing the others didn't show up."

It had sounded like a good idea, back when it first struck her. "Barry crossed the line by *stealing* power, but can't the rest of us 'borrow' powers of our own from the gods we've temped for to stop him?" Ilana looked to Ratatosk for approval. The squirrel nodded, giving official permission to the plan. Encouraged, Ilana went on. "The split second that Barry shows up, we pounce before he can even *think* about making trouble."

"Yeah, but don't forget, you'll be busy with maid of honor stuff," Corey pointed out. "We'll be working shorthanded."

That was when Ilana got Good Idea, Version 1.5. "Let's ask some of the gods to help, too!"

Some turned out to be *two*. Not even Mrs. Atatosk could contact gods who had other plans, especially on such a great beach day. All calls to the Fates went straight to voice mail; Max hadn't heard from Eros all summer; Corey's hero-employers were cowards when it came to commitment ceremonies like weddings; Sophie said that her boss, Athena, promised to come but was vague about *when*. The only ones who'd responded were any-excuse-for-a-party Dionysus and Circe, fussy about furniture but always sincere in supporting "her" temps.

Just as well, Ilana thought, surveying the terrain like a seasoned general.

It wasn't supposed to be a big wedding, but "big" was a relative term, especially when Ilana's family was involved. They were all enjoying the pre-ceremony party while waiting for the organist to play the traditional sit-down-and-shut-up-we're-going-to-start music. Uncle Gary was trying to teach the bartender the *right* way to mix a martini; his wife, Cynthia, was trying to drag him away so the poor bartender could do his job in peace; five-year-old Cousin Missy, the flower girl, was having a tantrum; her twin brothers Evan and Pete were pelting each other with crab puffs; and from time to time the general hubbub was drowned out by an earsplitting yowl from deep inside the house as Dyllin pitched the mother of all conniption fits because the wedding programs had been printed with a border of lilies, not daisies.

If Chaos got loose around here, how could we tell? Ilana thought.

"Ilana, dear?" Mrs. Atatosk, no longer in squirrel form, came up out of nowhere and touched her arm. Ilana squeaked and shot skyward in spite of her heavy maid of honor dress. "Gracious, I'm sorry. I didn't mean to startle you."

"No, it's okay, really." Ilana took a big gulp of sultry air. "I've got to pay attention. If you'd been Barry—"

Mrs. Atatosk clasped both of Ilana's hands. "Dear, repeat after me: We have done everything in our power to be ready if Barry shows up. There is nothing more for us to do. The situation is under control. It is going to be a lovely wedding. Breathe."

"Do I have to?" Ilana managed a weak smile.

"Have to what? Breathe?"

"Repeat all that. I'd rather go see if Dyllin needs me for anything. You know, bring her some tissues, get her a drink of water, straighten her veil, shoot her with an elephant tranquilizer—all the little things sisters do."

Mrs. Atatosk giggled. "Run along, then."

The instant Ilana stepped over the threshold, she was engulfed by her family like a bunny by a python.

"Where have you *been*?" Dyllin desperately clutched her bridal bouquet as if it were Ilana's throat.

"I hope you have a good reason for keeping us waiting, young lady," Dad said sternly, over Mom's my-baby's-getting-married sobs. "Do you realize that I'm paying for an open bar *by the hour*?"

"Is it time?" Ilana asked.

"What, are you *blind*?" Dyllin demanded. "The minister's in place. Ras has been standing beside him for three million years already!"

"Not to exaggerate or anything," Ilana muttered under her breath. Aloud she said, "I thought the organist was supposed to give the start signal."

"Oh my God, he *didn't*?" Dyllin squealed. "Is he even there? I knew it! He didn't show up. He's sick. I can't walk down the aisle in *silence*. My life is ruined!"

Ilana let out a short, sharp snarl of frustration. "Dyllin, he's fine, but if you don't shut up for two seconds, we'll never hear the music."

But Dyllin was off in another direction. "Oh no, where's Missy? She's going to wreck everything, I know it! That awful little brat's probably going to do something idiotic like eat her flower petals."

"Probably," Ilana said. Then she grinned, glanced over her sister's shoulder and said, "Hi, Aunt Betty, we didn't see you standing there. Is Missy ready to go?"

Dyllin turned in time to get the full force of the world's iciest stare as Missy's mother said, "Yes, that 'awful little brat' is." She gave her daughter a gentle push forward before pivoting on her heel and sweeping out of the house, leaving a trail of frost crystals in her wake.

Dyllin turned on her sister. "This is all *your* fault," she cried.

"Sure, why not?" said Ilana.

○ ○ ○

Much as Ilana hated to admit it, it *was* a lovely wedding. The organist played flawlessly. Missy scattered petals like a pro. Mom managed to keep from wailing like a banshee when Dyllin went down the aisle on Dad's arm. Best of all, there was no sign of Barry.

I guess he decided to do the right thing after all, Ilana thought as she stood beside Dyllin under the arbor. *Or maybe he just got wind of what we had planned and pulled a strategic retreat. Smart choice, Barry. Remind me to thank you for it next Friday.*

The last notes of the processional died; the minister cleared his throat and directed the bride and groom to join hands. Dyllin passed her bouquet to Ilana, who as maid of honor had to look after it, the ring, and her own flowers. It was quite a juggling act.

"Let me help you with that," said a sassy voice at Ilana's elbow. A pastel-pink polished fingernail with a smiling kitten decal touched Dyllin's bouquet. The flowers flared up as if they'd been thrust into a blast furnace. The little blond teenager in the fluffy pink dress grabbed a fistful of the ashes out of midair and smeared them under her eyes, commando-style. Then she grinned and waved a scorpion-tipped whip at the flabbergasted wedding guests.

"Hi!" she said, perky as a poodle. "I'm Meg and I hope you all kept your gift receipts. Catch!" She grabbed Ilana's bouquet and threw it high into the sun. It soared like a rocket, trailing white petals, green smoke, and purple sparks, before exploding in a shower of mice. Dyllin's mouth hung open so wide that it was a miracle none of the squeaky little horrors landed in it.

The wedding guests were dancing around, frantically brushing rodents out of their hair, when the sky opened and Barry arrived fashionably late.

ALL WORK AND NO PLAY

"Stand back, all of you!" Barry shouted as he descended from on high, brandishing a wooden staff with two golden snakes twined around it. "This is a Caduceus and I'm not afraid to use it!" He wore nothing but a loincloth and a dish-shaped helmet adorned with tiny wings, while winged sandals let him glide gracefully to earth.

"Well, now we know which god got robbed," Ilana muttered. "But why did Barry steal the powers of *Hermes*? He's only the messenger of the gods. That's kind of lame. What's he going to do, text-message Dyllin until she loves him?"

A large black squirrel zoomed up her dress to perch on her shoulder. Barry's arrival packed enough stress to startle Mrs.

Atatosk back into her true shape. "Hermes is more than a message-bearer," she said. "He's diabolically clever and the patron of thieves. He wasn't even one day old when he stole Apollo's cattle and covered up the crime by making the poor beasts walk backward into a cave with pine branches tied to their hooves."

"I guess that explains why he was too embarrassed to admit that this time *he* got ripped off. Except I don't think Barry's here for our cows," Ilana said. "Max! Sophie! Corey! Protect Dyllin!"

The temps fought through the crush of fleeing wedding guests up the aisle. Corey transformed as he ran, his jacket, tie and slacks melting away, becoming the tunic and lion's pelt of Hercules. The hero's favorite weapon, a club big as a tree branch, materialized in his hand. Corey never could have lifted it, but the ability to "borrow" skills from temping for the great hero also let him "borrow" abilities. His shoes became sandals, and with every step those sandals took, a new set of muscles erupted on his body. It was like watching a slick time-lapse commercial for a gym. He joined Max and Sophie in a human wall around the bride.

It wasn't a very *good* wall.

"Dyllin, who are these people?" Mr. Newhouse shoved his way past the three temps to glare at Barry and Meg. "This is *my* home and *my* daughter's wedding. You two are rude, irresponsible, and trespassing. Gather up every last one of your verminous pets and leave immediately or I'll call your parents. And you—!" He rounded on the organist. "I'm not paying you to sit there with your mouth hanging open. *Play!*"

Trembling, the organist obeyed, but he was so badly rattled

that instead of soothing classical music, he ran through a medley of cartoon theme songs.

"Stop!" Barry waved the Caduceus like a baton. "I have something to say to Dyllin and I don't want to have to shout over *The Simpsons* to make myself heard!"

"You have *nothing* to say to her." Ras strode forward. Like Mr. Newhouse, he plowed through the temps.

Ilana groaned. Her friends' idea of a defensive wall was more like a swinging door.

"You tell him, Ras darling!" Dyllin gazed at him with hero worship in her eyes.

Ras blew her a kiss, then turned back to deal with Barry. "You had your chance and you never took it. Now she's marrying me, and you know damned well there's no way you can ever hope to—*squeak!*"

"Oooooh!" cried little Missy, who had stood her ground even while grown-ups ran away. *"Gerbil!"* She pounced on the tiny creature that poofed into existence at the precise moment that a flash from Barry's Caduceus engulfed Erastus Ames. The gerbil thrashed angrily, tangled up in Ras's abruptly abandoned suit, until Missy grabbed him by his tufted tail and dropped him into her flower basket.

Dyllin screamed.

"Oh my!" Mrs. Newhouse gasped, looking around anxiously. "What happened to the groom?"

"There, there, dear," her husband said confidently. "I'm sure there's a perfectly logical explanation for this."

"But that awful boy turned him into a gerbil!" She pointed

vaguely across the lawn where Dyllin was racing zigzag after Missy, shouting at the little girl to bring back her groom. Ilana's well-meaning Protect Dyllin order was officially a flop.

"Don't be silly," Mr. Newhouse said. "People do not turn other people into gerbils at weddings. That's a field mouse. Ras has probably run to fetch a broom to shoo it away before our other guests see it and panic."

"Um, Daddy?" Ilana said. "It's a little late for that."

"Nonsense, Ilana." It was Mrs. Newhouse's turn to be the voice of reason. "They're not panicking, they're *socializing*. Yoo-hoo!" she called after her fleeing guests. "Don't wander off or you'll miss the party!"

"Miss the *party*?" Dionysus echoed. "Not on my watch! Okay, people, hold it right there!" Grapevines shot out of the earth, their stems and tendrils twisting into an impenetrable barricade that surrounded the Newhouse property, trapping everyone inside.

The organist lost his nerve and took to heels right in the middle of the theme from *Scooby-Doo*. He was so eager to escape Barry's shadow that he ran right into the bride, who was too focused on catching Missy to see him coming. The impact propelled Dyllin into one of the two rented punch-spewing fountains. Three tiers of silvery basins splashed down, sending her staggering backward into the arbor. She toppled over in an avalanche of splintering slats and wilting roses, her bridal headpiece crushed, her gown stained pink, her hairstyle soaked in fruit juice.

"That does it." Dyllin grimly got back on her feet. "Nobody wrecks my wedding *or* my hair." She picked up a piece of the shattered arbor and threw it at Barry like a javelin.

It was a fight to remember. Most of the guests were too terrified to do more than scream and run around like headless chickens, but a few had the true hero's attitude: Help now, ask for explanations later. Dyllin fired the first shot, and they all joined in. Missy's brothers repeated their crowd-pleasing use of crab puffs as missiles, bombarding Barry relentlessly. Grandma Newhouse took a swing at him with her purse until Aunt Betty dragged the old woman away. Cousin Donny—Ras's best man in the absence of any attendees from the groom's side—grabbed an empty serving tray and flung it like a Frisbee, knocking Barry's winged helmet into the other fruit punch fountain.

"What did you just do?" Meg appeared almost nose-to-nose with Donny as Barry retrieved his hat. Her voice was disturbingly calm.

"Back off, little girl," Donny directed.

Meg's brows came together. "I am not a 'little girl,' I am Megaera the Jealous One, and I have placed my awesome powers of vengeance in the service of *that* man." She gestured at Barry.

"That jerk?" Donny's brows rose. "Jeez, *why*?"

"Well, because he's, like, *jealous,* silly." Meg made a face. *"Duh!"* She cracked her scorpion-tipped whip, but Donny ducked. She was drawing it back for a second try when a large floral centerpiece came sailing through the air and knocked the Fury off her feet. Megaera and her scorpion whip went down with a shriek of "You made me break a naaaaaaiiiilllllll!"

"Don't you *dare* raise a hand to my son!" Donny's mother shouted, reaching for another centerpiece.

Barry recovered his winged helmet from the punch and flew back to his beloved. "Dyllin, please, I just want to talk to you!"

"And I *don't* want to talk to you!" Dyllin turned her back on him and stalked away, calling for Missy to bring back that gerbil *now*, or else.

Ilana and the other temps waded through the wedding guests. "Dyllin's protecting herself just fine, but we still need to catch Barry," she said, wiping her brow. "This dress is so heavy, I'm sweating like a pig."

Circe overheard. "What a *good* idea," she said, pulling out her wand.

"Circe, your spells won't work on him," Ratatosk called to her from high up in an oak tree. "The Caduceus protects him!"

"You never know what's possible until you try," Circe replied, aiming her wand at Barry.

She was an enchantress, not a sharpshooter, and she had no experience hitting distant, moving targets, especially ones that flew. Spell after spell missed its mark, fizzled out, or hit someone else. When she finally scored a direct hit, Barry flew on, unchanged.

"Drat. Oh well, no harm done," said Circe, and was promptly lifted off her feet by a wild stampede of former wedding guests, all oinking madly.

Dodging swine, Arachne scuttled up to Ilana. "This just in: Your maid of honor gig is on hold, so how about spinning something *besides* your wheels?"

"Spinning—? Oh! Right, right." Ilana wasn't sure how she could use Barry's life-thread to make him back off and clear out, but she had to do *something*. She stuck out her hand and called for his spindle, loud and clear.

Her hand stayed empty.

Arachne tsk-tsked. "I was afraid of this. He's a lot more than plain old Barry now; it'll take more than a plain old temp to summon his spindle."

"I can't be more than what I am," Ilana protested.

"Says you," the spider countered. "Take a lesson from your boyfriend." She nodded in Corey's direction.

"He's not my— Oh, forget it. Corey!" Ilana yelled. Still wearing Hercules' form, he appeared at her side. "Quick, tell me how you did that." She pointed to the club, the lionskin, the muscles. "How do you *become* the ones you temp for?"

"You just— I don't know— you just do your job, that's all," Corey said. "You focus on what you know about it, call out to every scrap of power that you've 'borrowed' while working for the gods, and then you— you— You know, this is a bad time for a learning experience, Ilana."

"It's the only time!"

Ilana closed her eyes, clenched her hands and concentrated fiercely. She thought about all she'd seen and done and learned and accomplished that summer. She thought of the office and the spindle room, the life-threads and the death receipts, the Oopsie and the Scry-o-Tron 9000. Most of all, she thought of the bulletin board, and the cards and newspaper clippings displayed there.

I did all that! she thought. *All by myself, and that means I can do* this *too.* She felt transformation sweep over her like a breaking wave.

"Wow! Look at you!" Arachne's admiring exclamation snapped her back into the moment.

"What happened?" Ilana cried. She looked down. Her revolting maid of honor dress was now a dazzling white robe tied with a jeweled sash. Golden sandals were on her feet and a glittering crystal spindle was in her hand. She gazed at it in wonder.

Arachne scrambled onto her shoulder and grinned with satisfaction. "Now *that's* what I call an extreme makeover!"

DO YOU WANT A JOB OR A CAREER?

"*This* is Barry's life-thread?" Ilana asked, eyes fixed on the crystal spindle.

"It is now," the black squirrel replied.

"It's . . . humming."

"Maybe it doesn't know the words," Arachne suggested.

"It's humming *like a high-tension wire*," Ilana specified, scowling at the spider.

"That's what happens when you merge a mortal's life-thread with unlawful godly powers," Ratatosk said. "If you can't return it to normal—"

"*Bzzt*! I know, I know." Ilana pressed her lips together and looked determined. Clutching the crystal spindle, she marched forward, declaring, "Okay, Barry, first *and* last warning. This is your life-thread; if you value it, leave Dyllin alo—!"

A huge chunk of wedding cake zipped through the air, missing her head by inches.

"I was wondering how long it would be before someone did that," said Arachne, watching a second piece of wedding cake go flying. "And by 'someone' I mean your sister."

"Why am I the only sane person in my family?" Ilana asked plaintively.

Bridal veil in tatters, gown soaked in fruit punch, Dyllin stood beside the seven-tiered wedding cake, thrust her frosting-drenched hands into its heart, and flung a lump at Barry. Her aim at a moving target was about as good as Circe's.

"Looks like she doesn't believe in 'No dessert till after dinner,'" Arachne remarked.

"Dyllin, what are you doing?" Mrs. Newhouse ran to her wild-eyed daughter's side, fluttering her hands uselessly. "That cake is for your wedding guests!"

"*What wedding?* My groom is a gerbil, and it's all because of *him!*" Dyllin threw another fistful of cake.

Ilana couldn't help feeling proud as she watched her sister make Barry dodge glob after glob of fancy baked goods. *Now* that's *the Dyllin I know: a fighter, not some silly Eek-help-save-me girl. If Barry didn't have Hermes' powers and the Fury for backup, I bet she'd dunk that jerk in the swimming pool so fast—!*

"Ilana, are you *nuts?*" Heather zoomed in out of nowhere and dragged her away behind a large oak tree at the edge of the yard. She struck so unexpectedly that Arachne tumbled off Ilana's shoulder and bounced when she hit the ground. Corey scrambled to save her before she could be trampled.

"What are you *doing*?" Ilana yanked free of her friend's grasp.

"Cake, eggs, allergy, you do the math," Heather told her. "And you're welcome."

"Allergy, overprotective parents, *egg-free* wedding cake," Ilana countered. "But thanks."

Heather looked disappointed. "You mean I didn't need to save you? Rats. I thought I'd finally found a way to *help*, even without cool 'borrowed' powers."

"Hey, you're cool enough for me." Max's voice came from the oak tree's crown, followed by a rustling as he emerged from the overhanging branches. A huge pair of swan's wings stretched out behind him, the same dazzling white as his rather skimpy loincloth. He glided slowly down and hovered in front of the girls.

"You've got *wings*, Max." The more Ilana stared at him, the higher her eyebrows rose. "Not a lot of clothes, but *wings*."

"I temp for Eros, what I'm wearing is bigger than a lot of European bathing suits, and it's my *official uniform*, okay?" Max blushed and went on the defensive. "What's more important, what I'm wearing or the fact that I came up with the way to stop Barry?"

"You did? What is it?"

Max preened. "It was under our noses the whole time. The answer"—he paused for dramatic effect—"is *love*." A shining ivory bow and a gold-tipped arrow appeared in his hands. "Love will make him see he's being creepy, selfish, and W-R-O-N-G. After that, he'll apologize and surrender. Simple *and* beautiful, right? And I know beautiful." He winked at Heather and tapped his cheek. "How about a kiss for luck?"

Heather didn't need to be asked twice, and when Max pulled the old trick of turning his head at the last minute so her kiss landed right on his lips, she didn't object.

"Thank you, fair damsel." Max flourished his right wing like a cape and wheeled around, ready to take on the world.

"Hold it." Ilana grabbed Max by the tip of one wing. "Forget my-friend-the-fair-damsel, what's all this 'the answer is *love*' junk? You can*not* stop Barry with something out of a fortune cookie!"

"It's not junk and I didn't get it out of a fortune cookie," Max replied haughtily, removing his wing from Ilana's grip. "I got it from watching TV. Now if you *don't* mind—"

He took off in a blink, leaving Heather and Ilana standing on the far side of the oak. Before they could move, they heard the beating of his mighty wings, the twang of a bowstring, and Max's voice declaring, "*Feel* the love, stupid!"

It was followed by a boom of suddenly released energy, a brief lull, a bleat of dismay, a delicate fluttering, and mocking laughter. Just as they stepped out from behind the oak, they heard Dyllin yell, "That was *nasty*, Barry, even for you!"

"Where's Max?" Frantic, Heather looked here, there, everywhere. "What happened? Where is he?"

"I don't know." Ilana strained in vain for any sight of him.

Sophie and Corey came running up with Arachne riding on Corey's shoulder. "There you are!" he exclaimed. "Did you see all *that*?"

"We were back there." Ilana pointed at the tree. "All what?"

"Circe was trying to catch the wedding guests who need to be de-pigged, Dionysus's way of offering to help was saying 'Hey, little lady, let a *man* do that for you,' Circe started giving him a lecture about sexism, he turned himself into a cat and ducked into the vines to get away from her, she turned herself into *another* cat because nobody walks away from one of her lectures, and then—"

"*Forget* the gods!" Heather cried. "What happened to *Max*?"

"It's all right, dear," Ratatosk called down from the branches of the tree. "He's up here with me."

"Agh! Don't look at me!"

Everyone gasped. No bigger than a three-month-old infant, plump, curly-haired, and wearing even less clothing than before—no more than a wisp of pink gauze, to be precise—Max hovered in midair on stubby dove's wings.

"He turned me into a Cupid," he whimpered.

Arachne laughed so hard she fell off Corey's shoulder.

"And *that's* what happens when you fight cosmic forces with the wisdom of TV sitcoms," Ilana remarked.

Meanwhile, Dyllin had finally run out of cake and Barry was closing in on her, with Meg cheering him on.

"Back off, Barry!" Dyllin shouted. "There's nothing you can say that I want to hear!"

Barry sighed. "Have it your way." He scooped her up one-handed. Though she kicked and struggled fiercely, he held her to his chest and waved the Caduceus in a wide arc overhead. "Less talk, more wedding!"

With that, he let her go.

Ilana stared. *Why isn't she running away? Why is she looking at Barry like he's twenty gallons of chocolate ice cream? The only guy she ever looks at* that *way is—*

"Ras!" Dyllin exclaimed, throwing her arms around Barry's neck. "I'm so glad you're back. Let's get *married.*"

The temps watched in shock as an unnatural calm descended on the crowd. One by one, the guests filed back into their seats docilely, including the pigs. The minister, the organist, the best man, the mother and father of the bride all moved into their proper places like zombies. The only absent members of the original wedding party were Ilana and Missy.

"How's he doing that?" Ilana couldn't believe it.

"Illusion," said Ratatosk. "He's using Hermes' powers as a trickster and a thief to steal their ability to see the truth."

"But where's Missy?" Ilana asked, scanning the crowd. "Why isn't she up there with them?"

"Children have the power to see the truth no matter how many illusions stand in the way." The squirrel looked solemn until Ilana's sharp, skeptical look made her add, "Oh, all right, I made that up because it sounded good. She's probably just out of range."

"Like us?"

"*Active* temps are under the direct protection of the gods and immune to Hermes' power—"

"Says you!" Max cut in. He smelled like roses.

"—of *illusion*," Ratatosk finished. "The power that the Caduceus gives him to cause *physical* transformation is another story."

"You mean the stick with the snakes?" Heather asked.

"That 'stick with the snakes' is the stolen emblem of the god himself," the squirrel replied. "It symbolizes and directs Hermes' power. The longer Barry holds it, the harder it will be for him to recall he's only a mortal."

"So, break his grip on the stick and you break his grip on the power." Heather nodded. "Why didn't you say so?" She grabbed Hercules' club from Corey's hands and raced toward the wedding before anyone could react. "I want to help and I *like* breaking things!" she called over one shoulder. Ratatosk's distressed chittering went right over her head as she charged, yelling, "This is for what you did to Max, loser!"

Barry turned, a lazy smile on his lips. Heather was less than ten steps away when he gave the Caduceus a casual flick, engulfing her in a blast of pink and silver light. The dazzle died, revealing a bewildered white poodle holding the hero's club in her jaws.

Meg squealed with delight. "Ooh, *cute*!" She moved toward the poodle, making little kissy-noises.

"Stop that!" The unexpectedly thunderous sound of Barry's voice brought Meg up short. "Make yourself useful, girl. Collar the beast."

Meg pouted. "You're just lucky you're *that* cute when you're jealous or else I'd—"

"*Now!*"

"*Whatever.*" She tossed one loop of her scorpion whip around the poodle's neck. Heather cringed in terror.

"Oh dear," said Ratatosk. "He's actually *giving orders* to one of the Furies. He's acting as if he were—"

"A god?" Corey said.

"What he *is,* is dogmeat," Ilana stated. "That's my friend he's got on a leash!" She grabbed the loose end of Barry's life-thread, scooped up a fallen lump of wedding cake, and angrily squashed the two together.

A massive chunk of cake appeared out of nowhere and smacked Barry right in the face.

"Score!" Max exclaimed. He tried high-fiving Corey, but with his pudgy little arm he was hopelessly unequal to the task, and rebounded halfway to the swimming pool.

"And there's more where that came from!" Ilana shouted, glorying in an easy win. "I told you, Barry, this is your *life-thread.* Now give up, or I'll show you what I can *really* do with one of these babies!"

"You'll do *nothing*!" Barry wiped cake from his eyes, then aimed the Caduceus at Heather. The poodle whined, and the piteous sound made him smile. "Nothing except keep your distance. One more of your silly little tricks and I'll show you what *I* can do with *this* baby."

His threat froze Ilana where she stood. "Well?" he added.

"What are you waiting for? Want to see what I turn her into next? A lizard? A worm? A puff of air? Or are you just too stupid to move? Did Dyllin get all the looks *and* brains in your family?" His scornful laughter flew after her when Ilana finally turned and ran.

She didn't stop running until she was out of Barry's sight and around the corner of the house where her mother's rock-edged flower bed bloomed. "Hold my friend hostage, will you?" she muttered as she flung the spindle to the ground and dropped to her knees. "'Silly little tricks,' huh, Barry? Is that all you think I can do to a life-thread?" She uprooted an apple-sized stone from the garden border, and raised it high above the crystal spindle. "How's *this* for silly?"

A strong hand closed around her wrist. She looked up and saw Corey, Arachne on his shoulder. "Don't do it, Ilana," he said.

"I'm only going to hit the life-thread hard enough to knock him out!" she cried, struggling to free her hand. "I have to do *something* to stop him!"

"Not if it turns out to be something that's too much," Corey said. "What if you shatter the spindle?"

"I don't care!"

"I don't believe that." He let go of her wrist.

She lowered the rock to her lap. "I can't just give up, Corey."

"I'm not asking you to do that."

"Yes, you are! You're a hero; you *need* people to be helpless or you're out of a job! Sorry, but I'm not going to lose another friend by waiting for someone else to rescue her."

"*Another* friend?" Corey echoed.

Ilana looked away. "Atifa."

"The one who died in the epidemic. I remember; you told me." Corey took a deep breath. "Ilana, you *couldn't* do anything to save her."

"Maybe not," Ilana said, grimly raising the rock a second time. "But I can save Heather. And I can rescue Dyllin."

Arachne jumped from Corey's shoulder and scrambled onto the crystal spindle, firmly planting herself between the rock and Barry's life-thread. She looked up at Ilana. "Go ahead, hit it," she said. "You *probably* won't crush me like you *probably* won't crack Barry's spindle, but even if you do, hey! What's a little overreacting between friends?"

Ilana let the rock drop back into the dirt. "Why do I do these things?" she wondered aloud.

Corey hunkered down and touched Ilana's cheek gently in the place where she had once drawn the tiny image of a skull. "Because it's hard to feel helpless."

She nodded. "It's harder to feel guilty about it afterward."

"Even if there never was anything you *could* have done to help?"

"Especially then." Ilana shrugged. "It doesn't make sense, but that's how it is. I'm so damned scared of not being able to help, to fix things, to make everything right again, that I just *react* instead of thinking first." She smiled weakly at Corey and Arachne. "Maybe it's time I tried something different, for a change."

"Stand back, everybody!" Arachne announced. "She's got a brain and she's not afraid to use it!"

"Oh, I'm going to use something much more dangerous than a brain," Ilana replied. With the crystal spindle in one hand, she held out the other and pronounced her cousin Missy's name.

It only took a moment for Ilana to use Missy's life-thread to fetch the child herself, casting and reeling in the filament like a fishing line. She sent the spindle safely back the instant the little girl came skipping around the side of the house, her flower basket swinging, a very queasy-looking gerbil hanging over the side.

"Hiya!" Missy crowed, then thrust the gerbil at Ilana. "Say hi to Cousin 'Lana, Mr. Fluffybottom," she commanded. Ras squeaked and squirmed furiously.

"Missy, dear," Ilana said in her most wheedling voice. "Want to do something *fun* with Mr. Fluffybottom?"

Missy thought it over. "'Kay," she said, then picked a rose petal out of her basket and put it on the gerbil's head. "But he's gotta wear a hat."

○ ○ ○

"I'm tired, I'm thirsty, I'm bored," Meg griped. "Stupid mortals, stupid wedding, stupid, stupid, *stupid*." She swung Heather's leash back and forth petulantly. "When is it going to be *over*?"

"Shh!" Barry hissed, eyes on his bride. "Dyllin is still reading the love poem she wrote for me."

"You mean for *him*," Meg said spitefully. "*He's* the one she loves, big surprise."

"But *I'm* the one she's marrying." Barry leered. "So it's really all about me. Stop fidgeting. I looked at one of the programs and the vows are next. Once we're man and wife, she'll be mine and *you* can go to—"

"Hello, Barry," Ilana said.

Barry spun around so fast he almost lost his winged helmet yet again. "Where did *you* come from?" he snapped.

"Do you want the 'Mommy and Daddy loved each other very, very much' answer?" she replied. "Or the one about how some people just don't pay attention? You were so busy bickering with Meg that I could've driven up the aisle in an SUV and you wouldn't have noticed."

"And *some* people are too stupid to believe that I mean what I say!" Barry bellowed. He brandished the Caduceus and turned to where Meg stood holding Heather on the scorpion-whip leash. "Say good-bye to your friend."

"Bye, Heather," said Ilana, turning in the opposite direction and waving gleefully as the white poodle went bounding out of Caduceus-range.

Meg looked down and shrieked. "My whip!" The severed lash that had once collared Heather writhed at her feet, scorpions clattering their claws in rage. It had been chewed clean off while the Fury's easily diverted attention was on Barry and Ilana. "Who did this?"

"Being a rodent is all about chewing through things *fast,*" Ilana replied. "Just ask Mrs. Atatosk. Or Ras." She snapped her fingers and the gerbil scaled her white dress like the world's smallest mountaineer.

"Here comes the groom, and he's still hungry." Ilana drew the crystal spindle from her belt, whipped out the loose end of the thread, dangled it in front of the gerbil, and very sweetly said, "Bon appétit."

Not even Hermes himself could anticipate having his life-thread chomped by a seriously enraged gerbil. Even if Ras didn't draw blood, he made a very deep impression.

At the first nip, Barry yelped and swung the Caduceus wildly, sending bursts of power in all directions. Two wedding guests were transformed into armadillos when the blasts hit them. Three more became lobsters. Barry's power kept everyone else serene in the illusion that the wedding was proceeding normally.

Still holding Ras and the crystal spindle, Ilana nimbly dodged the random flares, but Meg was not so lucky. A stray bolt of energy sizzled through her hair, leaving a bald patch the size of a saltine cracker. "*Eeee!*" She clapped one hand to the side of her head. "This is *your* fault, you meddling mortal; you and that icky little *rat.* I don't care who he really is, I'll stomp him like a cockroach. Drop him *now*!"

"Make me!" Ilana hollered, and swung the crystal spindle like a tennis racket. She hadn't played the game in years and she'd never been very good at it, but on the other hand, Meg's face was a lot bigger than a tennis ball.

"*Agh!* You broke it! You broke my nose, you big stinky!" The gods had golden ichor instead of blood in their veins, but it was just as squirty. Meg vanished, howling for Asclepius, god of healing.

"Ow!" Barry roared. The impact of his life-thread hitting Meg's face was too light to damage the crystal spindle, but more than enough to knock the wind from his lungs and the Caduceus from his hand. Ilana saw it fall and threw herself forward to capture it.

She was a little too eager. In her haste, she forgot that Ras was still clinging to the crystal spindle, literally by a thread. He lost his hold, and the gerbil and the Caduceus hit the ground within a heartbeat of each other.

"Ah-ha!" Ilana exclaimed, raising the Caduceus.

"Ah-ha yourself!" Barry snapped back, seizing the gerbil. "Foolish mortal, give me back what's mine or I'll crush this miserable beast like a grape!" He gave Ras a squeeze to make his point. The gerbil squeaked in fright.

"Barry, *you're* the foolish mortal," Ilana said. "And the Caduceus isn't yours; it belongs to—"

"You *dare* defy the gods?" Barry's grasp on Ras tightened, making his squeaks louder and more desperate. Though the crystal spindle's hum was becoming more intense by the moment, Ilana knew Ras's life was on the line.

She couldn't risk it. She placed the Caduceus back on the ground and said, "There. Now let him go."

Barry pounced on Hermes' symbol, but didn't release his

hold on Ras. "That was your last mistake, newbie," he said. Still kneeling, he lowered the Caduceus level with her heart.

"I want Mr. Fluffybottom!" Missy shrieked. The five-year-old came flying down the aisle and threw herself on Barry's back, sending him sprawling face-first into the dirt. Reflex made him tighten his hold on Ras and the Caduceus, but Missy was a force stronger than reflex. When he refused to let go of her beloved pet, she dug her tiny fingers into his wrist and bit him.

Barry screamed and dropped the gerbil, then stared at his wounded hand as if he were seeing something that simply could *not* be happening. "I'm . . . bleeding?"

"Yes, Barry," Ilana said gently. "Just like every other mortal. Remember?"

"Mortal . . ." Barry spoke like someone coming out of a deep dream. The Caduceus slipped from his hand and the world went white with light.

When the flash faded, the Caduceus was gone, and so were all the changes it had caused. The crystal spindle in Ilana's hand became an ordinary D. R. Temps one, no longer humming dangerously as it reeled up Barry's life-thread. She sent it back to the spindle room with a "Beat it, troublemaker," and a sigh of relief. Freed from Barry's illusions, the wedding attendees—including all the former pigs and the five who'd briefly been lobsters and armadillos—milled around as if they'd just returned from a group-rate alien abduction. Max gave a happy shout the minute his dinky wings vanished, his feet hit the ground, and he was no longer a Cupid. Rehumanized, Heather spat out the discarded shoe she'd been chewing to calm her nerves. And last of all, released from rodenthood, no longer small and brown and furry, Erastus Ames stood revealed to all in his true form.

Really revealed. He wasn't wearing anything but a pair of glorious white wings. He turned to the slack-jawed wedding guests and sheepishly said, "Hi, everyone. I can explain. Honest."

Missy burst into tears and ran to her mother's arms, howling for her lost pet.

"You can show some manners first, young man, instead of everything else!" A towering woman dressed in white came out of nowhere to stride down the aisle. She had a shining helmet on her head, a massive shield on one arm, a sword at her belt, and an owl on her shoulder.

"A-A-Aunt Athena?" In or out of his mortal disguise as Erastus Ames, the sight of the angry goddess of wisdom made her nephew Eros turn pale.

"Yes, 'Aunt Athena'!" the goddess shot back. "Don't act so surprised; this *is* a family occasion and besides, my temp, Sophie, asked me to be here. If I didn't say anything until now it was because I was taught that a good guest doesn't meddle. On the other hand, considering the antics I've seen here today, particularly *yours,* perhaps I should have."

She tried to strike an indignant pose, hands on hips, but her shield got in the way. "Sophie!" she called out. The meek little temp rushed up to take the shield from her employer. "*Most* particularly your antics," she repeated. "Even the god of love must obey the rules of public decency, Eros. *Put on some clothes!*"

"But I haven't got any—" he began. Then a look of perplexity flitted across his face. He looked down at his legs.

"*Agh!* A spider!"

"Oh, grow up," said Arachne. She continued to crawl up his left leg until she reached his hip bone. There she began spinning a web that became first a strategic scrap of fabric, then a loincloth, and finally a pair of Bermuda shorts complete with belt loops.

"Don't mention it," Arachne said as she jumped off his knee.

"*Look* at this mess, Eros!" Athena made a sweeping gesture over the devastated yard. "This is what happens when you avoid your responsibilities. Your power can conquer Zeus himself. Mortals fear you more than the Furies! But you got so careless that a second-rate temp was able to turn you into a hamster."

"Gerbil," Eros muttered. "And he couldn't have done it without the Fury on his side. They ganged up on me."

"You *let* them gang up on you," Athena scolded. The goddess of wisdom looked ready to work herself up into Stern Lecture Mode, but then she took a deep, centering breath and spoke more coolly. "There's nothing wrong with falling in love with mortals—Zeus did it all the time—but neglecting your *work* for her? Bad enough, but trying to marry her without telling her who you really are?" She shook her head. "I am extremely disappointed in you."

"Get in line," said Dyllin. She closed in on her former fiancé. "You *lied* to me!" she shouted in his face. "You lied to me, and you probably used your powers to keep me so dizzy in love with you that I'd never even try to *catch* you lying to me!"

"But baby, I *do* love you," Eros protested, turning on the full force of his charm.

"And *that's* supposed to make it all better? In your dreams. When were you going to tell me the truth? When we were honeymooning on Mount Olympus? If I can't trust you, I don't want you. We're through."

While Athena and Dyllin berated Eros, Corey laid hold of Barry to make sure he didn't slip away. But even the 'borrowed' strength of Hercules was no match for the determination of a man in love. As Dyllin stamped off, Barry tore himself out of Corey's hands and flung himself onto the train of her bridal gown. She dragged him five feet before she noticed he was there.

"Wait!" he cried, pulling himself up the dress hand over still-bleeding hand. "Give me another chance. I know I'm not a god, but I love you more than any god ever could and today I proved I'm willing to fight for that love. I don't care if you're too shallow to look into my heart and see my *true* worth—beautiful girls can't help being a little stupid—but there's still time for you to do the smart thing. I forgive you, darling. Say you'll be mine!"

There was a stunned silence. Ilana imagined her mouth had fallen open so wide that her lower jaw must be somewhere down around her knees. *Wow,* she thought. *Someone exists who can make Jeff Eylandt look good. What are the odds?* She looked at her sister, wondering whether it would be a good idea to make a preemptive call to 9-1-1 and get the ambulance on its way to pick up Barry *now.*

To her surprise, Dyllin was smiling. More than that, she was gazing at Barry tenderly. "Oh, dearest, why didn't you tell me all this before?" She helped him to his feet and clasped his hands. "No matter what you did—destroyed my wedding, tried to trick me into marrying you, used stolen powers to take away the last drop of my free will—it was all just *peachy* because you love me soooo much that nothing else matters. Who *wouldn't* give you a second chance?" Smiling demurely, she led him away.

"Did you see that?" Eros demanded indignantly. "After everything he did, she walks off with him?"

"Yes, she does," Ilana said. "In the direction of our swimming pool." She began a countdown under her breath: "Five, four, three, two—" The splash and Barry's yowl came before she got to *one*.

The sound of Barry's unscheduled plunge attracted the attention of Circe and Dionysus. They crept out of the grapevines, shed their feline forms, and laid aside their differences in order to set things to rights. Circe strolled among the wedding guests, turning pigs back into people. Dionysus made the living fence—fruit, leaf, and root—shrink back into the earth. Mr. Newhouse watched the wine god work for a while, then stepped forward. The light had finally dawned on him.

"So . . . you're a god," Mr. Newhouse said.

"Yep," said Dionysus.

"Lot of that going around here, lately. I suppose that explains why my daughter's wedding didn't go quite the way we planned. Not that I'm blaming *you*, of course."

"Thanks."

"From what I gather, both of my girls seem to know a lot of you people. Their mother and I never had a clue. Er, it is all right to call you 'people,' isn't it?"

"Fine by me." Dionysus made another part of the vine-fence vanish. "If you don't mind being devoured by panthers afterward, for insulting a god."

"Why don't I just let you finish your work," said Mr. Newhouse, as he headed for the safety of his house.

"Hey, everybody!" Circe had restored the last pig to human shape and now moved on to her next cleanup task. "Who wants coffee?" She stood beside a giant silver espresso machine and cast her enchantments out over the yard, drawing in every last one of the still-dazed wedding crowd. They lined up without protest, drank a cup of Circe's memory-altering brew, and went home peaceably, chatting about what a nice party it had been, even if the bride *had* gotten cold feet and called off the ceremony. These things happened.

Ilana stood in the shadow of the oak tree, watching Circe and Dionysus tidy up. She had a few final details to deal with herself, one of which was overseeing the reunion between Arachne and the goddess who'd turned her into a spider so long ago.

"I just wanted to thank you for what you did for Eros," Athena told Arachne. She squinted at the spider. "Hmm. You look familiar. Have we met before?"

"Think about it," Arachne said frostily. "It'll come to you."

Athena gave a little gasp. "Arachne! After all these years. It's a small world."

"Mine's smaller."

Athena looked momentarily uncomfortable. "You know, in view of what you did for my nephew, I think perhaps it might be time for me to let bygones be bygone." She picked up the spider and brought her to eye-level.

"If you're going to apologize, do it fast," Arachne snapped. "I don't like the way that owl of yours is looking at me."

"Oh, I'm not going to apologize," said the goddess. She took a deep breath and blew it out right into the spider's face.

Her breath turned to silvery threads of spider-silk that whipped themselves around Arachne and sent her sailing out of the goddess's hands. Before Arachne touched the ground, she was encased in a glimmering cocoon as large as a soccer ball. When it landed, it shattered into a whirlwind of feathery flakes, as a beautiful girl, fully human, sprang from its heart.

"Oh wow," said Ilana. "Now *you* need clothes."

RETIREMENT PLAN OPTIONS

"Yoo-hoo!" Tabby called as she and her sisters came into the Newhouse backyard. "We're here! Sorry to be so dreadfully late; Georgette had trouble getting a babysitter."

They found a scene that was a bizarre mix of devastation and industry. Ilana and Arachne were the only members of the extended D. R. Temps family there to welcome them, though they were far from the only people present. The gods had done their jobs and gone, but the mortal hired help were still cleaning up an impressive amount of rubble.

"Gracious," said Tabby. "Did we miss anything?"

"Not much," said Arachne, wiggling her toes in the grass. "I found out that Ilana and I are the same dress size, but that's about it." She twirled happily in place, showing off her fully restored human body.

"Yeah, that's all," Ilana said, catching Arachne when she got dizzy and fell over. "Except the part where the wedding *im*ploded, Dyllin almost *ex*ploded, and everyone found out Max has a tattoo on his—"

"Tsk. We knew *that*," Tabby said in that tone of voice that meant the news had taken her completely by surprise but she'd sooner kiss a newt than admit it.

"Including the part where Mrs. Atatosk fired Barry for misappropriation of powers, tore up his contract with D. R. Temps, and Dyllin made him eat the shreds?"

"We missed that," Dimity said in her measured monotone. "Curses. Oh well, this is summer. There are always reruns. I call first dibs on the Scry-o-Tron. Ha. Ha. Ha."

"Where's Dyllin?" Georgette asked anxiously.

"In the house, phoning the newspaper to cancel the wedding announcement, eating raw cookie dough, and waiting for the plumber," Ilana replied. "She tried to stuff her bridal gown down the garbage disposal. Dad says the repair's coming out of her own money; she says it was worth it."

"Logical," said Dimity. "I approve."

Corey joined them, carrying a box piled high with wedding favors. He peered over the mound of net-bagged Jordan almonds and said, "Hey, Ilana, got a second? Mrs. Atatosk wants Max to drive these back to the office for her. I don't care if she is the Dark Squirrel of Doom; if she eats all these, she's going to be sorry in the morning. Want to come try talking sense into her?"

Ilana followed Corey around the house and down the driveway. "I guess Max found his car," she remarked.

Corey set the box down. "No, he's still looking and everyone else is helping. Mrs. A. took off with Circe and Dionysus and forgot to tell him where she poofed it."

"So this—?" Ilana toed the box.

Corey shrugged. "Just my excuse to cut *you* out of the herd. Why should Max have all the skills?" He put his arms around her. "You okay?"

"In general?" Ilana asked. He was looking at her intensely, as if he couldn't see anything else in the world. It made her feel thrilled and awkward at the same time, so she coped with it the only way she knew how, by turning on a never-ending stream of snappy answers. "Or with what happened here? Or with Dyllin almost burning down the house when she set fire to all of Ras's photos in the bathroom sink? Or with the fact that we're going to be eating wedding leftovers for the next six months? Or—?"

He kissed her just in time. It made her head twirl like all the life-thread spindles in the world. Then he smiled and dashed off before either one of them could feel awkward about what had just changed between them.

Ilana was still grinning ear-to-ear when she returned to Arachne and the Fates. She expected the former spider to start teasing her about going off alone with Corey, but Arachne had other matters claiming her attention.

"You look wonderful Arachne," Tabby said, holding the former spider at arm's length and looking her over, head to toe. "How did this happen?"

Arachne shrugged. "I did something that pleased Athena and she realized what a bi . . . uh, big meanie she's been to me all these years. I guess even the goddess of wisdom can learn something new if you give her enough centuries."

"Athena is *very* hard to impress," Tabby said. "You must have done something spectacular."

"I made underpants for Love," Arachne gravely replied.

"Good for you, dear." Georgette patted her hand. "It's always nice to have a practical skill or two when you're starting out on your own."

"On my own?" Arachne raised one eyebrow.

"You are human again," Dimity stated. "A mortal. Mortals who live with gods too long run the risk of forgetting they are human. That is why it's forbidden."

"Unless they're mortals who are related to the gods by blood or marriage," Georgette was quick to add. "Like my precious family."

"I'm sorry, Arachne." Tabby fidgeted as she sought just the right words. "As long as you were carrying the full burden of a god's curse, you didn't count as a mortal. Now that the curse has been lifted and you're entirely human again, we'll expect you to move your things out of the office by Monday."

"What 'things'? Three dead flies and some leftover wasp's wings? I've got *nothing*: no home, no money, no relatives, no clothes of my own. Where the heck am I supposed to go?"

"Nowhere," Ilana said. "You're staying here; my house. We'll tell anyone who asks that you're our cousin from Los Angeles. *Everyone's* got a cousin from L.A."

"What about your parents?"

"No problem; I'll just take their life-threads, braid them with yours, mine, and Dyllin's, run the whole mess over a welcome mat or a Home-Sweet-Home sampler or something, and—"

"Ilana, dear, *how* could you have forgotten about *not* being allowed to alter the life-threads of your immediate family?" Tabby said. "Rules are rules."

In response, Ilana turned and casually asked, "Georgette, dear, *how* bad would it be if I didn't temp for you again before your kids go off to camp?"

Georgette's body trembled. Her eyes turned bloodred. She sucked in her breath, and her voice rang out with the dread finality of the black scissors as she decreed: "Rules are rules, Tabby, and exceptions are exceptions. *Make one!*"

"Y-yes, Georgette, dear," said Tabby.

○ ○ ○

Autumn had come. The grass in the Newhouse backyard had just recovered from the wedding when it was killed by the first frost. Ilana and Arachne kicked their way through drifts of fallen leaves as they came walking up the brick-paved path to the front door.

They were heading for the kitchen to get an after-school

snack when Ilana's mother called from the living room, "Come in here a moment, girls; we've got company."

Nestled into a large, cozy armchair, a cup of tea in one hand and a plate of nut bread and coffee cake in the other, Mrs. Atatosk perked up the instant she saw the girls. "Hello, children!" she chirped. "Arachne, you look wonderful. Your new life agrees with you?"

"Thanks to Ilana," the former spider admitted. "She's been taking the time to help me fit in."

"Isn't that nice." Mrs. Atatosk stuffed down two slices of nut bread. "And after all that time, Ilana dear, wouldn't it be nice if you could find a moment to, oh, *finally hand in your Waiver,* perhaps?"

Five minutes later, Mrs. Newhouse was simultaneously pouring tea, passing Mrs. Atatosk her second piece of cinnamon walnut coffee cake, and giving Ilana Lecture Number 982 on the subject of Personal Responsibility.

"And you *still* haven't turned in your Waiver? You know how important it is!"

Ilana's brow creased in perplexity. "*I* do. Why do *you*?"

Her mother tossed her head. "Honestly, Ilana, do you think I was *born* this age? I've had my share of summer jobs, too."

"You mean *you* used to work for—?"

Mrs. Newhouse plowed right over the question. "Mrs. Atatosk is a very busy person. You should be ashamed of yourself, making her come all the way from New Haven just because you're negligent." She turned to her guest and added, "I apologize for my daughter. I had no idea she was this unreliable."

"No need, dear," Mrs. Atatosk said, gobbling the last bite of coffee cake on her plate and reaching for a platter of peanut butter cookies. "She was reliable where it mattered most: on the job."

"Really?" Mrs. Newhouse brightened. "I'm so glad. A reference letter from a satisfied employer will be a great help to her when it's time to start applying to colleges."

"Oh, I'm certain that by the time Ilana's ready for that, she'll have all *sorts* of letters in her file," Mrs. Atatosk said cheerfully. "In fact, given her performance, we at D. R. Temps are already receiving calls from clients eager to secure her services for *next* summer."

Mrs. Newhouse sighed. "At least *someone* is planning ahead. That's not Ilana's strong suit, unfortunately. When her sister was this age, she was already studying college catalogs, but for some reason, Ilana just doesn't want to look to the future and—"

"I'm waiting to pick my early decision school until I know whether Harvard's got a better premed program than Yale," Ilana announced, interrupting her mother. "I want to become a doctor specializing in epidemiology and do hands-on work in Third World nations. You can't beat the Ivy League for prestige, but even if most of the Seven Sisters schools are co-ed now, I like the whole idea of going somewhere with a tradition of giving women the same educational opportunities as men."

"Ilana! Where did *that* come from?" Mrs. Newhouse couldn't

have been more surprised if her younger daughter had just announced plans to become a tap-dancing horse.

"A good summer job can really help you focus on the future," Arachne volunteered in a cheery, after-school-special tone of voice.

"A *great* summer job helps guarantee there'll *be* a future," Ilana added. The two girls giggled.

Mrs. Atatosk placed her purse on her cookie-crumb-strewn lap and reached inside. "And when you make those future plans, Ilana, we all hope D. R. Temps will be a part of them." She handed her a small blue box.

Ilana opened it and smiled. "Me, too," she said, fastening the golden pin with the little silver acorn charm right above her heart.